"So, Lucy, what about the position here at Capital Healthcare appeals to you?" asked the female interviewer with the frizzy hair and massive eyebrows.

Hmmm what doesn't? I thought. No shift work. I'm a total bitch with not enough sleep and besides, who can sleep during the day with a school next door? Bloody kids laughing and having fun and let's not forget the bell ringing several times a day, very insensitive really!

No horrid purple uniform that makes me look like Barney the freaking Dinosaur.

No crabby old doctors - so much for finding a hot young doctor to be my future husband at the hospital. Fail. Oh there was that one hot surgeon I thought could be a goer until I realised he had a wife who was just as hot as him. That was nothing if not an Alanis Morissette song waiting to be howled alone in my bedroom.

Oh bugger - I haven't answered the question and they are all staring at me.

"To be honest," I started, "I want to work in an environment like Capital Healthcare because I believe that everyone wants to come to a Doctor's surgery and not be just 'another number'. I want to make patients feel comfortable and have that personal rapport with them that is just unmanageable at a hospital where the number of patients and the fast turnaround is just so great. I want to work in a place where everybody knows your name and they're always glad you came."

Shitballs, did I just recite the Cheers theme song in a job interview?!?!

I'm talking out of a hole in my arse. Oh crap, just smile and hope they didn't notice...

Oh wait - Frizzy is smiling. Phew.

The three interviewers started packing up the folders on the table and the old male one took the lead this time.

"Well, thank you very much for your time Miss. James," he said, shaking my hand. "We endeavour to make our final decision in the next two days as we would really like to have the new nurse start as soon as possible, dependent obviously on how much notice needs to be given at their current job."

Geez, he's not giving much away...time for the big guns.

"Thank you Dr. Abbott," I said, "it was an absolute pleasure meeting you all. You have a wonderful atmosphere here and I have enjoyed the opportunity to even be considered for this position."

And then I smiled the most dazzling smile I could manage and aimed it at all three of them, one by one as I shook their hands.

Come on, come on, dazzle them or it's a never ending future of Barney jokes and rubber soled shoes...do it for all the pretty dresses I could be wearing to work. YES! Three smiles in return. And remember to smile at the receptionists as you leave, they could put their two cents in too.

And it's over. Big sigh of relief. Outside in the fresh air again - any longer in there and I would have ended up with sweaty pits to share with the interviewing panel. How not to get a job #1: sweaty pits in a job interview.

Bloody hell - I hope I had nothing stuck in my teeth!!

I threw my bag in the passenger side of my red Mazda (because sexy bitches drive red cars you know) and wondered what I should do for the rest of the day. I really should go to the gym - mind you I think I have sweated enough already today.

Maybe I'll just get a pie for lunch on the way home and then decide. *Mmmmm pie...*yep totally deserve it. Actually I think after that effort I deserve a sausage roll too. Awesome plan.

I started the car (or Henrietta as she is affectionately known) and the radio came on. YESSSS could the day get any better?! Britney on the radio...delicious pastry treats on the menu...man all I need is a magic bedroom-cleaning fairy and it would be perfect!

Meh. The bedroom can wait 'til another day, I thought as I turned Britney up loud and got my groove on, Henrietta styles.

~~~~~~~~~~~~~~~~~~~~~~~~~

"Hey chick are you home?" I yelled out as I walked in the house. Last thing I needed was to walk in on my flatmate Jess and her boyfriend going at it like rabbits on the kitchen table like I did a couple of weeks ago (not that I have ever seen rabbits having sex but can only imagine it was similar).

Haha, that table has seen so much action over the last couple of years – it's such a good height. Eww, now that I think about that, I don't think I want to take it if I move out.

"In the kitchen!" Jess called back. I assumed that meant she wasn't half naked with a big hairy man with a lily white ass on top of her (*God did you really need to remind yourself of that mental picture?!*) so I walked in. Immediately I was greeted - and not in a good way - with a revolting smell wafting out of the oven.

"Ummmm, what are you cooking?" I asked politely, trying not to screw my face up in disgust.

"Lunch! Homemade mini pizzas," she said, noticing the bakery bags in my hands, "but I see you're sorted already so it's all good."

"Yeah I got you a pie too," I said as she pulled her 'creation' out of the oven. I had to restrain myself from laughing and/or vomiting as I saw that the homemade pizzas were topped with tinned spaghetti, tinned salmon, jalapeno peppers and something orange and unidentifiable.

Oh god did she massacre a pumpkin in the making of that pizza??

"Oh thanks Goose, but I thought I would try something new," as she took a bite out of one of the pizzas. Her eyes widened, tears formed and her face went bright red at which point she forced herself to swallow.

"On second thoughts, steak and cheese I hope??" she asked and took the bakery bag I offered to her. "How was the interview? Did you dazzle them?"

"Can't talk. Eating pie." I replied with my mouth full of flaky pastry, meat and cheese - aka my own personal heaven.

After inhaling the pie (oh ok, and the sausage roll) I said "It was pretty good I think. The manager had horrific eyebrows and all I wanted to do was tell her it's not alright to walk around with a caterpillar on her face and the head GP was a bit old and proper but they seem ok. Oh, and I accidentally quoted the Cheers theme song but apart from that it wasn't too bad. They said they will be making a decision in the next couple of days."

"I'm sure you caned it, they would be silly to say no to you," Jess said (being an eternal optimist surely makes up for her complete lack of cooking skills?) "and besides, I'm sure they will think you are too young to remember Cheers so will totally think it was a random coincidence."

"Hmm good call. There probably aren't too many 26 year olds that love old school TV. Ahh MacGyver...Magnum PI...now they are real men. Dig the mo."

"Yes you are a special case...some even call you a freak. Oh oops I wasn't supposed to tell you that," Jess put her hand over her mouth and faked embarrassment.

"Shut up bi-arch. Go back to work you lazy tart," I laughed and threw my rubbish at her.

"Ugh don't remind me it's my last day off. Gutted much." Jess worked as a primary school teacher so had to deal with whiny, feral children all day – worst job *ever* in my opinion. Oh wait, I have to give wrinkly old people sponge baths on a regular basis. Hmm, didn't think that one through.

"I have to admit I'm devastated that the holidays are almost over," I said with a sad face, "I mean, who is going to make me delicious lunches every day?!"

I laughed as she pulled a face and said "Smart ass. You'll keep!"

"Is Ross the rooter coming round tonight?" I asked. "The poor bugger hasn't looked me in the eye since I walked in on you two!"

Jess laughed. "I know he's soooo embarrassed! I told him to get over it, I'm sure he will eventually."

"Tell him if it will make him feel better next time I get a shag I'll let him walk in on us to make it even stevens. Mind you the rate I'm going that could be long time coming. No pun intended - haha."

"Awwww poor Goosey, have you revirginated?! Actually yeah - it has been awhile aye? Who was the last one? Rob the Builder??"

"Shit, revirginated and then some. Think it's closed over!!"

Ahhh, Rob the Builder. Way too much of a mama's boy that one - I wasted a whole year before realising that his shit-stirring, Tupperware-selling, bitch of a mother would never allow her 28 year old son to actually live his own life and that he would never grow any balls to stand up to her anyway.

Such a shame cause he had such nice teeth. Ohhh and his forearms...so toned and brown....stop it! The guy was a dick...mmmm his di-

"Oi Goose! Are you listening to me?!" I snapped out of my completely inappropriate thoughts to rejoin the conversation. "I was just saying Ross isn't coming over tonight so I'm gonna go get a DVD to watch later, I think the new Reese Witherspoon one is out. You keen?"

"Sounds like a plan stan. On one condition though," I said.

"What's that?" she asked.

"That I'm cooking dinner!"

May

Where the hell is that music coming from?? Damn it that dream was just getting good! Oh crap I changed my ring tone yesterday. Where is my bloody phone?! I fumbled around and found it in the last place I looked, on my bedside cabinet. Duh. Missed it.

Damn it, woken up for nothing. I looked at the clock. 7:32am.

7:32?! Who the hell is ringing this early??

Just then it started again:

*"Don't cha wish your girlfriend was hot like me?
Don't cha wish your girlfriend was a freak like me?
Don't cha?
Don't cha?
Don't cha wish your girlfriend was raw like me?
Don't cha wish your girlfriend was fun like me?
Don't cha?
Don't cha?"*

I LOVE this song! Oops suppose I better answer it.

"Hello?" I croaked.

"GOOSE!!!" I recognised my friend Dee's exuberant voice.

Far too happy for this time of the morning. Bitch must have got laid.

I looked at my cellphone again but it didn't show her name, just said 'Caller ID withheld.'

"Dee? Why's your number blocked?"

"Oh haha forgot about that! I blocked it so I could crank call Jason last night. I obviously forgot to change it back. My bad."

Jason, her ex, is learning the hard way that Dee is not a girl you cross if you want to keep your balls intact. Silly bastard.

Dee's full name is Indiana Jones. No bull – we have decided that either:

a) her parents didn't like her or

b) they were on drugs when it came time to name her or

c) they wished their baby was a puppy.

Personally I think it may have been d) all of the above.

Dee is one of my best friends and is totally awesome - like doesn't shave her legs for 3 weeks then goes to the pub to take a guy home for a one night stand but doesn't give a shit what he thinks kind of awesome.

"What you doing Lucy Goose??" she asked.

I checked the clock again. 7:35. Fully awake now. *God, it's going to be a long day.*

"It's half past seven in the morning. And it's Saturday. I was sleeping. Wait, what are *you* doing awake at this hour?!?"

"Oh, I'm on my way home...had such a ripper night. Totally rooted my boss on the pool table at his house after the staff BBQ," said Dee, who was never one to shy away from an overshare.

"Which boss?? Marcus?" I said, referring to the only single guy I could think of at her work. Dee works as a PA to several lawyers at a really flash law firm in the city.

"Hmm no...Alex..." her voice trailed off.

"INDIANA JONES!! Isn't he married?! With a kid?"

"Nah. Two kids."

"Dee! Are you crazy? Where was his wife??"

"Away visiting her parents with the kids. Apparently she is a real bitch and didn't want him to have the staff party at their house so she took off for the weekend. She totally sounds like a bitch you know," Dee justified.

"Hmm of course she is. So what's the haps now then? "

"Nothing. It was just a one off thing. Too much tequila. You know what I'm like on tequila." *And vodka, and bourbon, and rum...*

"Speaking of tequila," she continued, "I've got a minger of a headache so I totally need to get to sleep." *Lucky for some.* "But see you later for dinner and a full overview of last night's events? You will *so* laugh, he was totally trying to give me anal but kept pretending it was an accident!"

God help me that is far too much information for 7:39 in the morning!

We said goodbye and I unsuccessfully tried to bury my face in the pillow and will sleep to come back to me but then some completely inconsiderate mongrel of a neighbour decided it was time to start their lawnmower.

Asshole! I groaned, rolled over and heard a pained meow as I rolled on my poor innocent cat (totally her fault for hiding under the covers though). I pulled them back to see my beautiful kitty with a rather pissed off expression on her face - getting flattened by someone twenty something times your weight would probably do that to you. Lucky I didn't kill the poor bitch really.

"Aww my baby girl... my milkshake brings all the boys to the yard,
And they're like
It's better than yours,
Damn right it's better than yours,
I can teach you,
But I have to charge," I sang to her, as I do most mornings. And afternoons. And evenings. The joys of having a cat called Milkshake. La la-la la la.

I dragged myself out of bed (climbing over the mountain of clean washing needing to be folded that seems to permanently covering one side of the bed – but hey, at least it's clean) and headed out to the kitchen to feed Milkshake.

Note to self: get a boyfriend so I have to fold the washing and put it away.

My other flatmate Andrew was already in the kitchen drinking coffee - such a shame he isn't anything to look at (although he loves to think he is). Mind you it's been so long since I've seen some action it might not be long until he starts looking attractive.

Note to self: get a boyfriend so I don't start fancying Andy.

"Morning Andy."

"Hey Goose. You're up early."

"Hmm. Dee rang to fill me in on her escapades. So are you - what are you up to?"

He laughed. "I've got to head in to work unfortunately. Have got a big presentation on Monday and I've barely started it and...blah blah blah blah blah blah blah blah..." Well this is what I heard anyway.

Andy has a very important job as a technical advisor (or something like that) to some big company who does big business deals with some big overseas companies. I smiled and nodded and pretended I understood what he was saying - or at least like I care a slight bit. Really I don't. Too many big words. I turned my back to him to spoon cat food into Milkshake's bowl so I could stifle a yawn.

Bugger it, I'm going back to bed.

~~~~~~~~~~~~~~~~~~~~~~~~~

May 27th. How did that happen? It's like the middle of the month

just disappears into some alternate universe. Like it jumps from the 1st of the month to the end of the month and feels like about 3 days.

So I have been at the new job for about about six weeks now and it's been pretty great really. *So* loving not doing shift work but it's taken me ages to get used to dragging my ass out of bed before 7am every morning as I'm used to sleep ins until at least 10am on a regular basis.

But I have to get up early to make sure I'm presentable – tame my fro, cover my bags, conceal any pimples that may have erupted overnight – people probably think I'm high maintenance. If only I could be one of those people who really doesn't care about their appearance and doesn't wear makeup or straighten their hair (or even wash it for that matter). Although, on second thoughts, I'd rather be high maintenance than be a minger...

And in positive news, Frizzy from the interview (her real name is Alice, she's the centre manager and she's only 34 – I thought she was about 40!!!!) must have been between eyebrow wax appointments when she was interviewing me cause I was so pleased to see freshly shaped eyebrows when I started there. Phew. That could have made for an uncomfortable work environment when all I wanted was to tell her that Bert from Sesame Street called because he wants his eyebrows back.

Now all I have to do is drop the benefits of GhD's into the conversation and smuggle some hair dye and makeup into her bag and I may be able to save her from an eternity of premature fugliness.

I'm not a bitch honestly, and I'm certainly not a supermodel, I just don't think there is any excuse for a woman to let herself go. I don't care if you have got a bit of extra weight on or have just had a baby and feel like a fat blob, pour yourself into some suck-in undies, take off your ugly ass trackie pants and your slippers, put some makeup on and wash your hair. But that's just my opinion. It makes me sad to see what could be a reasonably attractive woman slobbing around in trackies and baggy t-shirts with zits on her face. Cover those bitches, chuck on some jeans and a push up bra and you'll be good to go girlfriend!

And I do know what I'm talking about, I'm a fat girl trapped inside a skinny(ish) body. I don't like salad. I hate exercise more than anything else in the world. But I have to force myself to eat shrubbery and sweat like a pig at the gym to control the fatty inside who would jump out screaming like Xena Warrior Princess with a mouthful of pie if I let her.

Anyway, back to the matter at hand. I'm going to a party tonight.

My friend Emma is turning 30. Poor old bitch. I used to work with Emma at the hospital - she's a midwife so sees up women's foofoos all the time. And even worse, sees babies come out of them. The closest I've come to seeing a birth is watching a YouTube clip of it with Dee and even *that* sent me into the corner of the room rocking in the foetal position for about an hour. Maybe I will be one of those 'too posh to push' mothers when my time comes. IF my time comes that is.

Note to self: get a boyfriend so not to be a spinster with no babies and 15 cats.

Why don't I have anything to wear? I thought, pulling everything out of my wardrobe for the second time. *Where is my black dress with the white lacy bit at the bottom?* I racked my brain (didn't take long) and still couldn't think where it was. Bugger.

"Jess??" I went into the hallway and called out. "Want to come shopping??"

I caught sight of myself in the hallway mirror. These girls at school once said my hair is 'dirty blonde' in colour. I thought that was really rude so being that one considered herself 'strawberry blonde' I informed her that there is no such thing as a strawberry blonde, there are only Gingas in denial. And then the brunette other one I referred to as 'dog shit brown'. That shut them up pretty quick.

I scrutinised my reflection again and wrinkled my nose up. "And maybe a session at the gym??"

~~~~~~~~~~~~~~~~~~~~~~~

Six hours later Jess and I had completed a marathon shop in which I bought a fricking amazing little blue dress to wear to Emma's party.

Ooh, must remember to shave my underarms in the shower.

We skipped the gym workout (mainly because we ate so much Chinese at the smorgasbord for lunch that we could barely even walk around the mall let alone on a treadmill) but we discussed it at length and decided it was ok because we would make up for it and do a double workout tomorrow.

"Goose?" Jess came into my bedroom. "Are you going to have a shower so I can put the fake lashes on for you?"

"Yep getting there! I'm just texting Leo to see what time he is picking me up. Thank God he is going too, I *hate* walking into places by myself and feeling like Nigel No-mates."

"Me too. But there are going to be heaps of people from the hospital there aren't there?"

Leo is our gay friend who is a nurse in the Emergency Department at the hospital. He never fails to crack me up - he is such a total bitch. But also completely lovable at the same time.

"Yeah he is. He doesn't even like Emma that much, thinks she's a bit of an incense burning hippie. But you know what he's like, free piss and he'll be anyone's best friend!" I laughed as my phone signalled I had a text.

My phone makes the sound of Darth Vadar breathing which almost

scares the crap out of me every time it happens but I love having it for the mere fact that it scares the crap out of everybody else too.

"God I hate that!!!" Jess exclaimed after nearly falling off her perch on the end of the bed. "I'm going to steal your phone and change it when you're not looking!"

"That's nothing - you should hear it when I forget to put it on silent and it goes off at 4am in the morning. Now THAT'S what I call a skiddy undies moment," I replied with a laugh and headed off to the bathroom to have a shower.

Afterwards, I turned the shower off and stepped out only to realise that I hadn't brought a towel in with me.

Shit! And I didn't shave my pits! Back into the shower I went and finished my de-furring.

After getting out the second time and unsuccessfully calling out for Jess to bring me a towel, I decided a nuddy run to my bedroom (the furthest away from the bathroom of course) was on the cards as Jess obviously hadn't heard my SOS calls.

Don't come out of your room Andy. Don't come out of your room Andy.

I cracked the door open and could still hear Incubus playing from Andy's stereo. The coast was clear. I put one arm across my chest and one covering my lady bits and ran for it - and bowled right into Andy who was coming out of the kitchen eating a bag of chippies.

Oh my effing God. Shame....

I could feel my cheeks flaming red - the ones on my face I mean, the other ones are decidedly white (as Andy obviously just discovered).

"Shit! Sorry!!!" I yelled as I kept running to the safety of my bedroom and could hear Andy and Jess pissing themselves laughing as I slammed the door shut.

"So hot right now Goose!" I heard Jess' muffled call through the door.

A minute later there was a knock on my door and the door opened a crack (no pun intended) and Jess' hand came into sight – holding a towel. "Forget something?"

She came in a minute later, still looking like she was about to burst out laughing.

"Shame! Poor Andy!" I said, pulling my pyjama pants on.

"As if! That was the biggest thrill he has had for ages. You should have seen his face! He was speechless!"

"I aim to please," I said with a smile.

"Now lie down while I put your fake lashes on," Jess said.

"Ok...but are you sure you know what you're doing with them?"

"How hard can it be? Oh my God Goose! Your bed! You've folded all your washing and put it away! Holy shit! Is tonight going to be a big night??"

"Haha maybe...I did have my brazzy wax yesterday so it would be rude to waste it. Again." I said.

"Woo hoo – back on the horse aye. You go girl!" my own personal cheerleader chirped away.

"Sure sure. We'll see. There might not be any talent there, I might end up in bed with you!"

"Well, I'm sure after your display just before, Andy wouldn't be complaining if *he* got a midnight visitor," Jess laughed and then accidentally stabbed me in the eye with the tweezers.

~~~~~~~~~~~~~~~~~~~~~~~~~

"Oh helloooo Miss Lucy...seriously hot man checking you out at 3 o'clock...don't look! Show some restraint you desperate bitch! That's not 3 o'clock you egg that's 9 o'clock. Ooh yes he's still looking at you...cause you're looking all hot in your sexy blue dress...yeah baby somebody wants a Goose sandwich tonight..." the ever dramatic Leo announced.

I turned to the real 3 o'clock. *Oh helloooo is right. This party just got a whole heap better.*

"No visible wedding ring. No bald spot that I can see. And unfortunately not a hint of gay damn it. Would you bloody well stop playing with your eyelashes you're starting to look a bit spastic. Ooooh he's coming over," Leo said excitedly and pinched me on the ass.

How much glue did Jess put on these freaking things?! Holy shit he IS coming over.

"Helloooo, I'm Leo," Leo introduced himself with a flamboyant curtsy, "and you are?"

"Adam," the hottest guy I have ever seen in real life said. "Nice to meet you Leo."

Then "Hi," he directed at me with a dazzling smile. *Holy crap, I thought I knew how to dazzle.*

"And soooo nice to meet YOU," Leo continued. "Oh thank GOD you have those granny suck-in undies on Goose – or they would be down round your knees already!"

Oh my God. Did he honestly just say that?!

"So, Goose is it?" Adam asked inquisitively. "Granny knickers - sounds interesting. Maybe you could show me them later," he said with a wink. "Can I get you guys a drink?"

"Um, it's Lucy," I stammered and blushed in quick succession, "yes please." *Oh fuck.* "Oh, um, I mean yes to the drink that is!"

Leo just about pissed himself laughing to which I elbowed him in the side and he took that as his cue to leave. "Well I'm off to see who else is here...have fun darling..." his voice trailed off as he walked away backwards making blow job faces at me behind Adam's back.

Fuck me. He looks like a fucking model. Oh fuck. Eight months without sex and I've turned into a stammering idiot who can't have a simple conversation with a man. Not to mention the potty mouth.

Fuuuuuuuuck he really is hot though....

~~~~~~~~~~~~~~~

A few hours later, I opened the taxi door and just about assed over in the gutter. I giggled as Adam helped me right myself.

*Yep still unbelievably hot...*I determined as I looked up at his sexy green eyes. The numerous vodkas I had consumed at the bar definitely did wonders for helping me forget that while being unbelievably hot he is actually a complete dickhead.

I figured that out after the first vodka so spent the remaining 5 (or was it 6?) half listening to his inane conversation about how brilliant and awesome he is and how his boss at the advertising firm he works at thinks he is, yep you guessed it, brilliant and awesome. Instead I just imagined how amazing he would look naked on my bed.

"Have you got your key?" he asked me as I stumbled up the steps to my front door.

I giggled again as I rifled through my bag. "Yep here they are!" I exclaimed loudly. "Oops...ssshhh," I lowered my voice and whispered. "Oh shit," I giggled again when I realised I was holding a mini flashlight with a keyring on the end of it but there were no keys attached to it. "It's all good. I'll ring my flatmate she will let us in," I over-enunciated in an attempt to sound sober and completely desirable.

Just then the door opened and Jess was standing there in an oversized t-shirt (Ross the Rooter's I'm guessing).

"JESS!! I was just going to ring you! Oops. Ssssshhh, sorry."

"You left your keys on the table. All good I was awake anyway. Hellooo," she said to Adam, raising her eyebrows at me in a "Damn girl you did good" kind of way.

"Have fun..." she said and headed back to her room.

We went into mine and I turned the light on. Milkshake was stretched out on the bed and opened one eye and yawned.

"I just have to go to the bathroom, make yourself comfortable I won't be a minute," I tried to sound seductive as he lay down on the bed and started patting Milkshake.

Oh good Lord, an unbelievably sexy, insanely hot guy is lying on my bed stroking my pussy. Breathe. Remain calm.

I kicked off my high heels and attempted to not crash into anything in the hallway on my way to the bathroom. Once inside, I quickly and stealthily removed my suck in undies (and by quickly and stealthily I actually mean hopping on one foot and crashing into the toilet while trying to forcibly extricate my stomach from the giant knickers that I *finally* got off just as I was beginning to think I may have to have them surgically removed) and then I opened the bathroom drawers to find the much sexier ones I had hidden in my drawer earlier for an emergency such as this.

I checked my face in the mirror (drag queen lashes still adhered and makeup still acceptable, excellent) pushed up my C cups in my push up bra, shut the drawers and pulled my dress back down, praying he wouldn't notice I was returning with a few more lumps and bumps than what I left with.

I got back to my room and flicked the light off as I entered so that he wouldn't notice that my svelte figure had been left behind in the bathroom. As my eyes adjusted to the dark I saw that he was still lying on the bed.

Here goes...back on the horse....

We didn't waste any time and started fooling around. Back on the horse was right – except he was more like a stallion - his body was so incredible and so smooth. *Hmmm I wonder if he waxes?*

Just then I felt a little poke. And when I say little poke I don't mean 'is that a banana in your pocket,' I mean 'is that a toothpick in your pants' kind of poke.

"Ooh yeah baby you love it don't you, yeah feel that rock hard steel," he grunted.

Oh. My. God. Is he actually IN?!?!

Approximately 97 seconds later he grunted again and rolled over.

Is he finished?!? Oh my god. I think he's finished!!! Surely he's going to make excuses and say he's not usually that quick.

"That was great," he said with a smug, satisfied look on his face.

What a tosser! Stallion my ass!!

I got up, hunted round in the dark for my knickers and pulled on a t-shirt then when I turned around to politely suggest I could call him a taxi I discovered the bastard was already asleep *and* on my favourite side of the bed. Grrr.

I sighed, fluffed up the pillow, lay down and Milkshake promptly jumped back on the bed with a quiet thud and promptly started purring.

Show off. Little tart got more action than I did.

I woke with a start, lifted my head off the pillow and opened one eye. *Phew, he's gone.* No uncomfortable morning after moment. The relief of an embarrassing situation being averted quickly turned to confusion when I attempted to open my other eye.

What the hell?! Oh shitballs...

I got up and rushed to the mirror to find that my left eye was glued shut from the porn star lashes Jess had put on me last night.

"Ow ow ow ow ow," I muttered as I attempted to prise my eye open slowly. Just then my bedroom door flew open, giving me a hell of a fright and in so doing, I pulled the fake lash completely off leaving a searing pain on my eyelid.

"Owwww," I cried out with my hand over my eye then noticed with my good eye that it was Adam who had burst into the room wearing nothing but a towel and with wet hair.

Geez could this day start any worse?? God damn it. How can he look so frigging amazing in a towel but be such an epic fuckwit?!

"I thought you had left." *I wish you had left.*

"I knew you would want to see me before I did," he said with a cocky smile. *Piss off!*

"I'm sure you don't mind that I used your shower, I have to go straight out to a game of golf with my boss. I'm sure he wants to talk about a promotion you know." I watched him get dressed. *Is that a tattoo of a tree on his arm?!*

A TREE?! Like, what the hell??

"Hmm great. Better not be late then." I said with as much enthusiasm as I could muster.

"Last night was great. I'll call you."

Haha asshole you don't have my number!

He looked at his watch. "Lucky you put your number in my phone last night, I've really got to run now."

Damn it. Leo was right - I am a desperate bitch!

~~~~~~~~~~~~~~~~~~~~

I waggled my little finger in response to Leo's question.

"NO WAY. Are you serious? I don't believe you! Are you lying to me? No man that sexy can have a pretzel dick. No. I just don't believe it!" He shook his head vehemently.

"Such a crack up. Tell him how long it took too!" interjected Jess as she came back into the lounge carrying chips and dip.

Leo had come over for a post-root debrief but was struggling to comprehend the fact that Adam was not actually the sex god we had both assumed he would be. He began a discussion about why I should give him another go as maybe it was a one-off poor performance and even though he was a totally up himself prick (and such a little prick at that – hahaha) he was so gorgeous it would be worth keeping him around just for eye candy for awhile.

"He might not even call me so it might not even be an issue," I interrupted his impassioned argument with a mouthful of chips.

"Shit you're all class Goose. By the way, what is wrong with your bloody eye?? You look like you've got pinkeye or something. Eww did you get his gizz in your eye?? I had that happen to me once. It was sooooo painful," Leo screwed his nose up.

I took a swig of my Coke. "No!! I can thank my tryhard lash lady over there for looking like a conjunctivitis sufferer." Then I burped. "Pardon me."

"I pity the fool who marries you someday you filthy tart."

"Sweet. I guess that means I can take you off my bridesmaid list then," I smiled at him sweetly.

"Oh let's not make hasty decisions darling. Your complete lack of class can be quite endearing sometimes."

I burped again. "You know it biarch. Be nice to me or I'll make you wear orange!"

Just then Andy walked in, holding something up gingerly with two fingers and asked "Umm, who put these enormous undies in my bathroom drawer?"

Oh the shame...

June

As it turned out, Adam did ring. Two days after our earth shattering sexual encounter (yeah right) he rang wanting to catch up for a drink on the upcoming Friday night. I weighed up the options - and as the only other choices for that evening were going to be cleaning my room or hanging out with Jess while she babysat her niece – I decided to give him another go.

He picked me up in his massive shiny black penis mobile – oops, I mean 4WD truck, and we went to a bar for a couple of drinks. After the second one I realised that if I continued to see him I would have to become a borderline alcoholic as nothing short of excessive amounts of alcohol could make his obnoxious personality bearable.

Mind you I have to admit I did love the attention I got from other girls who were obviously totally jealous that I was there with such a hot ass guy. It did cross my mind that they were possibly wondering what such a sexy guy was doing with someone not nearly as attractive as him but, whatever the reason, I decided to take one for the team and started knocking back the drinks.

By the time we made it back to his apartment I had gone to my Vodka induced happy place and we barely made it up the stairs before I jumped him. Totally loved the fact that he lifted me up with my legs around his waist and carried me to the bed though (have seen that in movies before and always wanted to do that – SO HOT!!!)

And then so not. Quick as a flash it was over. Again.

At least he was happy with himself - can a man really be that selfish that he doesn't care about a woman's needs?! In fact, I think he may have set a new record and, for his effort (or rather, lack of) we have nicknamed him the One Minute Man and for any future references he shall be called this.

I have since deflected his numerous advances (ok, two texts) and I figure since I haven't heard from him in the last two weeks that he and the stupid tree on his arm have moved on to greener pastures.

Oh well, at least I didn't waste my Brazilian wax this time. My beautician will be pleased when I tell her – actually to be honest she probably won't give a shit, but I pay her so she will no doubt pretend she does.

~~~~~~~~~~~~~~~

"Ros bro cup wi me," I heard the sobbing voice on the end of the phone say.

"What? Jess? What's wrong?" I asked her, trying to decipher what she was saying.

"ROSS BRO CUP WIT ME!" she hiccupped through her tears.

Oh shit. Ross broke up with her?

"Oh no Jess. I'm on my way home I'll be there soon ok??"

All I heard in response was a hiccup and a sob. I hung up and quickly added two blocks of Caramello chocolate and a 2 litre tub of Cookies and Cream ice cream into my trolley (Jess is an emotional eater just like me) then did a rally car drive to the checkout.

On my drive home from the supermarket all I could think was how I didn't see this coming. *Not as much as Jess I bet though. Oh my poor chicken.*

Jess and Ross were honestly such a cute couple – not like nauseatingly cute and all over each other all the time but just so well suited, like really considerate of each other and seemed to just fit. I honestly thought they would get married and have babies and I would get to be bridesmaid and be Aunty Goose to all their kids.

Oh man, if they can't make it then what hope in hell do I have to get into a lasting relationship?? Oh my God I'm such a bitch. I can't believe I'm thinking about myself right now...

I pulled into our driveway and turned Henrietta off, grabbing the bag with the chocolate and other break up necessities in it. I found Jess in her bedroom sobbing into her pillow. She sat up when I opened the door and I saw her mascara and tear stained face and my heart broke a little bit. There is nothing worse than seeing a friend in pain and knowing there is nothing you can do to make it better.

As we ate our way through both blocks of chocolate and half the tub of ice cream she managed to calm down enough to tell me that Ross had been acting funny for a couple of weeks but she didn't think much of it as he had been quite stressed at work lately. But then they had been out for lunch with his family for his Nana's 80th and everything had been fine – until they got home and he dropped his bombshell on her.

Basically he told her that he wasn't ready to settle down, didn't want to get married or have kids (I totally got that wrong!!) and didn't even want to move in with her. Pretty rough after almost 2 years together.

"I don't get it. I wasn't even putting the pressure on him for any of that. Well I don't think I was anyway," she said dejectedly.

"You probably weren't but maybe he thought you would have expectations for what the next steps would be seeing as you have been together for awhile now. Maybe he's having a turning 30 crisis?"

"Or maybe he's met someone else!! One of those sluts from his work I bet!" she burst into tears again.

Bugger, of all the times to run out of chocolate!

I comforted her to the best of my abilities for the next few hours (had to have a quick mission out to get McDonalds – nothing like a large Big Mac combo and an apple pie to cheer a girl up) and by about 11pm that night she fell asleep out of pure emotional exhaustion. I tucked her in, watched her sleep peacefully until I realised I was being a bit of a Single White Female, and then went into my bedroom to get into my pyjamas.

I picked up my cellphone to text Leo to fill him in on the dramas and there was a text from my brother Matt asking if I could pick him up on my way to lunch at our parents house tomorrow because his car had crapped out again.

Crap! Forgot about lunch! I groaned.

I wondered if Jess' emotional crisis was a good enough reason to skip it. I then concluded my life probably wouldn't be worth living if I did as my mother already whinges and moans that she doesn't see us enough as it is, God knows I don't need to give her more ammo.

Yep pick you up at 12, k? I texted back.

Then I texted Leo and told him that Ross had broken up with Jess and she was totally gutted. Darth went off twice in quick succession. So popular haha.

Fucker! I knew he was dodgy. Anyone with a forehead that big can't be trusted! came Leo's response. God I love him.

Choice wrote my brother. A man of few words.

I left my phone in my room, brushed my teeth, grabbed my pillow and Milkshake and got into bed with her and Jess, who was still sleeping as soundly as when I left her. I figure nobody should wake up alone after they have been viciously dumped by the man of their dreams.

Ross the Rooter = Official bastard.

~~~~~~~~~~~~~~~~~

I woke up just before 9am to find Jess was already up and in the bathroom. I got up and fed Milkshake (the very reason I was awake – impatient little minx) and decided I would cook bacon and eggs for breakfast.

Ooh I think we have hash browns in the freezer. Yesss! Hellooo hash browns - come to Mummy.

While I was cooking Jess came out with red eyes, wet hair and a sheepish look on her face.

"Sorry about ruining your night last night Goose. Thanks so much for everything - I can't believe you slept in there with me too. You're just the best, honestly you really are."

I shrugged her compliment off with a smile. "Don't be a dick. You would do it for me. How are you feeling anyway?"

Just then the smoke alarm went off so we both raced around trying to turn the bloody thing off before it woke Andy.

Too late. A minute later he came into the kitchen.

"I'm guessing you're cooking bacon, Goose?" he said with a yawn.

"Bloody bacon. I don't know what it is about bacon that always sets the stupid smoke alarm off. And seriously, who puts a smoke alarm that close to the kitchen anyway?!"

"Dude, it's out in the hallway." Andy said as he helped himself to a piece of bacon. "But at least the bacon tastes good."

We sat and had breakfast (the hash browns were AMAZING) and while we ate Andy gave his opinion on the breakup. He told Jess that she was way too good for Ross and if he wasn't going to commit after that amount of time together then he never would have anyway. He also agreed with Jess' theory about Ross possibly hooking up with one of the sluts from work – as he put it, Ross is a 'chicken shit who didn't want to commit but also wouldn't want to be alone so it would make sense he would line someone else up first, especially some skank who wasn't looking for commitment.'

Wow, who knew Andy could be so insightful? AND he didn't even make her cry. Awesome!

After we had done the dishes I unsuccessfully tried to convince Jess to come with me to my parents for lunch so she didn't have to be by herself. And lunch with my family was always entertaining - at least that was a nice way of putting it. She declined the invite, saying she was fine and had heaps of marking to do for school and that I didn't need to worry about her.

I didn't push the issue and left her to it. I went and had a shower, put my makeup on and tried to mentally prepare myself for my family lunch.

My mother, Pauline, is 54 (or is she 55? No, definitely 54) and my dad Roy is 59. Mum used to be a real estate agent and Dad used to be an accountant but for the last five years they have owned dog kennels which are about 45 minutes away out in the semi wop wops. Wearing gumboots and cleaning up dog shit is not my idea of fun but I do love going and having cuddles with all the beautiful doggies when I go to visit them. Oh I do love small furry creatures.

The kennels are named 'The Doggery' which I convinced them to name it after having a lengthy discussion about why we call a place for cats a cattery, yet we call a place for dogs kennels, not the logical choice of a doggery. I even Googled it once to see if it could shed some light on the controversial subject (yes I am well aware I have no life) and even Google had no answer for me. It remains a mystery to this day.

My mum is a bit of a worrier and hates not being closer to us, but in some respects it's probably better as she would drive us crazy if she were on our doorsteps all the time. She could talk the ear off a lop-eared rabbit if given half the chance and not even pause for a breath. My dad is lovely but very shy – he is definitely more comfortable around the animals than he is around people, which I think suits Mum fine as she does more than enough talking for the two of them.

My brother Matt (or Matty J as he is also known) is three years younger than me and he is currently working as a bartender at a club in the city. He dropped out of University about two years ago and has been mucking around doing odd jobs since (he did a stint at building which is how I met Rob the Builder) and seems to be enjoying himself. I think good on him for taking some time to figure out what he wants to do with his life, he is *only* 23. But not everyone in the family feels the same as me.

Which brings me to my sister. My older sister Renee is a class A bitch. She thinks she is hot shit and better than everyone else, when really she is nothing more than a stuck up trollop with an opinion on absolutely everything – most of which she knows nothing about.

Renee is 29 and is an accountant at a firm in the city, which is where she met her fiancé David - who she quickly emasculated and has since had him trailing behind her like a sad little puppy dog. I used to feel sorry for him, but then figured if the guy has no balls to stand up to her and continues to allow himself to be treated like a doormat by my troll of a sister then he really doesn't deserve my sympathy.

She also thinks she is God's gift and that David should count his lucky stars to have someone as gorgeous as her (I guess in some ways he should, he's a Ginga, a bit on the chubs side and has bad teeth) but then she isn't exactly model material - she's got a J-Lo ass but nowhere near a J-Lo face. I can't wait for the day when they have Ginga kids with big asses and bad teeth. Actually I'm going to piss my pants laughing.

They are getting married next January - *SHIT!! I forgot I was supposed to have a list of makeup artists ready to give to her at lunch today!!* - bugger it. Now she will pick on me for being a crappy bridesmaid.

As if I even want to be her bridesmaid. I can't think of anything worse actually. I wanted to turn her down but Mum said I just had to suck it up (well not in those words exactly) and do it as it was nice to be asked.

Nice to be asked?! Piss off, the witch pretty much demanded that I would be and made out like it was some big honour. Matt and I still reckon it was because she doesn't have enough friends to make up numbers as David is having his three brothers as groomsmen.

Bet that will be a gingtastic wedding party. Haha.

Shitballs it's quarter to twelve! Better not add being late and keeping the Troll Queen waiting to my list of sins. I grabbed my purse and my keys, went and checked on Jess - who wasn't doing her marking but was instead watching Days of Our Lives.

Oh crap she really is in a bad way!

After I picked Matt up we made our way out to Mum and Dad's — first stopping at the shops cause Matt desperately needed a Red Bull as he had been working until about 3am and by the looks of him, had partaken in a few staff drinks afterwards too. On our way we discussed who we thought would bear the brunt of Renee's bitchiness today (usually she picked on only one person at a time – far too much effort to be a total cow to everyone in one go apparently).

I voted for myself as I had forgotten to get the makeup lady details and that would surely be worth a few personal attacks. Matt reckoned it would be him because he looks like shit and it's fairly obvious he's only had about 3 hours sleep so no doubt that will give her heaps of reason to hassle his job choice/immaturity/general appearance.

When we got there we noticed Renee and David's black Lexus was already parked in the parking area and Dad was coming back from the kennels in his gumboots. I could hear the barking from the various dogs that were staying and figured he must have just locked them back in after their exercise time. Am totally going to have to have some doggy cuddles before we leave – will help calm me down after having to endure the afternoon with my witch of a sister.

Here we go...

"Hi Dad!" we made it over to the back door where he was about to take his gumboots off.

He gave us a hug each. "Hi Goose how are you sweetheart? Hi Matty how are you bud?"

We went inside and I could immediately smell lunch.

Mmmmmm roast beef. Yummo.

"Hi Mum!"

She turned around and came rushing over like a mother hen.

"Hello darling! How are you my little Lucy Goose? Oh honey you look a bit pale. Have you had your iron levels checked lately? Roy, doesn't she look a bit pale?" Dad shrugged.

"Maybe it's just because you are wearing black, don't you have some lovely coloured tops you could wear instead of black? It just makes you look a bit tired. Are you eating properly?" she continued.

"I'm fine Mum, honestly." I don't think she even waited to hear my response as she had already turned her attention to Matt.

"Matthew Alan James. Don't you know how to pick up a phone to call your mother? I get so worried about you kids when I don't hear from you. Just wait until you lot have kids of your own then you will know how it feels to be a poor old parent who gives up their life for their kids only to be forgotten about when they grow up- "

She was interrupted by Renee. "Well maybe if Matt actually DID something with his life rather than just being a bum he might have some news to share every now and then. I hope when *we* have kids they don't look up to *you* as a role model that's for sure."

Troll!! I pity your unborn ginger children!!

Two minutes in and she's already started. That seriously could be a new record as we didn't even get an unenthusiastic greeting before she started in on him this time.

"I have a job Renee. Just cause I'm not doing something as totally boring and mind numbing as you doesn't mean I don't have a life."

Wow, he restrained himself. Go Matty J!

"What, pouring drinks at a pub?? Oh WOW, how stimulating that must be. Actually, I can see how great it is by looking at you – you look like shit. Did you even have a shower this morning??"

"Cut it out Renee. At least he has a job. He's got heaps of time to figure out what he wants to do," I interjected as I could see Matt probably wouldn't restrain himself much longer and I could smell the roast potatoes beckoning me.

"Whatever Lucy. You know it's a shit job. And what about *you* – can't you get a boyfriend?? At your age David and I were already living together!"

"Now kids that's enough. Lunch is ready, let's all just calm down and have a nice civilised lunch, can we?" Mum interrupted cheerfully. Mum doesn't like confrontation so tends to ignore it and change the subject quite frequently.

One thing I have learnt from my family is God help me I will *never* have more than two children. I hate being the middle child as I always feel like I need to stand up for Matt seeing as he is the baby and am always looked down upon by Renee. Not only that, three is an odd number and I just don't like odd numbers – and three or more kids would mean I'd have to drive a people mover mini van and that is never going to happen. I would rather eat one of my young than drive a Mum bus.

I often wonder what growing up would have been like if there were only two of us (as in me and Matt – Renee could have been the retarded sperm that swam the wrong way) or even four, cause then me and Matt could have had another ally in our fight against our evil big sister. Ugh, unless we ended up with another one like her.

Fuck that. I'm having two kids.

We all sullenly filed into the dining room, following Mum who was jabbering on about the neighbour down the road who had given her a new recipe for the Lime and coconut tart she had made for pudding.

Mmmm lime tart...

Renee actually handled the fact that I had forgotten to do my wedding research quite well, she retorted with "I figured as much, lucky my other bridesmaids are on top of it" and informed me that I would need to be available for a dress fitting in three weeks time and it was most likely going to cost me around $300 to have the dress made. I just about choked on the roast beef I was shovelling into my mouth at the time until Mum announced loudly that she and Dad would be paying for not only my dress and Matt's suit, but Renee's dress as well. They are going to have to pick up a *lot* of dog shit to pay for all of that - one thing my sister doesn't have is inexpensive taste.

I smiled at the mental image of the witch in her wedding dress falling over in a pile of dog shit.

"Lucy, are you even listening??" she interrupted the particularly pleasant thought with a scowl.

"Uh yep of course," I lied and I heard Matt snort across the table so I flicked him a death stare. "So, where were we?"

~~~~~~~~~~~~~~

Two hours later I had had quite enough of listening to Mum and Renee discuss wedding plans and Renee bitching about her friend Amy, who was going to be one of her bridesmaids until she had the complete *nerve* to get pregnant and be due around the same time as the wedding (what a clever bitch! So should have thought of that!) which meant Renee then had to ask her other friend Jody to be the third bridesmaid, which she didn't want to do cause Jody is "fat and might ruin her wedding pictures if she doesn't lose weight in time."

She is such a treasure my sister. In fact, I'd love to know where she buys her mirrors cause has she not seen her giant whoop ass lately??

Before we left, Matt and I went and saw all the dogs and I had cuddles with a few of them (Milkshake was not going to be happy that I cheated on her) and Matt had to stop me from attempting to take a Labrador home - then I had to stop him from putting dog shit under Renee's car door handles.

I really hate being a grown up sometimes.

July

"Hi Helen, my name is Lucy and I will be doing your smear test today," I smiled at the girl that was waiting in the treatment room.

"If you would like to go behind the curtain, remove your underwear and make yourself comfortable on the bed with the towel over you that would be great and I will pop back in a minute to get started."

I left the room and waited a minute or so then knocked on the door.

"Come in," I heard her call out.

"Awesome. I'm just going to get a couple of things ready. Are you having a good day so far?" I asked her. She looked about my age, was quite pretty really.

"Yeah, it's been nice. Just spent the morning with my boyfriend."

God help me she better have had a shower if she just had a root...

"Have you had a smear test before Helen?" I asked her politely.

"Yes a few times," she replied from her position on the bed.

"Great, so you know what to expect?" I asked as I put gloves on and unwrapped a speculum.

"Yeah I guess so it's never fun aye."

"That's true but definitely worth doing. If I can just get you to spread your legs and put your feet together that will be great.

I will slowly insert the speculum, just let me know if it's uncomfortable or painful, ok?"

HOLY MOTHER OF GOD!!!!!!!!!!!!!

As she chatted away about the weather, I couldn't help but be completely distracted by the vast, unruly forest of pubes I was faced with. Thankfully she was lying down and couldn't see the look on my face, which was probably something between sheer terror and complete amazement that a girl of her age could have something as frightening as that contained in her knickers.

What does she think this is? The 70s?!

Oh my god she has a BOYFRIEND!! How the hell does he find that shit attractive?? Ewwwww and what if he went down on her – all he would get is a mouthful of bush! Eww eww eww!

Should I say something? No of course not.

 I looked again.

Oh man maybe I should. Imagine if she gets pregnant, there is no way a poor baby could fight its way out of there. Think of the poor babies.

No! Stop looking! Talk to her. Turn away Lucy. TURN AWAY.

"All done Helen. You can put your pants back on."

PLEASE PLEASE PLEASE put your pants back on!

"And if you just pull back the curtain when you're dressed, I'll just be cleaning up over here."

"Cool thanks! I hardly felt that at all." she replied.

I'm not surprised! Get a wax get a wax get a wax!

When she pulled back the curtains I thanked her and let her know we would notify her of the results, all the while finding it hard to look her in the eye.

She left the treatment room to head out to reception and I tried to mentally erase the all too vivid picture of her mammoth muff from my brain.

Two of my workmates, Laura and Chelsea, walked in. "What's up Goose?" Chelsea said with a smirk.

"Oh dear God, you won't believe what I just saw. I think I'm scarred for life."

They burst out laughing. "Why do you think we booked her in with *you* today??"

Laura looped her arm in mine. "Come and have some lunch Goose. I promise the image will fade – in about two years when it's time for her next one!!"

~~~~~~~~~~~~~~~

After lunch I had to give some vaccinations for a set of twins (stuff that – one baby would be hard enough I reckon) and a 15 month old little boy who I swear looked exactly like Fonzie out of Happy Days. The teenage mother of the kid just stared at me blankly when I commented on the likeness.

I went out to the reception after checking the Fonz's injection site and Chelsea was at the front desk signing the form for the courier who was picking up the blood tests.

"Hi," the courier smiled at me when I walked over.

"Hello," I smiled back. "Ow! What was that for?" I said as Chelsea elbowed me in the side.

"Oh nothing LUCY. Thanks for that NICK, we *will* see you tomorrow, won't we?" she said to him.

"Sure will," he said with a grin. "Have a nice afternoon ladies." He smiled again and walked out.

"Ooooooh!! He likes you!" Chelsea sing songed.

"Who? The courier?" I asked, confused. I had never seen him before today.

"NICK. And he's not a courier, he's a lab tech. He totally fancies you!"

"Sorry to burst your bubble Chels, but I don't think so. I'm not quite amazing enough to have had him at hello."

Chelsea is one of the receptionists at work. She's 30, engaged and loves the idea of being a matchmaker – and unfortunately I'm the only single female at work so she has given herself the mission of finding me a husband.

"Haven't you seen him come in every day this week? The lab doesn't have a courier at the mo so he has been picking up the bloods. He's seen you and he liiiiikeeees you....he always looks around to see if you're here. He's 28 and single. He's quite hot aye?" she continued.

"Sure sure, whatever you say," I brushed her off but had to admit her comments cheered me up a bit, despite whether they were true or not.

At about ten past five, Laura (who's a nurse too) and I left and I dropped her home on my way. Laura is 33, married and she and her husband Jeremy are desperately trying for a baby. She is such a lovely person and she would do anything for anyone (one of those selfless bitches that put the rest of us to shame).

I know she is getting anxious about not getting pregnant as they have been trying for over a year - but she doesn't really say much as she hates burdening people with her problems. She is always more inclined to listen to people's problems rather than broadcast her own.

Unlike Chelsea, who will tell her problems - which are often no more earth shattering than the fact that her fiancé doesn't put the seat down after he pees - to anyone that will listen.

After I dropped Laura home I drove to the gym to meet Jess for a workout - to be honest getting changed into my gym gear was quite enough workout for me - but I struggled through 30 minutes of cardio, looking at the timer on the cross trainer every five minutes and being disappointed every time to find that actually only 37 seconds had passed each time I looked. Gutted.

I went over to where Jess was literally pounding the crap out of a boxing bag, sweat pouring off her with a determined look on her face.

"Geez girlfriend, go hard! Did someone piss you off at school today??"

"No. Ross. Rang. Me. Before." She managed to get out between puffs.

"No shit! What did he want?" I sat down on a weights bench and watched her pulverise the bag.

"Stupid. Fucking. Prick." She stopped boxing and wiped her face with a towel. "He told me he is seeing someone new. Thought he should tell me in case I found out from someone else."

I looked at her face. She didn't look like she was going to cry. In fact, she looked like a pitbull with anger management issues.

"What a saint," I snorted. "How do you feel about that?" I asked, a teensy bit nervous of what her reaction might be.

She took off the boxing gloves and wiped her face again. "I actually don't care. The stupid bitch can have the hairy asshole. You know what? I've realised I can do so much better than him. I wasted over 18 months on someone who never intended to commit to me but I kept hoping he would magically turn into the perfect man. I'm just embarrassed that I didn't see it sooner. And I'm pissed off that he sounded so smug on the phone – like he was all that cause he moved on before I did. So I told him he was a shit root. Mature aye!"

I laughed. Totally what I would have done. "That's awesome!! I'm so proud of you!"

"Let's go get some dinner," she said and grabbed her bag.

She didn't have to tell me twice, I was already halfway to the exit.

~~~~~~~~~~~~~~~~~~

I told her about Nick the lab tech at work over our Thai takeaways. I said how Chelsea reckoned he fancies me but I wasn't sure as he might have just been a friendly guy.

"Was he nice looking?" Jess asked.

"Umm, he had a nice smile. I don't know really – I didn't pay *that* much attention and he left pretty quickly. He definitely wasn't uggers though."

"Ha, I bet you will be paying more attention tomorrow! Man, Chelsea hard out wants to get you a boyfriend aye? She will have to find me one once she is finished with you!"

"Yeah she's hard out. Trouble is I'm not sure she has her standards set very high for me, I'm pretty sure she was eyeing up that smelly dude that works at the cafe near my work the other day," I screwed my nose up at the thought.

"Ha ha time will tell aye. Are we still on for dinner and drinks with Dee and Leo on Saturday?"

"Yep for sure. Dee gets back tomorrow."

Dee was away on holiday for her cousin's wedding and no doubt, Dee being Dee, she would have more than a few stories to share.

"Awesome," Jess said with a smile. "And don't forget we have got our brazzy wax appointments on Saturday morning too."

I laughed and as I did I sprayed Coke Zero out of my left nostril. "Holy shit Jess, that reminds me!!" I managed to choke. "You won't believe what I saw today!!!!"

~~~~~~~~~~~~~~~~~

The next morning I took extra time to straighten my hair (not sure why I bother really as the minute I step outside it looks like a fro) and as I applied my lipstick, I had to wonder what it is about us women that the minute we think there is a man sniffing around, we automatically put so much more effort into looking hot.

Hmmm, not too bad, I thought as I smoothed my skirt down and examined my reflection in the mirror. I grabbed my purse and keys and walked out to Henrietta, willing my hair to stay looking fabulous for awhile. It didn't hear me apparently.

When I got to work I managed to stealthily find out that Nick the lab tech came twice a day to pick up the bloods – around 11am and at about 4pm. I kept one eye on the door every time I was in reception (not at all confirming Leo's beliefs that I am a desperate bitch) and at 11:07am Nick arrived.

I played it cool with a bit of a hair flip and a smile. Chelsea didn't.

"Oh hi Nick!!! Look who's here Goose!!! You remember Nick don't you?!?" she exclaimed. "Ooh I have to go! Goose can you sign the release form for Nick please?" she smirked and scurried away to a vantage point about 15 metres away. Subtlety is not one of her strong points.

I blushed and took the clipboard from him and scrawled my signature where he pointed. He wasn't bad looking and made me a bit nervous. He had blonde hair and a really nice smile and the muscles in his forearm flexed as he took the clipboard from me.

I have no idea why forearms are so appealing to me but they are just are. And his really are quite distracting...

"So, I get the feeling that Chelsea is trying to set us up?" he remarked and nodded in her direction. She was peering at us from around the corner where the filing cabinets are kept.

Oh shame! I felt my face turn beetroot red instantly.

"Ummmm," I stammered, trying to think of some reason to give that wouldn't make me look like the single, desperate bitch everyone already thinks I am.

He laughed. "So do you want to go out for a drink sometime? You know it would be rude to say no after all the trouble Chelsea has gone to."

I nodded and said "Uh huh."

Uh huh?!? Frigging awesome. He probably thinks Chelsea is trying to get her retarded friend a date and he feels sorry for me.

He smiled again. "So...are you going to give me your number?"

"Uh huh." *What the hell is that my new favourite word or something?!*

I quickly wrote down my cellphone number on a Post it I found on the desk and gave it to him. I did manage to smile at him (possibly looked a bit retarded when I did though) and he folded it and popped it in the pocket of his shirt. Showing off his forearms quite nicely as he did I might add.

"I'll call you for that drink," he said. He called out "Bye Chelsea," then winked at me and left.

I exhaled and felt my face returning to its normal shade as Chelsea came bounding back.

"Ooooooooh Goose has got a date! Goose has got a date!"

"Shut up! Oh my God that was embarrassing. I bet he won't ring he probably thinks I'm a mutant now."

"Whatever. Far out I'm such a good matchmaker. Maybe I should start a matchmaking service – think of all the desperate and lonely people I could help!" she exclaimed.

"Hey! I'm not desperate and lonely!" *Much...*

"Oh ha ha. OF COURSE I didn't mean YOU Goose!" she said, laughing it off.

Lying is not one of her strong points either apparently...

~~~~~~~~~~~~~~~~~~~~

The next night Jess and I made our way into Tequila Mockingbird, our favourite pub, where we were meeting Leo and Dee for dinner and drinks. It's not the flashest of places but I *love* the name and the logo is a drunk cartoon bird - and there is nothing funnier than a drunk cartoon animal.

Except maybe my bitch of a sister falling in a pile of dog shit in her wedding dress (still holding out hope).

At Tequila Mockingbird they do some seriously kick ass food and we all know that's the most important thing to me – in fact Jess and I had already discussed the Cookies and Cream cheesecake they have on the dessert menu and I was almost salivating at the mere thought of it.

Leo and Dee hadn't arrived yet so we got a table and ordered drinks. I had offered to be sober driver for the night, mainly cause Jess often does and I thought it was about time that she had a good night out without being Mother Hen to the rest of us.

Just realised that must make me Mother Goose tonight. Man I quack myself up.

That and my period had started that afternoon (oh the joys of being a woman) and I don't know if you have ever tried to change a tampon in a pub toilet when you've consumed copious amounts of alcohol but let me tell you, it's far from a pretty sight.

My Coke Zero came, along with Jess' Margarita (it would be rude not to in a place with Tequila in the title really) and we started people watching. Fairly soon after Dee and Leo arrived in their usual hurricane styles.

"Oh Goose darling, your tits look fabulous," Leo said but then sympathetically patted my stomach, "but I think you need to stop feeding your food baby now."

"Shut up! I've got my period so I'm just bloated. You try bleeding like a stuck pig for several days and see how sexy you look."

He grimaced. "Thanks *sooo* much for that mental picture. Eww if I wasn't already gay you would have singlehandedly just turned me - oooh there's the waitress. I need some alcohol!!"

After their drinks came, we ordered garlic bread for starters (it would go against my morals to starve any kind of baby, even a food one) and Dee started telling us about her trip.

When Dee talks, people listen. She is absolutely stunning – she has got long dark hair and big chocolate brown eyes with these amazing long lashes and she is one of those naturally thin people I hate.

We had an in depth discussion one night about who would play us in a movie about our lives (stuff world politics when there is important shit like that to discuss) and we decided on Mila Kunis for Dee. Mine would be either Reese Witherspoon or Anna Faris (am totally ok with both those options) and Jess' would be Natalie Portman after she's eaten a few pies.

Leo decided Jake Gyllenhaal would be perfect to play him but we outvoted him because there was no physical resemblance to base that on, it was only because he thinks Jake Gyllenhaal is totally sexy. We thought the dude that plays Harry Potter would be perfect - he didn't speak to us for about an hour after we told him that.

"So there I am on a three hour flight home holding in a ripper fart the whole way. I finally get off the plane so as soon as I made it to the baggage claim area I let it rip," Dee paused while the waitress put the garlic bread down on the table.

"Then next thing I know this fucking beagle makes a beeline for me and starts sniffing around me hard out, it was practically slobbering all over me it was so excited. The customs guy or whatever he is that was with the dog was all like "I'm sorry miss but you must have food or something in your bags for him to have had that reaction, I need to check your bags please," so he did, and the whole time this dog is still trying to mount me with excitement."

We all listened while we ate the garlic bread. *Mmmmm garlic butter I love you.*

Dee continued. "So in the end I had enough and I said to the guy, "for God's sake there is no food in my bag, I just snuck over here so I could do a bloody fart in private!" and he started pissing himself laughing. FYI he asked me out and we're going out next Friday night!"

We all laughed – only Dee could admit to a guy she had farted in public and then get asked out. She truly is one of a kind.

We ordered our mains and I decided to go with the BBQ spare ribs that are one of Tequila Mockingbird's specialities. Totally unclassy to eat but I figured since I was already looking like a bloated minger I might as well act like one too. There is nothing quite like wearing a bib in public.

Jess brought up the topic of Nick the lab tech so I had to fill the others in on that whole saga and admit that I hadn't heard from him yet.

"I'm not surprised darling. He probably thinks you're a helmet wearing window licker after his last encounter with you," Leo said matter-of-factly.

"A *WHAT*??" the three of us exclaimed.

"Oh my god you three are hopeless. A helmet wearing window licker. A retard. Google it – in fact you will probably find a picture of you Goose," he laughed.

I started laughing so hard I had tears streaming down my face. "That is the funniest thing I have ever heard! Window licker!"

I tried to calm myself down but every time I did I had a mental picture of someone wearing a helmet trying to lick a window and it started me off again. Finally, with mascara streaks running down my face (so much for it being waterproof, bloody liars) I managed to stop laughing uncontrollably just as the waitress brought the food over.

She looked at me like I was, well, a helmet wearing window licker (oh how I love it!!!) and I might have taken offence had it not been for the MASSIVE plate of BBQ ribs she put down in front of me.

"Damn girl, you'll have food *triplets* after all that!!" exclaimed Leo.

~~~~~~~~~~~~~~~~~~~~~~~~

Later, after I had finished my stack of ribs and removed my bib (Leo actually referred to me as a 'savage beast' while I was eating – who needs enemies with friends like him really) I heard someone say "Hi Goose."

We all looked up to where none other than Rob the Builder had stopped next to our table.

Oh shit oh shit oh shit. Did I wipe all the BBQ sauce off my face? Is there anything stuck in my teeth??

"Oh my god, Rob! Hi!" I stood up as if I was going to hug him then realised I didn't know if that was appropriate or not so did an awkward foot hop from side to side.

"Hey Goose looking good!" said Dan, one of Rob's mates who was standing behind him.

"Hey Dee how YOU doing?" Dan did a Joey Tribbiani head nod to Dee. She 'accidentally' rooted him about a year and a half ago during a drunken evening and ever since he has thought he was in with a chance.

"Fine thanks," she said with a disinterested sigh.

"Hey Dan, thanks. You too," I said to him as Rob and I just stared at each other. "What are you guys up to tonight?"

Oh good God. His forearms. Don't look at his forearms.

I looked at his perfectly toned, tanned forearms.

Shit! Ok, don't blush. Don't blush.

I blushed.

"It's Dean's stag do tonight so we just had dinner and we're going out for a few drinks and things."

SHIT!! Where was he sitting? Did he see me obliterate the plate of ribs before?!

"I heard you changed jobs, that's awesome - no more Barney uniform aye?" he laughed. "Are you liking the new job?"

I laughed. "Yeah it's great. How's your family?" *How's your shit-stirring, Tupperware-selling, bitch of a mother?*

"Good! Katie is in the UK at the moment for a working holiday and I kind of doubt she will come back really," he replied.

Yeah, anything to get away from your shit-stirring, Tupperware-selling, bitch of a mother I bet!

"And I finally bought my own place so that's awesome. I move in a few weeks, it needs some renovations and stuff but obviously I can do all that over time," he continued.

"Oh wow that's so great! I'm so happy for you!"

And I actually meant it. Not only because it meant he was finally getting away from his shit-stirring, Tupperware-selling, bitch of a mother - but because he had been working so hard saving money for a deposit when we were together and I know how much he wanted to buy his own house.

We stood there smiling at each other for a bit until he gestured to his mates and said "Well, I guess I better go. It was really nice to see you."

"Yeah it was! Good luck with your move," I replied. "Have fun tonight."

"Bye guys," he said to my friends and walked over to his friends. As they left he looked back at me, grinned and did a small wave.

I sat down, where all my friends had been watching us and were now staring at me silently with their mouths half open.

"What?" I asked.

Then the silence was broken.

"What the fuck was that??" from Leo.

"Holy shit! How obvious could you guys be??" from Dee.

"Oh my God Goose!" from Jess.

"What are you guys talking about??" I responded as I quickly examined my appearance in my compact mirror.

Thank God. There was no sauce on my face or meat remnants in my teeth.

"Umm HELLO. You guys just had a moment. Like, a SERIOUS moment," Dee said.

"Shit, I thought you were about to start pashing right then," interjected Leo.

"It did look like you were both still completely into each other," Jess said gently.

"Pffft. Whatever," I waved their words away. "We just haven't seen each other in ages. It was nothing."

I blushed again, knowing full well they wouldn't believe me.

"Whatever Trevor. You still totally want to nail him you dirty little bitch," Leo exclaimed. "Mind you, I don't really blame you – he is looking GOOOOOD. Maybe all you need is a good hammering from old Rob the Builder aye Goosey?"

I just laughed it off, then proceeded in repulsing Leo by informing him I needed to change my tampon and made a rather hasty escape to the bathroom.

~~~~~~~~~~~~~~~~~~~~~~~

Ohhhhhhhh my head hurts....

I woke up to sun shining through the gap where I hadn't closed my curtains properly. I rolled over to look at the time on the clock beside my bed. 9:24am.

Ohhhhhhhh why does my head hurt so bad?? It seems rather unfair that I feel like I have a hangover yet I wasn't even drinking last night. Must have been the tequila fumes from the crapload of shots everyone else had consumed.

Haha I bet they have all got mean hangovers!

What a random night it ended up being. After the Rob the Builder incident they finally got off my back, thanks in part to a well-timed text from Nick the lab tech (woop woop I'm not a helmet wearing window licker after all!).

He asked if I was out and if I wanted to meet up for a drink – my initial response was a resounding hell no due to the fact that while my tits looked fabulous apparently, I also looked about 6 and a half months pregnant and sometime between the garlic bread and dessert *(mmmmmm cheesecake)* a rather prominent zit had erupted on my chin that even my heavy duty concealer couldn't conceal. Stealth little bastard.

BUT OF COURSE bloody Leo commandeered my phone and arranged for Nick to meet us at Tequila Mockingbird, ignoring my emphatic protests and borderline violent attempts to get my phone back.

"Ooh hi baby!" I said as Milkshake jumped up on me and smooched into my neck, purring.

"My milkshake brings all the boys to the yard, and they're like -OWWWWW!! Mongrel!!" I yelled after the little tart launched at me and sunk her teeth into my hand.

Still purring, she jumped off, her tail flicking. Little shit has totally got split personality issues.

I massaged my hand and rolled out of bed and made my way to the toilet.

There was no sign of life in the house. I figured Jess and Andy must still be asleep – we ended up picking Andy up from his work party on our way home too and he, like the rest of them, was fairly well sloshed. Thank god nobody spewed in Henrietta or that would have been my last offer to sober drive for those feral buggers.

Anyway, back to last night.

So Nick the lab tech showed up about half an hour after Leo had texted on my behalf and when he arrived I got the approving nod and nudge from both Leo and Dee and I have to admit he did look pretty good in jeans and a shirt with the sleeves rolled up.

Why does nobody wear long sleeved shirts these days? Just to torment me?!

We spent a couple of hours playing pool and it was all good. Dee found some random guys (as she does) who joined us and Jess actually really hit it off with one of them and I saw them exchange numbers at the end of the night.

Not long before we were going to leave I had excused myself to go to the toilet (to which an extremely drunk Dee yelled out "you going to change your plug Goose?!") and Nick said he would go with me and took my hand (to which an extremely drunk Leo started singing loudly "Goosey and Nick sitting in a tree K I S S I N G!").

No, my friends aren't embarrassing at all.

In the hallway outside the bathrooms he pulled me into the corner and told me how gorgeous I am (six months pregnant with a food baby AND a massive zit – shit my tits *must* have looked bloody fantastic!) and he started kissing me.

We had a full on pash session right there which is soooooo unlike me. I am not a pub pasher kind of girl, in fact I hate public displays of affection of any sort. It was a bit thrilling in a Mills and Boon kind of way but have to admit I was quite relieved that nobody chose to go to the bathroom at that particular time.

He wanted to come home with me but I was staunch and said no (partly cause I had Aunty Flow and partly cause I knew I had a week's worth of unfolded washing on my bed) and he even tried the puppy dog eyes on me.

But I remained strong and unwavering (I'm so impressive when I'm sober!) and he eventually settled for the promise of dinner on Wednesday night.

By this stage Dee had left with one of the randoms called Sam (I had taken a photo of him on my phone so I had something to show the police if she ended up murdered and buried in the forest) so Nick walked me, Leo and Jess to my car and proceeded in giving me another big pash when we got there.

Leo had a field day with that and I'm sure half the city heard him

squealing and yahooing. I was just pleased it was dark because my face had turned bright red and I couldn't get in the car fast enough.

Just then I heard the back door open and people laughing. I went out to the kitchen where both Jess and Andy were chatting and unpacking McDonalds breakfasts out of paper bags.

"Good morning!" Jess said, "we got you a McMuffin and a hash brown from Maccas."

"I love you. But how can you two be so bloody chipper after how much you drank last night? I feel like shit!"

"Harden up princess," laughed Andy.

"Yeah I reckon. Speaking of princesses, what time is your dress fitting with your sister today?" Jess asked.

FUUUUUUUCCCCKKKKKKK. Kill me now........

~~~~~~~~~~~~~~~~~

Two days later I had finally recovered from the dress fitting debacle in which my sister had managed to have a complete bitch fit at the dressmaker and make one of her bridesmaids cry all in the space of about ten minutes (she truly is quite talented).

I was gutted to find out that we would be wearing a frigging awful shade of pea green that was no doubt going to make the three of us look like blobs of snot. Not only is the colour foul but the style of dress is totally unflattering but I'm quite sure that is all be part of her master plan to make us look as ugly as possible next to her.

Sadly for her though she has obviously forgotten that, as she has got a massive whoop ass and a face like a rabid dog who has sucked about sixteen lemons in one go, I don't think she will succeed.

Nick had been texting heaps since Saturday night but the lab got a new courier so I haven't seen him since then. We arranged to catch up for dinner tomorrow night – because he lives with his sister he doesn't have a lot of privacy at his place so I offered to cook him dinner at mine.

"How about your lasagne?" asked Chelsea. "Your lasagne rocks."

We were sitting in the staffroom having lunch and discussing what I was going to cook for him.

"Nah not impressive enough. Anyone can make lasagne." (Not strictly true – Jess tried once and it was a dismal failure.)

"How about chicken fettucine?" she volunteered.

My phone started ringing and vibrating on the table. The screen read 'Caller ID withheld'.

"Don't cha wish your girlfriend was hot like me?
Don't cha wish your girlfriend was a freak like me?
Don't cha?
Don't cha?-"

"Hello?" I asked.

"Hi. Who's this?" asked a female's voice.

Ummm hello YOU are the one ringing ME...

"Lucy. Who's this?"

"I'm Nick's girlfriend. I don't know who the fuck you are LUCY but you need to fuck off and stop texting him! He would never be interested in a slut like you so give it up you stupid bitch!!"

Right...so much for living with his sister!

"Excuse me, whatever the hell your name is, but YOUR BOYFRIEND has been texting ME so he obviously likes sluts, sure explains what he sees in you anyway!" I replied angrily.

Chelsea's eyes widened and she mouthed "What the hell?"

"How dare you speak to me like that!!" the girlfriend screamed down the phone. "It's whores like you that break up happy relationships!!"

"Yeah ok, whatever champ. Maybe you need to ask Nick where he was on Saturday night and where he was planning on being tomorrow night before you start accusing ME of being a whore. He certainly didn't act like he was in a happy relationship when he was trying to get in my pants the other night!"

She started ranting again so I pushed the disconnect button on my phone and slammed it down on the table.

"Oh my God!" Chelsea exclaimed. "Nick's got a girlfriend?!?"

"What a tosser!!!!! I can't believe it!!! He told me he lives with his sister!!"

"I'm SO sorry Goose. He told me he was single when I was scoping him out for you!"

"It's fine Chels. It's not your fault. What a complete asswipe! Oh man I so have to text him!"

We spent the next couple of minutes composing the following text:

Your sister just rang. She called me a slut and a whore, not sure why?? ☹ Oh that's right, cause she's actually your GIRLFRIEND!!

About a minute later my phone started ringing. How ironic my ringtone turned out to be - I pressed the dismiss button before The Pussycat Dolls could tell me how hot I am compared to Nick's girlfriend (I may have read too much into that but I'll take it). About a minute later, Darth signalled I had a voicemail.

"Goose, can you ring me back and let me explain please? It's not what you think it is. Tamara and I have been on the rocks for ages and I really like you. I wasn't trying to be dodgy honestly. PLEASE ring me back, ok?? Otherwise I'll call again later."

I pressed repeat and handed the phone to Chelsea to listen to the message.

"Tamara?" she said. "Ugh such a skank name. What are you going to do?"

I shrugged. "Nothing. Even if he's serious and it's over between them who wants to be in a relationship with someone who has a psycho like that as an ex? She might kidnap Milkshake and boil her up!"

So I texted him back – as if I'm going to waste my free minutes on calling a cheater.

Don't bother calling again I don't want to be your slut on the side. Good luck with your nutter girlfriend I hope she doesn't axe you in your sleep.

About thirty seconds later Darth started breathing heavily again.

Please give me a chance I really like you and don't want to loose you. We could be great together!!

LOOSE me?!?!?!?!!?!

I showed it to Chelsea and she laughed. "Oh shit. He's fucked. I know how anal you are about spelling!"

I laughed. She was right though - I absolutely HATE bad spelling. I even broke up with a guy once for spelling 'grateful' wrong (he spelt it 'greatfull') and I honestly couldn't bring myself to have sex with him after that for the risk that I would get pregnant and have to have a kid to someone who I couldn't trust to help it with its spelling homework.

"I'll reply later. Or maybe I'll just *loose* his number. Haha. Shit we better get back to work," I said as I chucked my phone in my bag and threw it back in my locker and we headed back out to reception.

~~~~~~~~~~~~~~~~~

"So it was SO lucky I was staunch and didn't have sex with him the other night. I could have been the other woman!!" I told Leo, Jess and Andy later that night over the chicken curry I had cooked for dinner.

"Whatever Goose. You so would've gone there if you weren't on your rag and you know it you lying tart," Leo replied.

Jess laughed. "I believe you babe," she said to me and then she turned to the boys, shook her head and mouthed "No I don't."

"You guys are bitches. You just have no faith in me. Just wait - you'll see. I'm going to keep my undies firmly in place from now on until someone is completely worthy of getting them off," I said triumphantly.

Leo snorted. "Honey, we've all seen how big your undies are. They're going to stay firmly in place just because someone will need the jaws of life to get those bitches off!"

September

August seemed to fly by really. I didn't even go out much – there had been some bloody good TV shows on and to be honest, I'd rather sit and watch Grey's Anatomy and perve at McSteamy than search the pubs for a real one and be disappointed. Men are dicks. Even McSteamy is - but he is also unbelievably hot so he can park his slippers under my bed any day.

I even managed to force myself to go to the gym regularly (ugh) as the reminders from Renee that I better fit my bridesmaids dress or she 'will hate me forever' were coming in thick and fast. Not that I would care that much if she hated me forever, but a few hours at the gym was certainly a better option than the vengeful wrath of my sister.

I kept my undies firmly on (not that there was much demand for their removal) but Jess, on the other hand, had hooked up with Tom, the guy she met at Tequila Mockingbird, a couple of times. Even Leo had a couple of dates with a new guy he met at the hospital, Aaron. And Dee was still seeing, well, everyone.

And my birthday was looming. Normally I would have been looking forward to it but this year I just couldn't get excited. I was turning 27 which let's face it, is on the slippery slope to 30 and sadly, the pile of unfolded washing seemed to have taken up permanent residence on my bed.

A couple of my friends were even pregnant. I don't normally get clucky but I had to admit I was kind of jealous. But one of them was Laura from work (yay!) who was finally preggers so I was totally happy for her when she told me.

The other one, Sarah, I went to school with and I'm pretty sure she only got pregnant cause she wanted to stop her dropkick boyfriend from leaving her. Seriously – how could she not know that Band-Aid babies don't save relationships? Obviously she doesn't read Cosmo.

Anyway, a couple of weeks ago Andy had told me and Jess that he had been offered a job in Kuala Lumpur doing his technical advising crap to some company over there who deals a lot with the company he works with here. He decided to accept the job and he leaves in a week and a half so we now have the tedious job of finding another flatmate. Oh joy.

We decided to have a combined birthday party/going away party the following weekend and because I had to go away on a course for work and because Jess was on school holidays again, I had delegated the job of finding a flatmate to her. Sucker.

~~~~~~~~~~~~~~~~~~

One afternoon a week later, I was people watching at the airport while waiting for a flight home after my course. I had just watched a fat woman with big hair wearing a too-small turquoise tracksuit and a fanny pack (far too many things wrong with that picture!) with three hyperactive children have a complete psych out at her short, balding husband for putting her passport in the wrong pocket of their bag. I figured he was probably trying to lose her passport so he could leave her behind - I really wouldn't blame the poor bastard to be honest. Totally what Renee and David will be like in another 20 years.

I checked the time on my phone and noticed there was a text from Jess.

Grrr everyone that has looked at the flat can't move in for another 3 or 4 weeks!!! One guy can move in next week though should we just take him? I really don't want to have to cover the extra rent for 3 weeks do you?! ☹

Not really! Is he hot?! How old is he? I texted back.

28. Ummm not hot exactly but he is in the police so might have hot policemen friends!!! She replied.

Ooh I like her way of thinking...

Good call!! Yeah if you think he's ok that's sweet with me ☺

Cool...I'll invite him to the party on Saturday so we can get to know him aye?

Ooh yes. Tell him to bring some of his policeman mates too!! Ha ha ☺

For sure! Have a good flight. See you soon ☺

Good flight?? Ugh as if. I hate flying. I usually have the unfortunate luck of being seated next to people who either haven't had a shower for about three days, people who are so large they really require two seats, or people that have verbal diarrhoea and feel compelled to tell me their entire life stories.

Add that to chronic motion sickness and the completely over-the-top fear of plummeting to my death in a giant metal fireball and I think I can safely say that I will never be changing careers to become a flight attendant.

As I made my way to my seat in Row C near the front of the plane (I weighed up hitting the ground first if we crash with being able to get off the plane first if we made it safely - and getting off first won) and I was elated to see that I would be seated next to a tiny Asian lady. I smiled at her, sat down and started my pre-flight routine of checking for vomit bags and silently praying for my dear life.

"Excuse me, I'm in the window seat," I heard a man's voice say.

I looked up to find a hugely overweight man with greasy hair and sweaty pits standing over us.

Damn it. I groaned inwardly as he forced himself into the seat next to me. I closed my eyes, breathed through my mouth and tried to think about hot policemen. But all I could concentrate on was the random combination of BO, cat piss and curry from the seat next to me.

Oh bugger me where are the spew bags??

~~~~~~~~~~~~~~~~~~~~

"Looking goooood girlfriend!!" Leo came over and pinched my ass. I had to admit, the regular gym sessions I had been doing in preparation for the troll's wedding were been paying off and the low cut black dress I got on sale ($150 down to $80 - hello!) actually looked pretty decent on me. But I had to remember to stay away from the sausage rolls as I wasn't wearing any suck in undies - so there would be nothing to contain my gut if it made a spontaneous comeback.

In fact, I'd better not even *look* at the sausage rolls to be on the safe side.

I did have a bit of a fake tan botch up but I just hid the evidence by wearing knee high boots instead of the strappy heels I had planned to wear. Nobody would ever have to know that my legs were patchy and orange underneath.

"So who's the freak in the corner??" Leo asked, nodding his head towards our soon to be new flatmate Rupert.

"That would be Rupert. He answered our flatmate wanted ad and he moves in on Monday."

"Riiiiight. And did you not MEET him before you said he could move in??!"

"No, Jess did. She told me he is in the police – but what she neglected to mention was that he is in the *Community* Police, which is essentially nothing more than Neighbourhood Watch. AND of course that means he doesn't have any hot policeman friends – the only 'friend' he brought is his equally freaky brother, Kingsley."

Rupert and Kingsley had arrived at the party about 20 minutes prior, just about jumped out of their skins when we said hello to them, and then settled themselves into the corner of the lounge where they hadn't moved from since and were just staring at everyone and whispering between themselves.

At least Jess hadn't lied about him being good looking. The two of them were a bit hobbitish looking – short with big heads, beady eyes and big ears.

"But seeing as I'm not judgemental and am *such* a nice person, I will obviously give him a chance as he could be a really nice guy under the geeky exterior and poor first impression," I continued my spiel to Leo.

Far out, turning 27 is making me so mature! Or is it the wine?

"Well I'd be checking for peepholes in your wall before you get naked in your bedroom from now on Goose. Freak with a capital F." Leo shuddered and wandered off to get another drink.

"Happy birthday gorgeous!" I turned around and Dee had arrived with her latest conquest, Brett I think his name is. Or is it Brian? Not that it really matters as he probably won't be around long enough to meet him again anyway.

"Goose, this is Brent," she said.

Meh, close enough. Hmm where did I put my drink?

"And this is his friend Ben. He's just come back from London."

"Nice to meet you guys," I said to Brett, oops I mean Brent, and his friend. They smiled and Brent said "You too, happy birthday."

"Thanks! Help yourselves to drinks and stuff - everything is in the kitchen," I told them and they said thanks. I watched them as they walked off towards the kitchen.

Not bad looking, I thought. *But then I wouldn't expect any less from Dee.*

Jess brought me another drink as the doorbell rang. It was preggo Laura and Jeremy and Chelsea and her fiancé Damian. A couple of Andy's workmates arrived right after and then came some friends of mine from the hospital. I let them all in, directed them towards the food and drinks and someone turned up the music.

"I'm bringing sexy back
Them other boys don't know how to act..."

Mmmm Justin Timberlake. I want to have your babies. Oh damn. NOW where did I put my bloody drink?

~~~~~~~~~~~~~~~~~~

At about midnight the only ones left at our place were me, Jess, Leo, Aaron, Dee, Brent and Ben (who I found out is 29, was living in London for almost five years and came back about a month ago, is a graphic designer but hasn't found a job here yet so is currently living with his mother).

Andy and his workmates had gone out clubbing but Leo and Dee had decided that we were going to play drinking games. God help us all.

Ben and I had spent a lot of time talking throughout the night and I had to admit I was really attracted to him. He was a bit shorter than what I would normally go for but kind of looked like the lead singer of Simple Plan - and he had a cheeky smile that was pretty damn sexy.

And to top it off he laughed at all my jokes so obviously he has great taste - when I'm drunk I'm the funniest person in the world. In fact, I read a quote once that said 'I don't get drunk, I get awesome.' I am fairly certain it was written about me.

"Take off your fuck me boots and get comfortable Miss Lucy. You suck at drinking games so it will save someone doing it for you later!" Leo smirked.

"Fuck me boots?" Ben laughed.

"My name is Goose, not Boots. And maybe later..." I replied, fluttering my eyelashes at him.

Oh my god I'm awesome. So hot right now!

~~~~~~~~~~~~~~~~

About two hours later, after many shots had been consumed and I had been cracking jokes left right and centre and impressing everyone with my comedic wit, Jess flipped over an Ace.

"Waterfall!" Leo yelled and everyone started skulling.

Jess slammed her glass down on the table and said "God, I'm so fucked. I need to go to bed!" and stumbled off in the direction of her bedroom.

Dee said "We should get going too..." and grabbed Brent's hand and pulled him up. I giggled. The horny bitch had been practically molesting him all night I was surprised she had lasted that long.

"I'll call a taxi," said Brent. "Ben, do you want a ride? Or do you have other plans?" He smiled and looked in my direction.

I took that as my cue and sidled up to him like the sexy bitch that I am.

"You can stay here if you want," I purred seductively.

Man I'm on fire!

"Sweet," he replied and gave Brent a head nod and a one armed man hug. "Catch you tomorrow bro."

I pouted. *He could have been a bit more excited than that!*

"Lucky you had that Brazilian wax the other day aye Goosey??" Leo interrupted.

I giggled. Not even Leo could embarrass me - my alcohol induced awesomeness was just too strong. He was totally right though, luckily there was no hairy muff residing in my knickers. Money well spent.

The taxi arrived and everyone left together, leaving Ben and I standing in the lounge by ourselves.

"Sooooo, want to see my room?" I asked coyly.

He smiled his cheeky smile and replied "Lead the way."

I sashayed my hips in an attempt to make my ass look better as he followed me - not sure if he noticed though.

I managed to keep my knickers on until we got to my room but as soon as we shut the door we started fumbling with buttons and zips, clothes and shoes were flying everywhere and then it was all on like Donkey Kong.

Oh. My. God.

"Oh my god," he echoed my thoughts when we were finished. "That was awesome. We are so doing that again!"

Yesssss!! He's totally likes me!

We lay in bed talking and I found out the reason he came back from London because he split up with his girlfriend of three years. He didn't elaborate as to why they split up and I didn't want to seem like a pushy, nosy bitch so I restrained myself and didn't ask why (even though I am a pushy, nosy bitch and was *dying* to know).

After talking for ages we went for an encore root which was even better than the first. He fell asleep soon after and I snuck out to the bathroom to brush my teeth and reapply my makeup – then I lay super still while I went to sleep to make sure I would still look fab in the morning.

Best. Night. Ever.

~~~~~~~~~~~~

Three days later I picked up my cellphone and checked it for the fifth time in half an hour. Still nothing.

Damn it.

I replayed in my mind the events of the morning after the night with Ben.

When we had woken up things had been great, not uncomfortable or awkward at all. When I gave him my number he told me he had lost his cellphone and hadn't bought a new one yet but would be getting one in the next couple of days so would text me once he had. Then Brent arrived to pick him up so he kissed me and left.

Why didn't I get his home number??

I checked my phone again. Still nothing.

Is my phone working properly?!?

Jess walked in as I was prying the battery out of the back of the phone.

"I take it Ben hasn't called yet?" she asked.

"No! I don't get it. We had such a good time and I thought we got on so well!"

Just then a horrific thought entered my head. "Oh no Jess. What if he saw my orange legs in the morning?!?"

She laughed. "I'm sure you're overthinking it. Maybe he lost your number."

"Hmmmpf. Maybe I should ask Dee if he's mentioned me. That's a good idea. Do you think I should ask Dee?" I asked.

"Dee is about as subtle as a freight train. I wouldn't mention it to her unless you actually *want* her to embarrass you."

I buried my head in my hands. "Oh man I sound so desperate! What is wrong with me??"

She laughed again and patted me on the shoulder. "You're not desperate Goose, you obviously just like him. Don't worry, I'm sure he'll call you."

~~~~~~~~~~~~~~~~

Another two days later he still hadn't called (3 days + 2 days = total desperation) so I made an oh-so-casual phone call to Dee to see if she mentioned him.

"Hey Indiana Jones. How's your week been?"

"Lucy Goose! Good! Ugh actually I had a bit of a run in with one of the lawyers at work cause she told my boss that she thinks I dress too skanky at work. Stupid bitch. She's just jealous cause she's a total minger. And *as if* any of the *men* are going to complain that I dress too skanky!" she laughed. "Anyway, apart from that it's all good. How about you?"

Don't ask about Ben. Don't ask about Ben.

"Good!" is all I managed to answer. But at least I didn't ask about Ben.

"Ooh! Are you coming tomorrow night?" she asked.

"What's happening tomorrow night?" I asked, ever so casually but panicking on the inside.

"Hasn't Ben rung you??" she sounded surprised. "We're going out for drinks tomorrow night - you totally have to come! Actually bring Jess too. I think I will be outnumbered cause it's mainly guys going. Please tell me you'll come?!"

Make yourself sound popular in case it gets back to Ben...

"Oh, umm, I was going to umm..." *Shit I'm useless!* "Yeah ok then. I'll check with Jess but it should be sweet," I finished.

"Yay!" she exclaimed. "Oh shit I better go. Am at the Olds' for dinner and I snuck out for a smoke about ten minutes ago so no doubt they will be wondering where I am."

We said goodbye, hung up and I rushed off to find Jess – God help us we had a game plan to devise and less than 24 hours to do it.

~~~~~~~~~~~~~~

At about 8pm the following night Jess and I made our way to the pub that Dee told us to meet them at. I was really nervous but I got my cool, calm and collected face on and stopped to check my appearance in the shop window before we entered the pub.

Jess and I had had lengthy discussions over what I should wear and we had decided on tight-fitting jeans (had to take advantage of not having a muffin top at the moment) with a sexy halter neck top which showed off my cleavage quite nicely (Leo would be so proud).

I looked good - but then I had also looked good the previous Saturday when I'd had great conversation, heaps of laughs and amazing sex with Ben. And he still hadn't called me.

Oh crap. Maybe this was a bad idea.

"You look great babe. Let's go in," Jess had seen me scrutinising my appearance in the window.

I took a deep breath and we went in. I heard Dee shriek "Goose! Jess!" and she came bounding over and dragged us over to the table where Brent, Ben and a few of their friends were sitting around drinking and playing pool.

Play it cool Lucy...

"Hey Goose," Ben said with a cheeky smile and I blushed. "Come sit down." He gestured to the seat next to him.

The friend that was sitting there smirked and got up, leaving the seat empty.

For God's sake play it cool Lucy...

I sat down and when I did he leaned over, put his hand on my lower back and whispered in my ear "You look fucking hot tonight."

I turned about fourteen shades of red and laughed nervously. I said "Then how come you didn't call me? Don't you like me?" and instantly regretted it.

Shit! Way to play it cool!

He laughed. "I only got a new phone today and Brent told me you were coming tonight so I figured I'd see you here."

He does like me!! Yay yay yay yay!!!

"Oh sweet as. Wasn't a big deal or anything," I replied casually, with a wave of my hand and a flip of my hair to make him think he was an afterthought and I hadn't been sitting around waiting for his call like a desperate loser.

He laughed again. "Nice. Now let's get you girls some drinks!"

~~~~~~~~~~~~~~~

I managed to keep my desperation under wraps for the rest of the night – well, apart from when I grabbed his new phone and added myself as a contact and then texted myself off it so that I would have his number too. But I figured he might just think I was being helpful as it saved him from getting my number later.

It was another great night actually. I gave him space to hang with his friends yet kept myself in his eyesight most of the time (you know, to remind him how hot I am) and a few times I caught him sneaking looks at me. I charmed his friends, cracked witty jokes and was generally just the perfect girl.

I figured he would totally want me to be his girlfriend after seeing how easygoing, fun and quite simply, awesome I am.

We ended up back at my place sometime in the early hours of the morning and had another epic bedroom session. Afterwards we lay there, he had his arm around me and was stroking my arm while we talked.

"Do you want to get married and have kids someday?" I asked him.

"Yeah definitely. When you find the right person why wouldn't you want to aye?

"Uh-huh," I replied, smiling in the dark room. *Holy crap does that mean he wants to marry me and have babies? I think that's what he means!*

"Who do you think is the sexiest woman alive?" I asked.

"I don't know...maybe Anna Kournikova or Charlize Theron?" he replied.

Oh my god they are both blonde like me! Yes!

"Was your ex-girlfriend blonde?" I asked.

"Nah she wasn't actually. She was part Spanish."

Shitballs how can I compete with a frigging Eva Longoria lookalike!?

"Wow. I bet she was really pretty?" I felt my desperation returning.

Please say not as pretty as me...

"Yeah she was," he replied.

Damn it!

"But she's also a major bitch so let's not talk about her. I can think of better things to do," he continued as he rolled over and started kissing me.

Yes! He mustn't want to talk about HER cause he's falling in love with ME! Oh my God oh my God oh my God!! So happy right now!

~~~~~~~~~~~~~~~~~~

That feeling of elation didn't last long as by Wednesday I had turned back into the overthinking relentless phone checker I had been the previous week. I hadn't heard anything from Ben since he left on the Sunday morning and I had been resisting the urge to text him as I didn't want to appear too eager (or let's face it, desperate).

After work I trudged home. Milkshake gave me lots of smooches until I fed her - then she took off to find something better to do.

What a user...story of my life apparently...

I started cooking a dinner that would make any emotional eater salivate (chicken breasts stuffed with cream cheese, garlic and chives and wrapped with bacon nom nom) and not long after Jess arrived home and plonked herself down at the dining room table.

"How was your day?" she asked.

"Meh."

"Oh Goose. Have you still not heard from Ben?" she asked.

"No! I really thought he would've rung by now! He was totally giving me signals the other night. Well at least I thought he was," I said dejectedly.

"Oh babe. Why don't you just call him? You have his number don't you?" she asked.

"Yeah I guess I could but I just *really* don't want to look desperate. Do you think maybe he is a bit intimidated by me since I have a career and he hasn't found a job back here yet?" I replied. "Or maybe he likes me too much and is afraid of getting hurt again?"

"Is he your boyfriend?" piped up a male's voice.

"Holy shit Rupert! Where did you come from?" I cried after just about crapping my pants in surprise.

Far out he's a sneaky little bugger!

"Is who my boyfriend?" I asked.

"That guy you brought home the other night."

"Nah he's not," I replied.

"Oh, do you have sex with lots of guys that aren't your boyfriends?" he asked, almost innocently.

I heard Jess snort and I looked at her and had to stifle a laugh.

"Ummmm, not a lot. But yeah, sometimes I guess," I answered.

"Oh, ok then," he said and wandered off to his room.

Jess and I burst out laughing and Jess whispered, "Did he just ask if you're a slut?? Oh my God, I bet he was up at the wall with a glass listening to you have sex the other night!"

"Shut up skank! Ewwww - I am so moving my bed away from the wall later!"

"He is so weird! And I can't believe he has a single bed – I mean, what 28 year old still has a single bed?" Jess hissed.

"Well, he has *only just* moved out of his parents house and he works as a full time dish washer, he obviously hasn't had the need for a bigger bed. I'd be surprised if he has ever had a girlfriend before." I replied.

"True that!" she shuddered. "Anyway, back to Ben - I think you should text him. Suck it up girlfriend. Or you might never get to suck it again," she said and just about pissed herself laughing at her own joke.

Shit when she puts it like that...

~~~~~~~~~~~~~~~

Hey Ben it's Goose. How's your week going? ☺ I re-read the text I had sent to Ben the night before and saw nothing that screamed desperation.

So why hasn't he replied?!

I grabbed my bag out of my locker and Laura and Chelsea came into the staffroom.

"What's with the grumpy face?" asked Chelsea.

"I still haven't got a reply to my text from last night. Like seriously, what is his problem?"

"Maybe he's still hung up on his ex?" suggested Laura.

"Or maybe he's just an asshole," interjected Chelsea.

"Nah Chels, he's really cool. Funny, smart, good looking. I really think we could have something serious!"

"You mean if he *actually* replies to your message?!" chortled Chelsea. "I'm telling you Goose, you deserve better than that."

"Whatever, it's all good. I'm sure he's just busy job hunting and all

that," I replied, annoyed that Chelsea was being so negative. "Come on Laura, I'll drop you home."

~~~~~~~~~~~~~~~~~~

That night at about 7pm I *finally* got a reply to my text.

Hey Goose how's it going? Been really busy. My mum is away for a couple of nights...want to come over? ☺

I knew it! He does like me!!!

I made myself wait a torturous five minutes before I replied so he wouldn't know I had been carrying my phone around solely so I wouldn't miss his text - and I kept it simple so he wouldn't know how eager I was.

Sounds great...☺ What's your address?

I rushed off to get into the shower quickly, shaved my legs and my underarms and then put on a sexy red bra and g-string. Truth be told I hate g-strings but I wear them for effect only if I know I'm going to take them off pretty soon after. I checked my bum out in the mirror and gave my ass cheek a slap to make sure it didn't wobble like Homer Simpson on a treadmill. It didn't.

Thank you Renee for being a bitchy, demanding bridezilla!

I quickly got dressed and Darth signalled I had a text. It was from Ben, giving me directions to his mum's house.

Cool see you soon xx I sent back. I then noticed I had accidentally put kisses on the end of the text and felt instant panic.

Shit! Oh no I hope he doesn't think I am being too clingy!

I grabbed my bag and keys and headed out to Henrietta. I passed Jess on the porch, who was just getting home from Parent Teacher

Interviews.

"Whoa girlfriend! Where are you off to in such a hurry??" she asked.

"Ben texted! I'm going to his place!" I replied, breathless.

"Oh ok. Have fun. Be careful Goose," she said, with a concerned look on her face.

"I will!" I called as I pulled my car door shut and started backing out the driveway.

When I got to his house I walked up the path and saw a note stuck to the front door.

Come on in

Just in the shower ☺

I made my way inside and put my bag down in the lounge. I then walked up the hallway and heard the shower running.

The bathroom door was ajar so I knocked and poked my head through the gap.

"Ben? I'm here," I called out.

He pulled the shower curtain to one side, stuck his head out and smiled.

Ohhhhhh he's so hot.....

"I'll be out in a sec. Make yourself comfy in the lounge," he said.

"Ok," I smiled and wandered back out to the lounge and started looking at the DVDs on the bookshelf.

Effing g-string! I thought as I stuck my hand down the back of my jeans to try to dislodge it from going right up my crack and finding out what I had for breakfast.

Just as I was picking the wedgie from my ass, Ben walked in from the hallway. His hair was still wet from the shower and he was pulling a t-shirt on. He laughed as I quickly removed my hand from my pants and came over, put his arms around my waist and kissed me.

"Do you want me to do that for you?" he murmured.

Fuck! Shame! But mmmm minty fresh breath...

He went to the kitchen and came back with two beers and handed me one.

"Want to watch a movie?" he asked, gesturing to the DVDs on the shelves.

"Uh huh," I replied.

Oh awesome, I thought, *retard Goose who can't formulate sentences is back.*

"Cool...so how do you feel about a porno?" he asked.

I just about choked on the sip of beer I had just taken, blushed and managed to reply "Uh, what do you mean? Like, making one?"

He laughed. "If you want to," he replied and then obviously saw the look of pure terror on my face and said "nah I meant watching one. You keen?"

"Oh, ok, yeah. That's cool then," I said and relaxed back on the couch.

He put a DVD in, dimmed the lights and sat next to me. I kicked off my shoes and got comfortable – well, as comfortable as I could with dental floss up my bum anyway.

The main guy in the porno was ugly and fat, but a couple of the girls were quite hot and Ben seemed reasonably entranced with it. I noticed that one of the girls was a bit Spanish looking and started worrying that she might resemble his hot ex girlfriend.

We started fooling around and before long my g-string came off (oh the relief!) and pretty soon after we were having sex on rug on the lounge room floor. The moaning and grunting from the TV was quite distracting - I tried to ignore it but seeing as I happened to be facing the TV with Ben behind me, I couldn't help but see it.

At one stage he slapped my ass (which bloody well hurt) and I looked back at Ben expecting to find him looking at me with lust in his eyes, only to find he wasn't even looking at me - he was staring straight at the hot Spanish chick who was pretending to enjoy being ploughed by the ugly dude with the really big schlong.

Oh my God! He could be screwing anyone right now. Is he seriously more into the porn than me!?! No, surely not. He must have just glanced at the screen at the same time I looked at him. Yeah that must be it.

Not long after he grunted and it was all over. He sat back on the couch naked in all his glory, smirking at me.

"That was awesome. You're so cool," he said to me.

Yes! His ex mustn't have let him watch porn! He must like me even more now!!

I beamed. "Awww you're not so bad yourself," I replied as I put my top back on. "Where's the loo?"

"Down the hall, second on your right," he said. "Then meet me in the bedroom opposite the bathroom," he continued with a wink.

I looked at the clock and knew I really should get going as I had work in the morning. But I had to make him realise how stupid he would be to not want me to be his girlfriend - so I figured more incredible sex would be a great opportunity to help him realise how perfect I am for him.

Far out though, it's bloody tiring being a sexual goddess.

~~~~~~~~~~~~~~~

The next morning I woke up to the alarm on my phone vibrating. I turned it off and looked over to where Ben was sleeping soundly. I crawled out of bed and got dressed quietly and picked my necklace up from where I had put it beside the bed. I was about to put it on then I stopped.

Hmmm. If I leave it here, then he will have to call me to tell me I left it here. And then it will be a great excuse to see him again because I'll have to get it back....oh that's brilliant!

I left it on the bedside table and went out to the lounge to put my shoes on. I headed home to have a shower and get ready for work – all the while smiling because I knew this time I had a foolproof way of hearing from him.

I am like the MacGyver of dating.

~~~~~~~~~~~~~~~~~~~~

MacGyver my ass. Three days later my desperation was peaking again as I hadn't seen or heard from Ben since I had left his house on Friday morning (and arguably that didn't even count as he had been asleep anyway) so I had spent the weekend moping around like a social reject.

On Monday at lunchtime the desperation overpowered me and I texted him. I tried to keep my cool and not send a hysterical "Why don't you love me??" text so after re-writing it three times I sent:

Hey Ben! Hope you had a good weekend. Did I leave my necklace at your place? ☺

I was elated when I got a reply five minutes later. The elation didn't last long.

Hey yeah you did I went past your place this morning so dropped it off in your letterbox.

Damn...

Oh sweet as. Thanks! Want to catch up one night this week? I sent back, gutted that my plan had totally backfired but pleased he cared enough to drop it back.

I waited impatiently for a reply but by the time my lunch break finished I hadn't got one.

At 4:52pm I finally got a reply.

Sorry mate just really busy at the mo might be awhile before I have some spare time. Take it easy ☺

He was blowing me off - that much was clear. I felt my face drop and knew that tears may not be far away and of all the moments for Chelsea to appear in the doorway, she chose that one.

"Goose! Are you ok?" she came rushing over.

I didn't say anything, I just handed her my phone so she could read the text.

She handed the phone back to me with a concerned but knowing look on her face.

"I'm sorry Goose. I know you like him but it's been pretty obvious the whole way along that he's just not that into you."

Ouch don't hold back Chelsea....

"It wasn't obvious to me," I said, fighting back the tears. She grabbed a book out of her locker and handed it to me.

"I know hun. It sucks. But I think it's time you read this. It will put everything into perspective, I promise. Take it home ok?"

I glanced down at the book title. He's Just Not That Into You: The No-Excuses Guide to Understanding Guys.

Shame. She thinks I'm so useless with guys I need a handbook?!

I nodded and threw the book in my bag, partly because two other nurses came into the staffroom and partly to shut Chelsea up.

I said goodbye and walked numbly outside and headed home, not really focusing as I was driving but luckily making it home without running over any cats, dogs or old people.

When I walked into the lounge I was glad to see Jess was alone and Rupert was nowhere to be seen. She looked up at me with a smile and as soon as she saw my face she frowned and stood up.

She said "Goose what's wrong?" just as I burst into tears. Through my tears I showed her the texts and wailed "He really doesn't like me, does he?"

"Maybe he really is just busy babe," she consoled me.

"He called me 'mate'!! I've been such a dick! He must think I'm such a loser! I AM such a loser!"

I'm a loser baby, so why don't you kill me? Beck got it right when he sang that. He was talking about me.

"Who gives a shit what he thinks? You're awesome, he's the dipshit who's missing out!"

After about half an hour of weeping and wailing I pulled myself together as I noticed Rupert had arrived home and was hovering in the doorway. He looked kind of afraid of me and it wasn't until I looked in the mirror in my bedroom that it became obvious why.

My hair was a mess, I had mascara and makeup smudged all over my face, snot dripping out of my nose and my eyes were bloodshot. If I hadn't just been ruthlessly rejected by a guy I liked I may have even found my appearance funny.

I grabbed some tissues out of my bag to wipe my face and saw the book Chelsea gave me in there. I grabbed it out, cleaned myself up and started reading.

Chapter One: He's just not that into you if he's not asking you out: *Because if he likes you, trust me, he will ask you out.*

From the first page I was hooked. Jess came in about twenty minutes later with a pizza she had ordered for dinner and we sat on my bed, munching on Supreme pizza with extra pepperoni and laughing our asses off reading out excerpts of the book.

"Ooh check this one out," I said. *"'Oh sure, they say they're busy. They say that they didn't have even a moment in their insanely busy day to pick up the phone. It was just that crazy. All lies. With the advent of cell phones and speed dialing, it is almost impossible not to call you. Sometimes I call people from my pants pocket when I don't even mean to. If I were into you, you would be the bright spot in my horribly busy day. Which would be a day that I would never be too busy to call you.'"*

Jess laughed. "Oh seriously. This shit is magic!"

"I know!" I cried. "Listen to this, *'but what I can do is paint you a picture of what you'll never see when you're with a guy who's really into you: You'll never see you staring maniacally at your phone, willing it to ring. You'll never see you ruining an evening with friends because you're calling for your messages every fifteen seconds. You'll never see you hating yourself for calling him when you know you shouldn't have. What you will see is you being treated so well that no phone antics will be necessary. You'll be too busy being adored.'* I AM SO EMBARRASSED! I can't believe what a complete muppet I have been for the last ten years!"

"This is the honestly the best book ever written. Our lives are never going to be the same again, you do realise that aye Goose? No more dropping our pants for men that *just aren't that into us* anymore!" Jess clapped with delight.

"For sure girlfriend. Starting with Ben! What an asshole," I said as a thought dawned on me. "Oh crapballs, SHAME. I can't believe I thought he liked me TOO MUCH!"

We laughed and read more until the pizza was gone and we had eaten our way through an entire packet of chocolate biscuits and a bag of Pineapple Lumps.

And then we went to bed happy. And empowered - there's nothing like realising just how simple men are to see things in a new light.

And Ben, well, he was too short for my liking anyway.

November

I looked at the clock beside my bed. 2:18am. Weird, something must have woken me up. I patted Milkshake and just then I heard the floorboards creak so I sat up with a start.

"RUPERT! What the hell?!" I yelled as I saw him standing at the end of my bed, staring at me.

"I, uh, I brought Milkshake in for you," he said, gesturing to my cat who had been curled up next to me, sound asleep, until I yelled and was now moving hastily towards the end of the bed.

"What?! Oh, whatever. Shut the door on your way out please!" I watched as he left and pulled the door shut and I lay back down, my heart racing a little bit.

Calm down. Maybe he did bring Milkshake in? She looked fairly settled when I woke up though. Ewww how long had he been watching me for? I shuddered.

I finally fell back into a fitful sleep and had a strange dream about hobbits swimming in chocolate milk.

~~~~~~~~~~~~~~~

The next morning was a Saturday and Rupert had left early for work so I told Jess what had happened over breakfast.

"Ewww that's scary," she screwed up her face. "He really is so weird. I just don't get how he has no life outside of work. Have you ever seen him go out anytime that isn't for work or Community Patrol??"

"Nope. I just hope he hasn't been watching me sleep on a regular basis. Maybe we *should* be checking our walls for peepholes after all!" I replied. "Oh, and by the way, did those two pairs of knickers I can't find show up in your washing by any chance?"

"Nah still haven't seen them," Jess shrugged her shoulders. "Hang on a sec, what if Rupert has nicked off with them?? No pun intended."

"Ugh no way. He wouldn't. Would he?!?"

"Shit I don't know. Do you think we should have a look in his room in case he's got them?"

"I guess we could..." I trailed off. "Yeah damn it. I like those knickers."

We made our way to his closed bedroom door and opened it. His room was immaculate. Like freakishly so. No pictures or photos on the wall or anything personal.

"Far out. Do you think his mum comes and cleans his room when we're at work?" Jess asked.

"Damn, if she does I need to get her to do mine too!"

We looked around his room and under his single bed and opened the drawers, which contained perfectly folded clothes.

"Nope, no knickers," I said.

"He might be wearing them," Jess suggested.

"Oh gross!" I cried and just then I spied a piece of paper poking out from under his pillow.

I pulled it out and read it quickly then burst out laughing and handed it to Jess to read.

She read it aloud. "'28 year old man looking for a large lady for cuddles and companionship. Must like cooking and Star Wars...' What the hell?? It's got a receipt with it – holy shit he must have put it in the newspaper!"

"Why wouldn't he just go on a dating website?" I asked.

"Have you ever seen him on a computer?" Jess replied.

"Oh true, nah. Classic! Let's have a look in the paper!" I called as I was already halfway to the lounge to find the paper I had seen in there earlier.

We found it and trawled through the personals section until we saw the same ad.

"Is that his cellphone number?!" Jess asked me.

"God knows. I didn't even know he had a cellphone! I've never seen him use one!"

"Oh this is hilarious, Rupert is a chubby chaser! But he's so tiny a fat chick would squash him if they rooted!" Jess exclaimed.

"Wait a sec, if he likes fat chicks, then why is he watching ME sleep and stealing MY undies?! He must think I'M a lard ass!" I said.

"As if. Maybe he likes fatties cause they remind him of his mum?" Jess laughed. "I wonder if he's had any replies to the ad? We SO need to find out. Shit, we better put it back under his pillow so he doesn't suspect anything."

"True that. I think I'm going to go to the gym before lunch," I replied with a frown.

∼∼∼∼∼∼∼∼∼∼∼∼∼∼

As it turned out, we didn't have to wait long to find out if he's had any replies to his ad. The very next day while Leo, Jess and I were gossiping over coffee at the dining room table and Rupert was playing Playstation in the lounge, we heard the beep of a text message.

We all silently watched as Rupert pulled a cellphone out of his

pocket, read the message, smiled and then slowly one-finger texted a reply. Jess and I looked at each other.

"I'm just going to go to the mall to do uh, some, uh, shopping," Rupert announced and disappeared into his bedroom.

"The MALL? Shopping?!" Jess hissed. "He never goes to the mall!"

"Want to follow him?" I whispered.

Rupert reappeared, smelling like he had spilled an entire bottle of aftershave on himself then said goodbye as he went out the back door to his car.

"Hell yes!" Jess and Leo both answered and we grabbed our bags and jumped into my car, maintaining a safe distance between my Henrietta and Rupert's crappy old Honda Civic.

We arrived at the mall and managed to park two rows of cars away from his Honda and followed him into the mall.

"Slow down!" I hissed at Jess. "Don't you watch CSI?! Don't get too close or he might spot us!"

We needn't have worried. A couple of minutes later he stopped outside an ice cream shop and checked his watch.

Not long after, an extremely large girl tapped him on the shoulder and he turned around. They both smiled and it looked as though they were introducing themselves.

"Bloody hell! Someone ate all the pies! He's going to need a bigger bed!" remarked Leo.

"Sssh. Be nice. You might get fat one day," I chastised him.

They then disappeared into the ice cream shop and came out a few minutes later carrying triple scoop cones of what looked like Caramel Fudge ice cream. They started walking towards us.

Mmmmmmm caramel fudge ice cream... oh wait, is it actually Rum and Raisin? Ewww...

"Oh shit! Hide!" I suddenly realised he might see us so I quickly pushed Jess and Leo behind a pillar and we all watched as they walked past. As we looked at them from behind, I couldn't help but laugh at Rupert's tiny little frame walking next to the girl who was about twice as tall and about five times wider than him.

"Awww, he's all grown up now," I said.

"Shit, the poor bastard better hope that the ice cream fills her up – otherwise she might be having *him* for seconds!" Leo exclaimed.

"Mmmm I feel like ice cream, let's go," I said and turned around and walked smack bang into Rob the Builder.

"Hey Goose," he said with a perfect smile.

"Hi!" I replied, blushing. (Because let's face it, that's what I do.)

Just then I noticed a girl was standing next to him. She was quite plain looking, a wee bit chubby and desperately in need of an eyebrow tint. And she was giving me the death stare. I heard Leo snigger behind me.

"Oh, Goose, this is Abby. Abby, this is Goose, Jess and Leo," he introduced us all and we said hi and stood around in uncomfortable silence.

"So, how's your new place?" I asked him, trying to avoid the evil eye Abby was giving me.

"Really good! How are you guys?"

"That's awesome," I replied, "We're good. Same old."

Abby cleared her throat, put her hand on Rob's arm, and said in a sickeningly sweet voice, "Robbie, we better go, the movie is going to start soon."

Robbie?!? Stupid bitch.

"Oh right. Yeah. I better go," he said, and almost sounded disappointed. "I'll see you guys later," he said with a smile. "Bye Goose."

"Bye *ROB*. Nice to meet you Abby!" I said, ever so sweetly.

I can be fake too bitch. And at least my jeans aren't two sizes too small for my fat ass.

After a parting glare from Abby they walked off and we continued on to the ice cream shop. For some reason I felt a bit sad as he walked away.

"What a minger. Flabby Abby!" exclaimed Leo.

"Yeah she was a bit," I said. "But at least he hasn't upgraded since we broke up I guess."

"Fuuuuuck no! She's batting way out of her league. He must have permanent beer goggles on or something!" he replied.

"You should totally go back there. It's obvious he still luuurves you."

"I doubt it – and he's obviously moved on so nothing I can do about it even if I wanted to." I said, trying to keep my voice light.

And I SOOO don't want to admit I really want to...

"Nah I agree with Leo. He was totally gutted he had to leave with her," added Jess. "He's really nice. And he always treated you well, not like some of the numbnuts you've met lately."

"I know, it wasn't HIM that was the problem. It's his shit-stirring, Tupperware-selling, bitch of a mother that I couldn't cope with. And the fact he couldn't stand up to her too I guess."

"Yeah I get that, but she *will* die someday you know," said Leo matter-of-factly.

"And maybe we could arrange a hitman to help it happen sooner?" added Jess with a smile.

Now THAT'S an idea...

I laughed. "I love you guys," I said. "But no more talk about Rob the Builder ok? He's got Scabby Abby now – she can have the fun job of dealing with his psycho mother."

And then I proceeded in doing what all women do when they see their ex with another woman...

I ate the equivalent of my body weight in caramel fudge ice cream.

By the next night I had successfully convinced myself that I didn't still have feelings for Rob the Builder. They quickly came flooding back though when, as Jess and I were finishing dinner (Rupert was out, presumably with his large lady who likes cuddles – ewww mental picture alert!) I got a text from none other than Rob himself.

"Hey Goose it's Rob. It was really good seeing you yesterday. I was wondering if you wanted to come over on Friday night and see the house? I could cook dinner if you're keen? And then a smiley face." I read it aloud to Jess and she shrieked.

"I KNEW IT! I knew he still fancies you and by the way you're blushing I'm assuming you still fancy him too!"

"Yeah well maybe I do a little bit. But he's obviously got a girlfriend now so he must mean he wants to catch up as mates," I replied.

"Oh right. You better ask about her - I don't think he would be trying to do a dodgy, do you? Oooooh, he's just so INTO YOU!" she laughed. So we composed my reply.

Hey Rob ☺ That sounds really nice but I'm not sure Abby would be too keen on me coming around?

I got a reply a couple of minutes later.

Oh haha nah all good Abby is just a friend! She's friends with Dan's new girlfriend so we were all going to the movies yesterday arvo. So what's the verdict? ☺

I snorted. "A friend that wants to root him senseless maybe!"

But I had to admit I felt relieved – and totally confused. But good old Jess gave me a pep talk so I decided to say yes. I mean really, what harm could come of it? We are both adults and it will just be two adults catching up over dinner.

Yes, it's all good.

~~~~~~~~~~~~~~~

"THIS IS SO NOT GOOD! What the hell was I thinking?" I cried and threw a dress down onto my bed.

It was Friday night and I was supposed to be leaving to go to Rob's - but instead I was standing in my bra and undies in my bedroom throwing a hissy fit because I couldn't decide what to wear and everything I had tried on made me look fat.

"Don't be an egg! You look awesome in all of them. Here, put these on." Jess said and handed me a black and blue top and jeans.

"That makes me look like a heffalump," I replied.

"For God's sake, shut up and get dressed woman!" Jess scolded me.

I did as I was told then looked in the mirror.

"See??" Jess said triumphantly, "you look great. Now piss off. And text me if you're not coming home tonight..." she said with a wink.

I hugged her. "Thank you."

I drove to the address Rob had given me and parked across the road.

It was a cute bungalow type house and his car was parked in the driveway.

Awww it's even got a picket fence...

I took a deep breath, got out of the car and walked up the path. I looked for a doorbell but couldn't see one so was just about to knock on the door when it opened and Rob was standing there, smiling. Looking hot.

So very hot.

Oh God this was NOT a good idea. Maybe I should make up an excuse and leave, but then-

"Come on in," he interrupted my train of thought and stepped aside so I could walk into the hallway.

Oh bugger it. I'm in now. And something smells seriously yummy.

He gave me a tour of the house and I made the appropriate positive comments about its potential. We ended the tour in the kitchen where he poured me a glass of wine - I sat on a bar stool and he leant on the other side of the counter while we chatted.

"So you don't have any flatmates?" I asked.

"Not at the moment. Dan and his girlfriend Kara are going to move in in a couple of weeks though," he replied.

"Oh...I'm surprised *ABBY* doesn't want to move in. You guys looked pretty chummy the other day..." I said in a semi mocking tone.

WHY did I say that?! Now he's just going to think I'm being a snarky bitch!

Luckily he chose to ignore the bitchy undertone to my comment.

"Abby's ok. But she's not really my type," he said.

"Well, she made it pretty obvious she likes you a lot. I got the death

stare the whole time we were talking at the mall," I replied with a scowl.

Would you bloody well shut up!?!

He laughed. "If I didn't know better I would have said you're jealous!" I blushed and tried to think of a witty reply but I couldn't so I just drank more wine. As you do.

We had dinner and it was delicious – I had forgotten what a good cook he was. In fact, as the evening continued, I was beginning to wonder why the hell I broke up with him in the first place. I mean, seriously, his mum wasn't *that* bad was she?!

We were sitting on the couch a few hours later, talking, laughing, drinking and having a merry time when shit suddenly got serious.

"I'm so glad you came tonight," Rob said.

I smiled. "Me too."

"I miss you Goose," he said and gently put his hand on my cheek.

"I miss you too," I said. He leaned in and kissed me.

And with that one kiss I was immediately picturing our future together - moving in to his house, painting the picket fence white, getting married and having his (two) babies.

Then our clothes started coming off and we didn't make it beyond the couch before we were consummating our future marriage.

Then we celebrated our anniversary on the dining room table.

And then renewed our vows when we finally made it to the bedroom.

"Did I mention I'm so glad you came tonight?" Rob laughed afterwards, as we lay in bed.

"No pun intended aye?" I said with a smirk.

He laughed. "Yeah well, that was just a bonus. I might have had to give Abby a call if you didn't put out…"

"Bastard!" I laughed and punched him on the arm. He laughed and pulled me on top of him.

And then we went on our second honeymoon.

~~~~~~~~~~~~~~~~~

I woke up the next morning to the sound of rain on the roof. I looked at the clock beside the bed – 9:18am.

"Good morning," Rob smiled and pulled me over to his side of the bed.

"Mmmm, good morning," I replied - and felt on my leg just how good a morning he thought it was.

Holy crap what a night! I must look like shit!!!

Not that he cared apparently as he started kissing my neck. Just then I heard a door open and footsteps.

"YOO HOO! Robbie? Are you up yet? I'll put the jug on," the unmistakable voice of his Wicked Witch mother called.

"Shit!" he cursed and quickly started to get up.

"What the hell?! Has your mother got a key?" I hissed as he hurriedly looked for his pants.

"Of course she does! I've got to get out there or she'll come in here to find me. And you *know* she will!" he whispered.

"I'm naked! All my clothes are in the lounge!" I screeched quietly, sitting up and clutching the sheet to my chest.

"Yeah, well, I have a fucking hard on! I win!" he whispered as he finished pulling his shirt on, kissed me quickly and darted out the door, closing it behind him.

I heard him greet his mother and I lay back on the pillow and covered my face with my hands. I could hear their muffled voices in the kitchen and she was obviously getting comfortable as I heard a chair scrape as she sat down at the kitchen table.

Shit! I need to piss!

Luckily the bedroom had an ensuite bathroom so I decided I would retreat into hiding in there – there was no way I was going to come face to face with his mother under these circumstances.

I swung my legs over the side of the bed and stood up on the floor, feeling something squelch under my foot.

Ewwwwww what the fuck was that?

I lifted my foot up to find a used condom stuck to it. Lovely.

I lifted my leg up and attempted to pull it off and in so doing, lost my balance and fell backwards, smashing my lower back on the bedside table and sending the clock, Rob's watch and a bottle of water tumbling to the floor with an almighty crash. I landed on the floor, stark naked and spread-eagled with the condom still attached to my foot.

Which is exactly what his shit-stirring, Tupperware-selling, bitch of a mother saw as she burst into the room, with Rob following closely behind.

The look of distaste on her face was fairly obvious as I finally managed to peel the condom off my foot and pulled the sheet down from the bed to partially cover me.

"Lucy. I'm surprised to see YOU again," she screwed her face up. "But I guess I should just be glad you used protection Robbie, *who knows where* she's been since you broke up." She gave me a lingering look of disapproval and then turned and walked back out to the kitchen.

I felt tears form in my eyes but I forced myself not to cry. I wouldn't give the bitch the satisfaction.

Rob rushed over and started to help me up off the floor. "I'm so sorry Goose!"

"Leave me alone!" I yelled and shrugged his hand away then clambered over to his drawers, almost tripping over the sheet I had wrapped around myself.

"Goose don't leave like this," he pleaded. I ignored him and grabbed one of his t-shirts and put it on - it barely covered my naked ass but at that point I really didn't care. I threw the sheet back on the bed and noticed the condom on the floor where I had thrown it. I scooped it up and stormed out.

His mother was sitting at the kitchen table, looking rather smug with her hands around a cup of tea. I went over to her and stood in front of her.

"I pity you," I said. "Because you are a sad, pathetic woman and you have nothing better to do than shit stir in everyone's lives. Oh, and you're a total bitch."

She looked shocked but didn't respond.

"Oh, and by the way, where your hands are *right now* is exactly where my naked ass was while your son was fucking me on that table last night," I continued my rant and then dropped the used condom into her full cup. "Enjoy your tea, won't you."

Then I strode off to the lounge, found my knickers and put them on then grabbed the rest of my clothes and my shoes and headed to the front door.

Rob followed me. "Goose, *please* don't leave like this. She doesn't mean what she says."

I turned around on his front steps. "Rob, wake up. She's a bitch and she's never going to like me. I was stupid to think it could have been different this time around. I really wish it could – but I can't be around someone so negative and controlling. And I don't know how you can either."

He looked at me with his eyes downcast, like a beaten man. "She's my mother," he said, as if that was all the justification he could give me.

"I know. And I feel sorry for you," I said, then turned and started walking away from him, only just managing to restrain from impaling myself on top of the picket fence that had held so much promise last night.

I made it to the car, wearing nothing but my knickers and his white t-shirt in the pouring rain. It was the ultimate walk of shame.

And damn it, I still needed to piss.

December

The rest of November had pretty much been a write off. After the disastrous end to the short-lived reunion with Rob the Builder and the time it took to heal my wounded heart and battered ego, we were well into December before I knew it.

Not that Rob hadn't tried to make it up to me – he had sent flowers, rung, texted and said all the right things but deep down I knew that any relationship we could potentially have would always be marred by the presence of his evil witch of a mother (oh and perhaps the fact that I had chucked a used condom in her cup of tea may have been a slight issue).

And unfortunately, I couldn't afford to hire a hitman so my dream of a white picket fenced future with him was over.

Christmas is coming. Fa la la la la la frigging la.

I think I lost the Christmas spirit around the time I realised the possibility of being a spinster with fifteen cats was becoming more and more likely and I would quite possibly die old and alone with shrivelled up ovaries.

But yay for two weeks holiday, even though most of it would be taken up with being bossed around by Renee as her wedding is now less than a month away. She's been really shitty lately because her fat bridesmaid Jody has been doing Weight Watchers and has lost bulk weight so now looks fantastic – that's got to be Karma right there (and a sensible eating plan).

I'm celebrating my first night of holidays by going out for pre-Christmas dinner and drinks with Leo, Jess and Dee. We are all single at the moment - which I'm sure will last all of about five minutes until Dee's next conquest comes along.

I so wish I could be more like her, use men for what I can get from them and then toss them aside. I bet *she* won't die old and alone with shrivelled up ovaries.

"Jess?" I called out as I walked out to the lounge.

"In my room!" I heard her muffled reply.

"Have you seen my pink knickers? The ones with the little black bow? I thought I'd wear a matching set tonight, you never know who might get to see my undies!" I asked from her doorway.

"Are you planning on scoring?" she asked.

"As if. More like just in case I fall over and my dress falls off like it did that time at Leo's birthday dinner."

"Shit that was *hilarious!*" she laughed. "No I haven't seen them...how many pairs are you missing now??"

"That's the third pair - I'm going to have to ask Santa for some new knickers at this rate! Hey, I wonder why they are called a *pair* of knickers when it's only one item of clothing? Random."

"Hmmm don't know," she said and then frowned, "do you think maybe we should check Rupert's room again just in case?"

"I don't know...I guess we could. But he'll be home soon so we'll need to hurry up if we're going to."

"Come on," Jess said and headed towards Rupert's room then slowly cracked the door open and peered in.

We went in and once again, the room was spotless. We channelled our inner Ninjas and quickly searched the room and found nothing - until Jess bent down and checked under the bed.

"Ooh what's in here?" she asked, pulling a shoe box out.

"At a guess, shoes??" I replied sarcastically.

"Ummmm no...look," she replied and stood up to show me the contents of the box.

WHAT THE FUCK?!!!

"Oh my god he's such a perve!" cried Jess.

Inside the box were not only my three missing pairs of undies but also a fourth pair - *so need to remember to Google why they're called a pair!* – and one of my bras that I hadn't even noticed was missing along with a scarf I thought I had lost at work.

"Oh my god they're my period undies!!!! Ewwwwww I hope they're clean!!" I squawked.

"*That's* what concerns you the most? Really?? Is now the time to tell you that your scarf has stains all over it and looks like it could be snapped in half???" Jess said with a disgusted look on her face.

"What do you mean by-ohhhhhhhh YUCK!!!" I said as I got what she was implying.

"Ewww ewww ewww," Jess groaned and then we heard the back door open.

"He's home!" I whispered.

"Right. Come on," Jess grabbed the box and headed out to the kitchen. "Rupert, we need to talk to you."

He saw the box in her hand and turned bright red like his face was going to implode.

Shit is that what I look like when I blush? Shame.

Then he burst into tears. "Please don't tell my parents!" he sobbed.

Jess and I looked at each other in disbelief. "Ummm okay..." said Jess, "but you know you have to move out don't you??"

He sobbed even harder and ran into his bedroom, leaving his door open, and threw himself on his single bed.

"Riiiight, that went well," Jess sniggered. Then his door slammed.

We made a coffee and decided to wait him out. There was no movement or noise coming from his bedroom.

"Shit, you don't think he's topped himself do you??" I asked, a bit concerned. Seeing a dead body wasn't quite what I had planned for my day when I woke up this morning.

The doorbell rang. We got up and walked out into the hallway and opened the front door. Rupert's parents were standing on the step with worried looks on their faces.

"Ummm hi. Come on in," Jess said and shot me a 'What the hell is going on here?' look.

Rupert's mum went into his bedroom and his dad followed us into the lounge. A minute later, his mum brought a red-eyed, sniffly Rupert into the lounge.

"Now girls, Rupert rang us and told us that you have asked him to move out," his mum said to us.

"Yes we have," replied Jess. "And we would like him to move out immediately."

"But why dear? Can't we work this out?"

I was happy to let Jess do the talking. I was still having disturbing visions of Rupert with his hobbit penis jacking off into my scarf.

"No, I'm sorry we can't. There are a number of reasons why it's not working out," Jess replied.

"I understand dear, but we've actually turned Rupert's bedroom into my sewing room so we really don't want him to have to move home," she explained, "so surely we can work something out so he can stay," she finished, a tad presumptuously.

"No, I'm sorry but we can't," Jess said firmly, "and we would like his stuff moved out this weekend please."

"But my sewing-"

"No buts. He's out," Jess interrupted her.

Shit she's awesome! She should have been a lawyer!

And so that was that. Rupert the little pervert was accompanied out of the house by his reluctant mother, bawling his beady little eyes out, with his apologetic dad promising to pick up his single bed the next day.

And my poor violated scarf went straight into the wheelie bin.

2007

January

"Shit shit buggery bollocks!" I cried as I looked down at the scales. I had put on 2.5kg over the Christmas and New Year holidays – a result of far too many temptations (frigging cheesecake) and absolutely no willpower to speak of. And not to mention the gym membership that I may or may not have neglected to utilise the entire holiday period.

I worked out that I had exactly 15 days to lose the offending two and a half kilos if I wanted to fit into my bridesmaids dress and avoid having my vile sister flip her lid at me. I guess that means it's time to start my annual post-Christmas diet. Oh joy.

"Goose are you home?" I heard Jess call, "I got us pizza for lunch!"

Ooh pizza!! Yum! I guess I'll start my diet tomorrow....

~~~~~~~~~~~~~~~~~

I hate the gym. I want to die.

~~~~~~~~~~~~~~~~~

I looked down at the scales. *Oh thank God.* 2.1kg down with one day to spare. If only I could celebrate with a king size block of Caramello chocolate – but I knew all my bastard fat cells were just waiting for me to succumb so they could come hurtling back with a vengeance.

I left the bathroom and ran into Leo in the hall. After Rupert's dishonourable discharge from the flat and our subsequent need to find a new flatmate, Leo decided he would move in with us since he spends so much time here anyway.

"Hey skank. Want to go to the movies? I feel the need for some Leonardo Di Caprio loving tonight," he asked.

"Bugger I'd love to but I've got the Troll Queen's wedding rehearsal soon and Mum wants us to all have dinner with David's family after," I screwed up my face.

"Ooh how fun," he said sarcastically, "if the rest of them are anything like him you're going to be in for a loooong night."

"Tell me about it!" I said in despair, "My dream of being hit by a car, breaking my leg in four places and being hospitalised so I have to miss the wedding hasn't come true unfortunately. So I better go make myself presentable – my life won't be worth living if I'm late to the rehearsal."

"It's not too late - I can still run you over in the driveway if you want. Anything for you darling," Leo offered.

"Awww thanks babe, you're a sweetheart to offer. But no, I'll get my happy face on and suck it up. I'm sure it won't be as bad as I think."

~~~~~~~~~~~~~~~~

I was wrong.

I got to the waterfront venue where the ceremony was taking place and I could already hear my sister shouting at someone.

Damn I SO should have taken Leo up on his offer...

"Hello darling!" my mum came rushing over to me and kissed me on the cheek. She handed me a small green packet. "Here are these motion sickness pills I was telling you about, they are just new out so hopefully they'll work better than all the other ones you have tried!"

I took the pack from her and thanked her. My wonderful sister had decided to have her wedding ceremony at a marina and then the reception on a harbour cruise - knowing full well I get insanely seasick of course.

"But darling, I really think you should limit your alcohol intake since you haven't tried these pills before," she continued.

"Mum, seriously, I think alcohol will be the only thing that will be able to make tomorrow bearable," I retorted.

"Oh honey Renee is just a bit stressed, she will be fine by tomorrow I'm sure and -" she was interrupted by a loud commotion a few metres away.

"For fucks sake David!! Can't you do anything right??! You are supposed to be standing on the left!!!" my sister screamed at her cowering fiancé.

I didn't need to say anything I just looked at my mother and raised an eyebrow.

"Well, ok, just try and not drink *too* much darling," she conceded with a frown.

~~~~~~~~~~~~~~~~~

After getting through the rehearsal reasonably unscathed we went to an Italian restaurant for dinner with my parents, Matty J, Renee and David and his parents and three brothers. My earlier predictions proved to be right and all three of his brothers were also Gingas and the older ones, Ginga 1 and Ginga 2 (I can't remember their names, they look the same to me) had about as much personality as David – i.e zilch. The younger one, Jamie, was pretty laidback though so Matt and I made sure we sat with him down one end of the table, away from the fun-suckers down the other end.

Jamie was over from London for the wedding and Matty J had announced a few weeks before Christmas that he was moving there a couple of weeks after the wedding (he wanted to leave before it but he knew Mum would have thrown a shit fit if he missed it) so they had struck up a conversation about that. I half listened to them while watching the goings-on at the rest of the table.

Poor Mum was attempting to have a conversation with David's mother, a skinny, mousy woman who looked almost afraid of her. And Dad was doing well chatting to one of the brothers who was also an accountant, while Renee was having a discussion with David about something. And by discussion I mean she was telling him off.

I wonder what he's done this time?

I excused myself to go to the bathroom and when I was walking back to the table, Jamie appeared next to me, carrying a pink cardigan.

"Nice jersey," I smiled, "but I hate to tell you it's not really your colour. Doesn't bring out your eyes," I joked.

He laughed. "It's my Mum's. Man, you're *nothing* like your sister," he gestured towards a sour-faced Renee.

"I'll take that as a compliment," I replied with a smile, "and I can say the same about you and your brothers."

"Yeah, it takes a few duds to make perfection aye?" he winked as we got back to the table.

I laughed. Poor bugger must have forgotten he's a Ginga!

~~~~~~~~~~~~~~~~

I read the back of the packet of the motion sickness pills Mum had given me. "Take two tablets with a large glass of water."

Hmmm. Four pills with a glass of wine - same diff.

We left the hotel we were all getting ready at a few minutes later, with Renee squawking to us to make sure we help her get out of the car when we arrive at the ceremony so she wouldn't trip over her dress.

Renee had been her usual demanding cow self all day. The poor hairdresser had received the brunt of her temper as apparently she had parted her hair on a different side for the hair trial *and* she had dared to take too long to do my hair.

Then poor Jody, Caroline (the other bridesmaid) and I came in a close second for no particular reason – although I'm fairly sure it's because Renee's cunning scheme to try and make us look ugly in our snot green dresses failed miserably because we all still looked way hotter than her.

BUT we did our bridesmaidly duties with smiles on our faces and helped the silly wench out of the car. I don't know about the others but *my* smile was as a result of the thought of Renee tripping, dress, shoes, tiara and all, into the water on her way down the aisle.

The other bridesmaids and I walked down the aisle to a Coldplay song (bloody hell I can't stand Coldplay! Slash my wrists and make it stop already!!) to where David and his brothers were waiting. Jamie gave me a wink and a smile as I took my place so I smiled back at him and then we turned to watch Renee walk down the aisle with Dad. I had to admit she actually scrubbed up alright – and it was nice to actually see her smiling for a change.

After the ceremony it was time to board the harbour cruise for the reception. I looked at the boat and it was gorgeous – a 3-level luxury private charter boat called the Golden Sunset. I silently prayed that the pills I had knocked back would work as I ascended the boarding ramp and left solid ground.

~~~~~~~~~~~~~~~

"Those pills are totally awesome Mum!" I exclaimed six hours later. The reception was nearing the end and we would be heading back to the marina soon. I had been a wee bit queasy most of the evening and therefore hadn't eaten much more than some pumpkin soup and bread, but had managed to partake in a fair amount of wine and hadn't spewed – so all in all, a highly successful cruise in my opinion.

"Good darling I'm so glad! Now excuse me I have to go and talk to Shirley I just *have* to ask her about her cousin Sonia – apparently she's got a new man who's only in his late 30s!" she prattled on and then made a beeline for her friend Shirley.

"Goose...there you are!" Jamie said as he sidled up to me and took my arm. "Come and do some shots with us," he continued and led me to the bar.

He had been flirting with me all night and I have to admit the attention was flattering. He wasn't the best looking guy in the world but he had a great personality and we had been getting on really well the whole evening and having lots of laughs. Besides, wouldn't it be against wedding protocol for a bridesmaid and groomsman not to hook up for the night?

We did some tequila shots with Matt and Ginga 2 (who evidently wasn't as boring as David and Ginga 1) and then Jamie whispered in my ear "Want to get some fresh air?"

I nodded and smiled, knowing full well what he meant by that, and he took my hand and led me outside and up the stairs to the third level.

Whoa, it's a bit rougher up here, I thought as the boat swayed and I felt my stomach flip.

There was nobody else up there so Jamie took full advantage of that and started kissing me. Before long he'd stuck his hand up my dress, trying to break through the impenetrable barricade my suck in undies were proving to be.

The boat rocked sideways again and I felt my stomach lurch as we were making out.

Oh shit I think I'm going to-

I barely made it away from him and to the side of the boat before I spewed. The tequila burned like a bitch as it came back up.

Jamie started laughing as I turned around, beetroot red and wiping my mouth.

"That's got to be the first time the thought of hooking up with me has made someone puke – well I hope so anyway!" he pissed himself laughing.

"I'm sorry!! It's not you I promise! Oh God I think my seasickness pills have worn off," I moaned and then heaved over the side again.

"It's all good. We're starting to dock, I think we should go downstairs and get you off. Off the boat I mean," he laughed again. "You're a cool chick Goose," he said and kissed me - on the forehead.

Shame!

He led me down to the main area where people were gathering as the boat docked. Renee and David were circulating, thanking the guests, hugging people and saying goodbye.

She reached me and in a moment of completely un-Renee like behaviour, smiled and said "Thanks for everything you did today."

I started to reply but as soon as I opened my mouth my stomach churned violently. I tried to turn away but I was hemmed in on every side by all the wedding well-wishers so I couldn't for the life of me stop what happened next...yep you guessed it.

I power chucked pumpkin coloured puke all over Renee and her beautiful white wedding dress.

Ohhhhhhhh shiiiit...

March

It's been over a month since the wedding night debacle and Renee still hasn't spoken to me. Mind you, the situation wasn't helped by the fact that David's friend Darren got the whole thing on video and uploaded it onto YouTube the very same night. I heart Darren.

Luckily for me, Darren happened to be standing *behind* me while he was filming the unfortunate incident so I am totally unrecognisable - I could be any blonde bridesmaid in an ugly green dress with a bit of back fat overhang (so not happy when I saw *that* captured on film).

But Renee is front and centre for all the power chuck action and, of course, the absolutely *spectacular* tanty she threw afterwards – you would have thought I'd done it on purpose the way she reacted.

So it certainly wasn't surprising to see that nobody gave her much sympathy afterwards, in fact everyone on the video can be seen laughing their asses off and at one point I even got a couple of high fives. I guess that's what happens when you treat people like total shit most of the time.

And of course I apologised profusely but still maintain she needs to take some of the responsibility as she chose to have the reception on a boat - so she really should have known the risk involved. I mean, she grew up with me spewing into Mum's handbag on long car journeys, puking into vomit bags on plane trips and even throwing up into the bushes after jumping on the trampoline for too long.

But if she wants to hold a grudge, she can go hard with her bad self. Matty J left the country a couple of weeks ago - and I always wanted to be an only child anyway.

"Hey guys, come on in," said Leigh. Jess and I were at Barbara's Beauty Boutique for our monthly brazilian waxes and Leigh was one of the girls who worked at the salon. Ironically there is nobody called Barbara that actually works there.

"Ugh you have to do me first today or I'm going to chicken out. SO not in the mood to have my pubes ripped out today," I said, taking my underwear off and clambering onto the bed.

"Oh harden up princess," Jess said and took a seat and moved it around to the head of the bed so she wouldn't be looking straight up my vagina. Good call.

"Why what's up?" Leigh asked.

"Oh, nothing really. Just going to a friend's wedding tomorrow and it's yet *another* reminder that I'm going to die old and alone." I said.

"I keep telling her there are plenty of other fish in the sea but she's not listening to me," interjected Jess.

"DUDE! Do you really have to talk about *fish* when the poor girl is waxing my poon?!" I exclaimed. "I had a shower, I promise," I said to Leigh as she ripped.

Oww! Mother of God that hurts!!

She laughed. "Mate you've got nothing to worry about, it's when you see me put a face mask on and spray air freshener that you should be worried!"

I laughed. "Owww!" I cried as she ripped off a particularly vicious bit.

"Sorry!" she said. "That bit didn't want to come off."

"Far out next time just leave it there. God knows why I'm bothering it's not like I'm going to be getting any action anyway," I said.

"There might be some sexy guys at Chelsea's wedding," Jess said, "and you just never know what *fish* you might be able to catch there..."

We laughed as I threw my balled up knickers at her.

"Owww!! Bloody hell!"

~~~~~~~~~~~~~~~~~~~~~~~~

As it turned out, there were no sexy available guys at Chelsea's wedding. There were a couple of single ones (friends of her now husband Damian) but nobody that particularly floated my boat.

It was a gorgeous wedding and Chelsea looked absolutely beautiful - and much to her immense relief I didn't puke on her at the reception.

A week after the wedding, Chelsea rang me while she was still away on her honeymoon.

"Goose!!!! My cousin has found you a butcher!!"

Huh?!

"What?? I don't need a butcher. I buy meat from the supermarket," I replied, confused.

"No Goose, a butcher *to go out with*," she said, exasperated.

"Why did your cousin find me a butcher to go out with?" I asked, even more confused than before.

"Oh my God Goose, were you that drunk you can't remember the conversation you had with her at the wedding?"

Shit I was that drunk I can't even remember her cousin!

"Ummm maybe? What conversation?"

"Oh my God you're a shocker. So you were talking to my cousin Amanda and her boyfriend Blair -"

Ahhhh yes Blair, hot blonde guy who looks like Channing Tatum with a sleeve tattoo. Mmmm Channing Tatum...still a bit fuzzy on Amanda though...

"-who is a butcher. You were admiring his forearms and told him you would love to go out with a butcher cause you think they're so manly and good with their hands," she continued, "so they've found you a butcher! I have his number here, you <u>so</u> have to ring him!"

Oh shame. Hitting on her cousin's boyfriend in front of her wasn't bad enough I had to make myself look like a desperate and dateless bitch too?!

"Thanks Chelsea, and say thanks to Amanda too but there is no way I am ringing some total stranger," I replied.

She ignored me. "His name is Chops, not sure what his real name is. And he's just turned 33, got no kids and owns his own business. Sounds like a total winner!" she continued her spiel.

Chops? Sounds like a serial killer more like it!

"Honestly Chels, I am not ringing someone I don't know - it's not going to happen. But thanks anyway," I said, hoping that she would get the hint to end this particular conversation.

She didn't. "Well, I'm texting you his number anyway. I totally think you should ring him," I could actually hear her pouting over the phone.

"Okay, okay," I conceded. "I'll think about it."

"Yay!" she perked up. "And Blair has given him *your* number too!"

~~~~~~~~~~~~~~~~~~~~~~

I forgot all about the butcher until Chelsea came back to work two days later and made a beeline for me.

"Have you heard from Chops yet?" she asked excitedly.

"What? Oh. No I haven't," I replied.

"You guys suck. Why won't you just text him?! He could be the man of your dreams!"

"Yeah, or a maniacal butcher with a meat cleaver who wants to chop me up into little pieces," I retorted. "A guy doesn't get the nickname Chops for nothing you know."

"Whatever, you still suck. I'm going to text Amanda and get Blair to find out why *he* hasn't texted *you* since *you're* such a chicken shit," she grumbled and walked off in a huff before I could convince her not to.

~~~~~~~~~~~~~~~~~~~~~~

Later that night, Leo, Jess and I were watching Desperate Housewives and eating M&Ms when my phone breathed.

"Damn girl I wish you would change that stupid thing!" Leo hurled an M&M at me. It smacked me in the boob and then slid down my cleavage.

"He shoots, he scores!" Leo cried and feigned a cheering crowd.

"Shit, that would have to be the closest thing to a tit shot you will ever get," I joked as I fished it out and ate it. It would be wrong to waste food when there are starving kids in the world.

I checked my message.

Hey Lucy this is Chops. I got your number from Blair. He said you have a butcher fetish that you needed to get out of your system? ☺

Oh crap, shame.

I read the text out to the others and they laughed.

"Serves you right for being such a desperate bitch when you're drunk," chortled Leo.

Hi Chops…so tell me, are you good with your meat then? ☺ I replied.

"**Ha ha, I've got a big sausage…oops I mean I make big sausages that is!** And then a winky face. **So I hear you're a nurse?**" I read out his reply.

"Ooh he sounds cool. And you're blushing!," Jess said.

"Ooh Goosey Goosey Gander where shall she wander, into Chops' bedroom his sausage she will conquer," sang Leo, dancing around the lounge and making rude hand gestures at me.

"Whatever, it's nothing," I laughed it off and changed the subject. But I didn't stop smiling for the rest of the night.

~~~~~~~~~~~~~~~~~~

We spent the next two days texting back and forth and he seemed like a really cool guy (not holding out too much hope though - I've thought that about guys before and they've turned out to be bastards!) and I found out he lives about ten minutes away from me in a different suburb and owns a butcher shop called For Chuck's Steak.

I had to text him back and ask if he was serious when he told me the name - and turns out he was. Apparently he came up with the name because after about two weeks of not being able to decide on a name, his mate Gav said "For fuck's sake, would you just choose a name already?" And so it became For Chuck's Steak - that's right up there on the list with Tequila Mockingbird for most awesome business names in my opinion. Totally scores points for originality.

Apparently the nickname Chops is not because he is a serial killer (as if he would admit it!) but actually because he was a really fat baby so people started calling him 'Porkchops' which over the years got shortened to Chops. And the fact that he then became a butcher was just ironic. His real name is Nathan Phillips. Of course I then started imagining myself as Lucy Phillips and thought it has a nice ring to it. Desperate much?!

After the two day texting marathon (of which Chelsea was witness to some of at work and now I'm deaf in one ear from her exuberant squealing) we had decided we would talk on the phone that night.

He rang me at about 8pm and we talked for ages. He had a deep voice and sounded quite sexy but then who can really tell – you always hear about the women who do phone sex hotlines for a job and in reality they are massively overweight with saggy boobs and hairy chins.

He told me he had been going out with a girl called Fiona for about three years and they were engaged but that had ended about eight months ago when he found out she had been cheating on him with a guy she worked with. I felt sorry for him until he admitted that it may have been karma biting him in the ass as *he* had cheated on his ex girlfriend *with* Fiona a couple of years before that.

Warning bells went off with the old saying 'once a cheater always a cheater' coming through loud and clear in my head but then he said something which made me think twice about writing him off as a philandering mongrel.

He said "The whole thing made me learn my lesson. I had no idea how much I'd hurt my girlfriend when I'd cheated but now I know exactly how it feels. I would never do it again, if I was unhappy in a relationship I would be honest and try and fix it rather than just go out looking for someone else."

Maybe I'm getting sucked in but that sounds pretty mature to me...

Then he told me his mum died of cancer about four years ago. I chastised myself as one of my first thoughts was of joy as that meant there could be no potential mother in law issues. (Rob the Builder's shit-stirring, Tupperware-selling, bitch of a mother has *a lot* to answer for!) He said that losing his mum was the worst thing he's ever gone through.

Awww. Note to self: ring mum tomorrow and tell her I love her.

His dad is still alive though and he also has an older sister, Cherie, who's married with two young boys and they all live about two hours away so he sees them every few weeks. He admitted Cherie has always been a wee bit overprotective of him and even more so since their mum died – and she *hated* Fiona so was totally stoked when they split up.

That made me a bit nervous but then the way he spoke about his little nephews was just so sweet that I forgot about his sister and instantly let my imagination run wild with thoughts of him being an amazing daddy to our kids someday.

Snap out of it girl! You haven't even met him yet - he could be massively overweight with saggy boobs and a hairy chin!

"Wow it's almost midnight," he interrupted my thoughts.

I looked at the clock by my bed. 11:57pm.

"Crazy! That's gone really fast! You better go, you have to get up in a few hours," I said. He had told me he leaves for work at 5am most mornings. Bugger that, I need my beauty sleep too much.

"So, I was thinking, do you want to meet tomorrow after work? I've got to go to a mate's house for dinner so we could, like, just meet up for a few minutes somewhere on my way so it's not too hard out – then we can always do a cut and run if we don't like each other and there'll be no pressure?" he asked.

Hmmm. Is he trying to tell me in a roundabout way that he's ugly? Or is he just worried that I might be ugly?

"Yeah, that sounds like a good plan," I replied.

"To be honest, I think even if we're not attracted to each other I think we could be really good friends," he said to me.

Awwwwwwww what a sweetheart! He's so mature!

"I think so too," I said and genuinely meant it.

We arranged a place and time to meet and we said goodnight and I hung up the phone with a smile.

Oh man. He's so cool. I really really REALLY hope he's not massively overweight with saggy boobs and a hairy chin...

I left work the next day and made Chelsea promise that she wasn't going to follow me. She crossed her heart and hoped to die but I didn't entirely believe her.

I felt surprisingly calm – normally I would be all frantic and nervy if I was going to meet a guy for the first time but strangely I felt quite at ease.

I pulled into the carpark that we had arranged to meet at and didn't see a black Subaru anywhere so I assumed he hadn't arrived yet. I checked my makeup in the rear vision mirror and then saw a black car pulling into the carpark at great speed.

It pulled up next to me and I craned my neck to see the driver but I couldn't see crap all through the tinted windows. I got out of Henrietta and his car door opened and a tall figure got out.

Tall? Check.

Dark hair and decent haircut? Check.

Handsome? Ummmm...

Not ugly? Check.

"Hey Goose," he came around the side of his car and smiled at me.

Awww he's got a nice smile...

I smiled at him. "Hey yourself. Nice to meet you in person."

"You too," he replied with a grin. "You actually look really familiar," he said, "but I can't think why."

We had been talking for a few minutes when he snapped his fingers. "That's it! I saw you a few months back at Tequila Mockingbird. You were chowing down on a massive stack of BBQ ribs!"

Oh dear God NOOOOOO!

My cheeks burst into flames and I managed to respond with "Umm why on earth do you remember that??"

He laughed. "Cause me and my mates had a bet on whether you would finish them all. I won!"

He must have noticed my burning face then because he said "Oh shit, sorry. Don't be embarrassed! We have total respect for any woman who can appreciate a decent slab of meat. Turns me on actually," he winked at me and I felt my face cool down a bit. He really is quite lovely.

We chatted for a few more minutes and then I reminded him he better go if he was going to his friend's house for dinner. He looked at his watch.

Nice forearms? Ooh yes. Check.

After a couple more minutes we said goodbye and got back into our cars. I watched him speed out of the carpark and then dialled Jess' cellphone number and waited impatiently while it rang.

"Ooh how'd it go?" she answered it on the fourth ring.

"Oh my God Jess! I think I've just met the man I'm going to marry and have babies with!"

~~~~~~~~~~~~~~~~~~~~

About half an hour later I had just gotten home from picking up Indian takeaways for dinner when I got a text.

So, did I pass the test? ☺ p.s you're cute when you blush...

I smiled and took the food inside and showed Jess and told her that unfortunately he had recognised me from the meat massacre at Tequila Mockingbird.

"Well, it obviously didn't make him think less of you - you obviously passed *his* test!" she said.

Haha yeah maybe you did...so I passed yours too then? ☺ I sent back.

Oh yeah about that. I may have had an unfair advantage, Blair had already told me you were smoking hot!!

"Ooh EXCITING!" squealed Jess (with her mouth full of garlic naan bread) when she read his reply, "when are you going to see him again??"

"Say it don't spray it girlfriend!" I teased her. "Ummm, I don't know."

"Ooh I can't wait to meet him!" she replied enthusiastically.

"He's not as good looking as what I would normally go for," I told her, "oh my god I can't believe how shallow that sounds!!" I said, horrified at myself.

"So what?" said Jess. "Are you attracted to him?"

"Yeah I am," I admitted, blushing. "He's really nice too."

"Then that's all that matters babe. And compare him to the assholes you have hooked up with lately – they may have been really good looking but they were *total* dickheads! At least he seems like a good guy," she pep talked me. Then she smiled, "*AND* he didn't think you were a repulsive pig when he saw you hoeing into those ribs, that's got to count for something right??"

Oh God did she have to remind me? I'm NEVER eating ribs again!

~~~~~~~~~~~~~~~~~~

"So you should be pleased about what I'm cooking for dinner," Chops said with a sly smile after he had invited me into the small two bedroom house where he lived with his cat Prozac. "Pork ribs marinated in honey, garlic and ginger."

It was our official first date – we had talked on the phone every night but this was the first time we had seen each other since our first meeting in the carpark.

"Oh my God, *seriously*?" I asked, blushing. "You really want to witness a re-enactment of the massacre close up?"

"I told you, it turns me on," he laughed and winked at me.

Prozac came sauntering over and rubbed against my leg. I bent down and patted him and he purred and head-butted against my hand.

"Be careful," Chops warned. "He'll be all lovey dovey with you until he's had enough and then he'll violently attack. Hence his name."

"He would get along with Milkshake then," I replied as I kept patting him. "Oh yes you *would*, you bootiful boy. *Aren't* you a just a bootiful little bubba boy?" I said to the cat in a completely retarded baby voice that for the life of me I couldn't stop. Shame.

Prozac wandered off as Chops handed me a glass of wine. I thanked him and mentally reminded myself that:

a) I was not going to get drunk. And

b) under no circumstances was I going to have sex with him tonight.

I had even worn ugly knickers as a deterrent - they were big and green with an elastic waist and were usually reserved for period undies (they were a birthday present from my Grandma a few years ago, bless her ugly knicker picking heart).

Nope this time it was going to be different. No rushing into things and rooting on the first date and no acting like a desperate bitch who's afraid of dying alone with shrivelled up ovaries. Cool, calm and collected, that's the new Goose.

Now all I have to figure out is how to eat ribs without looking like a savage beast. Crap.

~~~~~~~~~~~~~~~~

I failed *miserably* at attempting to look like anything other than a ferocious lioness devouring an innocent wildebeest during dinner - not really my fault though they were just so delicious I couldn't stop myself. Not that Chops seemed to mind (maybe he was serious when he said it turns him on?!) and I figured even if we never made it to a second date I probably gave him a good story to tell his mates. That's me, always thinking of other people. I'm a saint really.

After dinner we cleaned up, all the while the conversation flowed easily and we got ready to watch a DVD. I chose Miami

Vice out of the three options Chops gave me and he dimmed the lights and sat next to me on the couch.

I was a bit nervous as he was sitting so close I could feel the warmth of his body but I tried to concentrate on the movie. I usually love movies with lots of shit getting blown up.

Eww what happened to Colin Farrell? He looks foul in this movie! Mind you I'd probably still give him one- ooh! My thoughts were interrupted by Chops doing the old have a stretch and put his arm around me trick.

Oh my God! Should I make a move? Or will he?!

He didn't. We sat there in silence for a few minutes but as I was fairly certain neither of us was concentrating on the movie, I turned my face to his and we kissed.

"I've been wanting to do that all night," he said as he touched my cheek and then he kissed me again.

UGLY UNDIES UGLY UNDIES UGLY UNDIES!! My internal alarm system screamed as I lay back on the couch and pulled him towards me.

Ow! What the hell is that?! I thought as I felt a sharp jab in my lower back. I quickly jerked my bum and leg up so I could reach behind me to grab the offending object, at the very same time he was moving to get on top of me - so my knee slammed full force straight into his groin.

"Fuuuuucccck!!" he exclaimed, clutching his man bits and moaning as he doubled over and rolled sideways off the couch.

"Oh no! I'm so sorry!!" I cried, pulling my hand from behind me to find that the TV remote was what had been under me and caused the mid air collision of knee vs. nuts. And judging from the figure writhing in pain on the floor the score is definitely Knee 1, Nuts 0.

He moaned again and managed to get himself back up onto the couch.

"What should I do? Should I get ice? Is it broken?" I asked in a panic. "I'm SO sorry!"

"You know, if you didn't want to hook up with me you could have just said so," he managed to exhale between deep breaths.

"No! It wasn't like that, honestly!!" I exclaimed.

"Goose, I'm kidding. It's ok, it's not broken. It's just really sore," he said with a half smile and then winced in pain again. He patted the seat next to him. "Come sit down, let's finish watching the movie."

So we did.

And in a hardly surprising ending to the night's events, Grandma's ugly knickers remained unseen - and likely never to be removed.

~~~~~~~~~~~~~~~

The next day I had convinced myself (after a two hour late night debrief with Jess and Leo while we inhaled a block of Caramello chocolate, two packets of Toffee Pops and a large packet of Twisties) that despite him kissing me goodnight when I left his house and saying that he would 'call tomorrow', that I would never hear from him again. And who could really blame him after the grievous bodily harm I had unintentionally caused him – bruised balls and a painful pecker would be a pretty acceptable reason for not wanting a second date!

So imagine my excitement when he actually DID ring like he had promised.

"How are you?" he asked.

"Ummm, I'm fine! How about your...ummm..." I replied.

"My frank and beans? My one eyed trouser snake? My heat-seeking love missile?" he asked.

I couldn't help but laugh. "Well, yeah, I was thinking more along the lines of your purple headed Cobra, but whatever."

He laughed. "It's all good. A bit tender but I will make sure I wear a protective cup next time I see you to be on the safe side."

Yessss! He wants to see me again!!!

"About that," he started, "do you want to go out for dinner tonight? You can always stay the night at mine afterwards if you don't want to drive home. You know, if you want to, I mean. No worries if you don't."

I grinned ear to ear. "I'd love to."

We made small talk for a few minutes and arranged that I would meet him at his house later and go out from there. I hung up the phone and immediately heard squealing so I turned around to find Jess and Leo already doing a victory dance in my honour.

"Oooooh Goosey's gonna get *naked* tonight!" Leo exclaimed. "I bet you're regretting eating all those Toffee Pops last night now aye Goose? Bloated much?"

Damn it. I bloody well hate it when he's right.

April

"So...ummm...am I your girlfriend?" I asked Chops as he got up and cleared our plates away.

We had been seeing each other for three whole weeks and we hadn't officially determined what our relationship status is - and he hadn't exactly been forthcoming with the desired info.

Are we in a relationship? Are we friends with benefits? Are we just casual and he can go out rooting other people if he wants? I mean it's not like I'm expecting a ring or anything silly like that (although I did see a beautiful white gold princess cut diamond ring while window shopping the other day) but seriously, the not knowing has been driving me *crazy*.

He looked a bit surprised. "Uh, yeah? I just assumed that you are. Do you want to be?"

I breathed a small sigh of relief and smiled. "Yep."

"Cool," he smiled back, "you're such an egg. Have you been wondering this whole time?"

"Oh nah of course not," I lied. "Just thought about it today and thought I better check before I start referring to you as my boyfriend." (I'm so totally full of shit, have been calling him that for the last two weeks and six days).

"Well, since you're now *officially* my girlfriend," he grinned, "I should probably break it to you that my sister wants to meet you."

The Jaws theme song instantly popped into my head while I had visions of his overprotective sister hating me as much as she hated his ex girlfriend and I started feeling panicked.

"Oh, um, right. I guess, um, yeah," I stammered.

"You don't need to be scared of Cherie," he put his arm around me, "I've told her how awesome you are – she'll love you I *know* she will. And you can meet my dad and my nephews. It'll be great!" he said enthusiastically.

I forced myself to smile. I haven't exactly got the best track record for getting on with my boyfriends' families after all and – *ooooh! YAY! He just called me his girlfriend! Woop woop!*

~~~~~~~~~~~~~~~~~~~~

The following Saturday I was waiting at Chops' house for him to get home from work so we could start the two hour drive to his sister's house for our overnight stay (like meeting his family wasn't scary enough on its own, I was going to have to unleash the beast and be seen by them without my makeup on in the morning! Now *that's* scary!).

Prozac was smooching into me on my lap – so far he hadn't lived up to his name and reputation and attacked me. What can I say, the cat has good taste.

He jumped off me as he heard the front door open and the sound of Chops walking up the hall. He came into the lounge in his work clothes, carrying his blue stripy butcher apron, and came over and kissed me on the cheek.

"Hey babe. Just going to have a quick shower and then we can get going."

The combined smell of raw meat, blood, sweat and sawdust hit my nostrils and I breathed in deeply. There is something so manly about that smell and for some completely unexplainable reason I find it incredibly sexy.

Damn he looks goooood right now...

I immediately stood up and put my arms around his neck.

"Hmmm, not so fast champ," I said and started unbuckling his jeans as I pulled him towards the bedroom.

"Goose, I haven't had a shower. I stink like pig carcass."

"Mmmmmmm I know...." I said, pulling his shirt up over his head and pushing him down onto the bed.

"Ok then, you asked for it!" he said, grabbing my ass cheeks under my dress and pulling me down towards him and his sexy butchery fragrance.

Oh my God yes...

You know, it's true what they say. You just can't beat a butcher's meat.

~~~~~~~~~~~~~~~~~

Not only did I survive meeting his family, I actually really enjoyed it too.

I did have to get him to pull over on the side of the road for me to spew my guts out on our way to his sister's house (only partly due to motion sickness - his only major downfall so far is that he is a scary hoon of a driver. I mean really, how hard is it to stick to the speed limit and check your blind spot?!) but he didn't seem to hold that against me. He even let me drive his prized Subaru on the way home to avoid a repeat performance.

Cherie and her husband Jon were lovely and made me feel completely welcome. She even hugged me and said before we left that their mum 'would have totally approved of you, thank

God Chops has *finally* found a nice girlfriend.' Yesss! Suck on that skanky ex Fiona!

His dad was hilarious, in fact he may even rival me as the funniest person in the world when I'm drunk. He hadn't even had that much to drink and he was whipping out some one-liners that had me in fits of laughter. Bit of an old hottie too, reminded me a bit of Bo from Dukes of Hazzard.

And the nephews. Oh, the nephews! Soooooo cute – there's little Nate who is 4 years old and the baby Eli who is only 14 months old. I believe I may have actually felt my uterus contract when Eli smiled a big gappy toothed smile and giggled at me. But luckily that very quickly passed when I saw the massive green shit he had done in his nappy and I had to stop myself from regurgitating my dinner.

Two weeks later I introduced him to my parents. The Ice Queen and her lackey were away for a work trip so of course, I was absolutely *devastated* to not be able to introduce Chops to them. Ha ha, as if.

My blush was on overdrive when I took Chops to The Doggery to meet them as my mother told every embarrassing story she could muster and then to top it off, she pulled out a photo album of photos of me when I was younger. To my horror, she showed him photos of me as a naked 5 year old wearing nothing but pink gumboots, an action shot of me spewing all over my 7th birthday cake and one of me as a 10 year old with a hideous fringe that I had cut myself.

Dad was his usual quiet self but he obviously approved of Chops as, while we were doing the dishes and Mum was talking Chops' ear off in the dining room about the price of lamb these days, he said to me "You've found a nice fella there Goose."

"I'm sooooo sorry about my mum," I said to him as we were driving home, "she loves talking and pretty much never shuts up. She means well but she can be a bit annoying sometimes!"

He laughed. "So can you - but that's one of the things I love about you."

I just about crashed the car. *OH MY GOD. Did he just say-*

"Love? You, um, love me??" I squeaked.

He looked embarrassed. "Well, um, yeah. That kind of slipped out. But yeah I guess I do," he smiled sheepishly.

YESSSSSSSSSSSS!!!!!

"I love you too!" I said excitedly and just about drove into a ditch for the second time.

He laughed. "Okay cool, now that we have established that, can you please watch where you are going?"

"Uh huh," I smiled happily. *He loves me he loves me...*

So there we have it. Six weeks into the relationship and my fears of dying alone with fifteen cats and shrivelled up ovaries have been well and truly replaced with daydreams of marrying Chops, buying a house with a white picket fence and having two cute little babies (but preferably ones that don't do massive green shits).

But I'm not totally insane, it's not like I have bought any bridal magazines or anything pathetic like that...oh ok, so there *may* be a couple under my bed...but only because I like reading the articles.

"Goodnight babe," Chops murmured and hugged me, him the big spoon to my little spoon. Truth be told I hate cuddling in bed – unless it's winter and then I'm a heat seeking skank.

"Night babe," I replied, I could hear Prozac purring and felt him nestling in further down the bed in between our legs.

I felt a stirring in my stomach and heard it gurgle.

Oh crap! I need to fart! Is he asleep yet? I listened to Chops'

breathing, which was slow and even. He usually falls asleep quickly but it was hard to be sure.

Oh man oh man oh man.

I was having trouble keeping it in and with every second that passed I felt my stomach cramping with the impending wind. Maybe it would squeeze out quietly? I had never farted in front of him before and the way my stomach was churning I didn't think I would make it out of the room in time to stop it happening now.

Oh no it's coming!

And then it came. I couldn't stop it - I let out a ripper of a fart that was so violent it actually vibrated with force against his thigh and sounded like a car backfiring. As Prozac took off like a shot, I felt a deep blush spreading across my cheeks and lay perfectly still, hoping it hadn't woken Chops.

"Shit was what that?" he asked in a sleepy voice.

Oh my God so embarrassing! He's going to think I'm such a minger!

"Uh, I think Prozac farted or something," I said casually, trying to hide the embarrassment in my voice.

As if he's going to fall for that...

"True that. Smelly bugger," he murmured, still half asleep.

Phew...

Crisis averted - and a poor defenceless animal who can never dob me in was blamed in the process. I am officially a bad person - but unofficially, what a freaking legend.

July

"Hi," the girl said as she walked past me on the path leading to Chops' front door.

"Hi," I replied and smiled at her. *Hmm, is it my imagination or did she just look me up and down?*

When I reached the front door I turned and watched her as she got into a white car that was parked across the street and then drive off.

I opened the door and called out "Hey babe!" and walked through into the kitchen where Chops was spooning cat food into Prozac's bowl.

"Helloooo baybeeeee how you doing?" I said to the cat and bent down and rubbed his head. "Was that chick trying to sell you something?" I asked Chops innocently.

"What chick?" he asked.

"The one I just saw leaving here. Was she selling something?"

"Oh. Um. No. Um, that was Fiona," he replied with a rather uncomfortable look on his face.

"What? Your cheating, slutty, ex Fiona?!" I asked, dumbfounded.

"Slutty is a bit harsh Goose," he replied, defensive.

Oh my God he's defending her?! What the hell is going on??! Oh shit was she pretty?! Damn damn damn I didn't pay enough attention! Hang on, what the hell was she doing here??

I took a deep breath before I spoke so I wouldn't sound like the high pitched, whiny psycho bitch I sounded like in my head.

"So, um, what was she doing here?" I asked him, a picture of angelic calmness.

Bitch Slut Skank Whore!!

"Umm, she came round to ask if I um, could help her move house in a couple of weeks," he stammered nervously.

She WHAT?!?!

"Okaaay," I replied, forcing my voice to remain at an even pitch, "and what did you tell her?"

"I said I'd check with you and let her know later."

SHIT!! So I get to be the neurotic, distrusting girlfriend and say no? Or say yes and send him back into the clutches of his skanky ex?? Shit shit shit!!! WAS SHE PRETTY?!?!

"Can't the guy *she left you for* help her move?" I asked ever-so-sweetly.

He opened the fridge to put the cat food back and emerged with a beer and a can of Coke Zero. "Nah they've split up apparently. Her brother is going to help but she needs someone else for the heavy lifting."

And that person has to be YOU?! Grrrrrrr.

"Well I guess if you really want to help the *woman who cheated on you* then I won't stop you..." I said to him as he handed me the Coke.

You better not help that bitch I swear to God I'll-

"Ok cool!" he interrupted my thoughts. "She's still got my TV cabinet so that'll be a good opportunity to get it back. Thanks babe," he kissed me on the forehead and wandered off to the lounge, beer in hand.

Hmmmph.

Reverse Psychology: FAIL.

~~~~~~~~~~~~~~~~~~~~

"What are you doing home? I thought you were staying at Chops' place tonight?" Jess asked as I walked into the lounge, threw my bag on the couch and slumped down next to it.

"I was going to. But I'm in a foul mood so don't feel like it."

"Oh awesome," Leo piped up, "so being the caring, sharing person you are you decided to grace us with your foul mood instead??"

I scowled at him as Jess asked "Why, what's up babe?"

"I'm so pissed off. His slut ex girlfriend was just leaving as I got there. She had 'popped around' to ask him to help her move house!"

"Ooh, was she hot?" Leo asked.

"I don't know. I think so," I replied dejectedly.

"Didn't you have your Magnum PI skills turned on? You're bloody useless!" he replied.

"Shut up! I didn't *know* she was his ex girlfriend when I saw her – I assumed she was trying to sell a vacuum cleaner or something."

"Was she carrying a vacuum cleaner?" Leo asked.

"Well, no," I replied.

"Then my initial judgement stands. You're bloody useless!"

"*Anyway*," Jess shot Leo a dirty look, "I assume he's going to help her?"

"Yes. What an arse. I totally made it clear I wasn't keen on the idea but he said it'll be a good opportunity to get his TV cabinet back. Pffft whatever," I said grumpily.

"I'm sure it doesn't mean anything Goose. You know he's a nice guy. Maybe she just doesn't have anyone else to help her," Jess said in a chirpy voice.

"Or maybe she wants to root him on top of the TV cabinet," Leo interjected.

"Shut up Leo. You're not helping my mood. I think I need a pie," I grumbled.

"Sweet, we haven't had dinner. I'll come with you," Jess said.

"Cool, I desperately need to drop the Cosby kids off at the pool first though," I half smiled. The thought of a pie in my near future was cheering me up immensely.

"Classy bitch! Have you *STILL* not had a shit at his house??" Leo asked in surprise. "What's it been, like three months or something??"

"Almost four. No. It's a bit hard you know, the bathroom is right next to the bedroom so he would totally hear me if I did!" I defended myself. "Besides, I only crap like twice a week so I haven't had that many opportunities to anyway."

"Overshare much?!" Leo screwed his nose up.

"I bet you still run water when you piss at his house too aye Goose?" Jess laughed, half joking.

Shame...she knows me so well.

Leo must have seen the look on my face and burst out laughing. "Holy shit that's *hilarious*. You're a tragic bitch you are. Poor Chops is going to have a heart attack the first time you take a dump at his place, he won't know what hit him!"

"Speaking of dumps, I'm turtle-heading so I better get a move on," I said and skipped to the door as both Jess and Leo groaned and screwed their faces up in disgust at my second overshare.

"Perfect timing," Jess called out, laughing, "you might make room for a sausage roll too!"

~~~~~~~~~~~~~~~~

Two weeks later we were sitting on the couch watching TV when Chops' phone buzzed, signalling that he had a message. My attention was fully on him as he read it.

"Who's that from?" I asked innocently, knowing full well it was probably from Fiona – who, much to my immense displeasure, had decided to become text buddies with him over the last few days.

"Fiona," he replied, "she's just giving me the address of where she's moving to tomorrow."

"Oh right," I scowled, which he either chose to ignore or was completely oblivious to.

He tossed his phone onto the coffee table. "I'm going to have a shower," he said and kissed me on the forehead, before getting up off the couch.

"Okay," I replied, smiling at him. I watched him wander off towards the bathroom and a couple of minutes later I heard the shower turn on. My attention turned to his cellphone he had left behind.

Don't be a crazy stalker! Don't do it!!

But the pull was too strong. I cocked my head, listening to make sure the shower was still running, and against all of my better judgements, my crazy stalker side won and I picked up the phone.

Awwwww he's got a picture of me as his screensaver! Oh, that's right. I put it there.

I quickly found his inbox and started scrolling through the messages, looking for the ones from Fiona. Much to my chagrin, there were a *lot* of them.

What the hell?? They've been having a grand old conversation apparently!

I read a few of them and they appeared to be reasonably harmless – she had a few too many smiley faces for my liking though. *Stupid happy bitch.* I opened the most recent one and started reading it.

24 Allenside Rd ☺ About 1pm, is that good for you? ☺ Fanks so much again for helping babe, you really are the BEST! ☺

BABE?!?! Grrrrrrrrr...and Fanks??? Who says Fanks!? What a stupid mole- oh shit!!

My murderous thoughts were interrupted as I became acutely aware that the shower had stopped running at some point. I hit the end button furiously until the main screen appeared and quickly put the phone back on the coffee table as I heard the bathroom door open. I attempted to make myself look comfortable on the couch and eyed the phone nervously as the screen was still lit up – a dead giveaway to my crazy stalkerish behaviour.

Chops came into the room wearing a towel around his waist just as the screen went dark.

Phew...

He picked his phone up off the table. "I'm going to head off to bed babe, I have to be at work extra early tomorrow since I'm helping Fiona in the afternoon."

I buried my angry thoughts – nobody likes an angry Goose – and realised if his slut ex wants him back, then it was time for DEFCON 1. Two can play her game...

I sidled up to him, knocking the cushion and the remote off the couch and almost tripping over the coffee table in the process. I batted my eyelashes at him, smiled and said "In that case, let me come with you. Pun intended." I took his hand to lead him to the bedroom, kicking my slippers off on the way.

"Oh yeah, it's on," Chops said and grabbed me around the waist, making me squeal like a little piglet (so *not* a sexy sound) and carried me to the bedroom - where I performed at my personal best to erase any thoughts he may have of reconciling with Fiona and her stupid smiley faces.

Oh yeah, it's ON.

<p align="center">~~~~~~~~~~~~~~~~</p>

The next day I had planned on a bit of retail therapy with Jess and Dee to keep my mind off the fact that Chops was helping Fiona move that afternoon, and therefore also to try and keep my mind off the fact that she might try to root him on the TV cabinet.

I continued with my plan to make Chops realise that I am the perfect girlfriend for him (not the crazy stalkerish one I really am) and baked some muffins to take to him and the guys at his work.

The door jangled as I walked in and Chops' workmate Blair (Chelsea's cousin's hot boyfriend with the sleeve tattoo) looked up from the counter where he was serving a customer and smiled at me. "Hey Goose, Chops is out the back, go on out."

"Thanks Blair! I made you guys some morning tea," I said and gave him a dazzling smile so as to ensure he would pass his opinion on how fabulous I am to Chops.

"Oh ace! You're the bomb!" he smiled back at me.

Why yes, yes I am. Please be sure to pass that along to your boss...

I walked out the back and was immediately hit with the sweet seductive smell of raw meat, blood and sawdust. Chops was slicing what appeared to be some sort of steak, looking all sexy in his blue apron and protective gloves, his arm muscles flexing as he sliced.

Ohhhhhh hellloooooo...

"Hey babe," I called out and headed over to him. "Hey Ollie," I called to his other workmate who was making their famous plum and sweet chilli sausages.

He looked up from the sausage he was holding. "Hey Goose," he called back.

Chops took his hand off his big slab of meat (hahaha I love butcher jokes) and smiled.

"Hey yourself. This is a nice surprise," he said.

"I made you guys some morning tea," I said, holding up the plate of triple chocolate muffins. "Plus I love seeing you at work, you know what this smell does to me," I said suggestively, running my hand along his forearm.

"You're awesome," he laughed. "Aren't you going out with Jess and Dee?"

"Yup. I'm going to meet them soon. I just wanted to see my big strong man before I do," I purred.

"What's gotten into you?" he laughed again. "Not that I'm complaining of course!"

Fiona is a slut. I am perfect for you. The telepathic thoughts I was sending him were hopefully getting through.

"Nothing babe. Just letting you know how much I love you, that's all," I replied, batting my eyelashes at him.

"Oh no have you got sawdust in your eye? I love you too," he said, smiling. "Thanks for the muffins babe they look awesome."

I stopped my failed attempt at batting my eyelashes. "I'll put them in the kitchen before I go. Will I see you tonight?" I tried to keep any high pitched whine out of my voice and sound calm.

"Not sure how long the moving will take, she's always been a bit of a hoarder and totally disorganised," he replied, "how about I just text you later and let you know what time I'll be finished?"

"Ok!" I squeaked, a little too enthusiastically.

"Cool, have fun with Dee and Jess," he said and kissed me on the forehead.

"Uh huh. See you later," I smiled serenely, resisting every urge to throw myself at him and beg him not to leave me for his ex.

But resist I did. What a superstar.

∼∼∼∼∼∼∼∼∼∼∼∼∼∼∼

However, I was not feeling particularly super about 9pm that night when I had not heard anything from Chops for six hours straight and I was turning into an emotionally charged bunny boiler with every second that passed.

His last text at 3pm had simply said **"This is going to take awhile! Will text you later xxx"**

"Don't worry Goose - maybe his battery has gone flat," the ever positive Jess said to me.

"If he's screwing his slut ex I'll kick his ass I swear," Dee interjected, "let's go for a drive and see if he's still at her new place."

"Nah, Dee, that's a bad idea," Jess said emphatically. "I'm *sure* nothing is going on - he might have just lost his phone or something."

"Fuck it let's go," I said and stood up and Dee did too. "Are you coming Jess?"

She hesitated. "I guess so. I'll drive. I *really* don't think this is a good idea though Goose..."

"I'd rather know now than in a couple of months when he's been sneaking around behind my back! Come on let's go."

So off we went. I realised once we reached Allenside Rd that I couldn't actually remember which house number she had moved to so it was a bit of a waste of time – but luckily we had stopped to get some chocolate from the petrol station on the way so it hadn't been a totally wasted trip.

Then we convinced Jess to drive past Chops' house on our way home just so we could see if he was home. But the house was dark as we pulled up outside and his car wasn't in the driveway.

"It could be in the garage," Jess said after I had wailed out that particular observation.

Dee snorted. "Once a cheater, always a cheater," she said matter of factly.

"Stop it Dee. It could be a misunderstanding. Besides, what's that saying about you? You've cheated on two of your boyfriends!" Jess exclaimed angrily.

"Three actually. And that's exactly my point Jess. I can't change what I am, no more than Chops can apparently." Dee took her seatbelt off. "Come on Goose. Let's see if the dickhead is home."

"No," I said dejectedly, "let's just go home." I felt like crying. My friends were fighting. I'd finally found an awesome guy and he had turned out to be just as bad as the rest of them. I had turned into a neurotic late night stalker. AND to top it all off I had eaten all my chocolate.

But I couldn't let it go. I composed yet another text, the fifth unanswered one of the evening. The first had been a casual "Hope it's all going well babe," and the fourth was a panicked "Where the hell are you???"

The fifth summed up my feelings quite nicely.

Thanks so much for considering my feelings tonight. Obviously you are too busy screwing your ex to even think about me or how I might feel about it. Hope it was worth it.

And then I cried.

~~~~~~~~~~~~~~~~~

"Now that it's raining more than ever
Know that we'll still have each other
You can stand under my umbrella
You can stand under my umbrella
(Ella ella, ay ay ay)"

I grabbed my ringing cellphone off my bedside table and looked at it with one eye, the other still buried in my pillow. Caller ID showed it was Chops. A quick glance at the clock showed it was 7:57am.

After a fast deliberation, I pushed the accept button and croaked "Hello?

"I'm SO SORRY Goose I swear to God nothing happened with Fiona last night my phone died while I was helping her move and then I was going to call you when I got home but then I realised your landline number was in my phone which was flat and while I waited for my phone to charge so I could text you I fell asleep on the couch cause I was shattered and I've only just woken up and turned my phone on and seen your messages now I promise nothing happened I wasn't trying to be dodgy!" He finally paused for a breath. "Honestly I'm *so* sorry I didn't mean to upset you."

So hang on, he didn't cheat on me?! Jess was right- his battery was flat? Or is Dee right – once a cheater always a cheater?! Oh I just don't know-

"Goose? Are you there?" I realised Chops' voice was echoing in my ear.

"Oh um yeah. I'm here."

"Honestly babe I am so sorry I know you weren't overly stoked about me helping her in the first place and now I've just fucked it all up. I really don't know what else to say to make you believe me."

"So you didn't root her on the TV cabinet?" I asked stupidly, still trying to sort everything out in my head.

"What??" he laughed. "No way! Why would I? I've got you now, Fiona was in the past and to be honest, we should have never been more than just friends anyway."

Oh great. His skank ex is going to be his new BFF now?!

But I realised that while I was totally butt hurt about the whole thing and not quite over the fact that I had spent the night in tears thinking he was shagging his ex, deep down I felt he was telling the truth.

So Team Jess was the winner. And I got flowers, chocolates and a week of sucking up to make up for it – and Fiona doesn't even have a TV cabinet anymore. Ha.

August

"I'll just grab some toilet paper," I said and veered the trolley over to the left.

"Oi! Watch it! You just about ran over my foot!" exclaimed Leo.

"*Sor-ry*," I said, not really sorry at all as I was nowhere near running over his foot - might have taken out his little toe if anything. Bloody drama queen.

"Why are you being such a speed demon anyway?" he asked grumpily. We were doing our weekly grocery shopping and I had commandeered the trolley, much to Leo's annoyance - as he liked taking his time perusing the aisles with a bunch of bananas sticking up out of the baby seat of the trolley in an attempt to find some hot single gay man to take home and make his bitch.

"I'm just hungry," I replied.

"Yeah well, you're mean when you're hungry."

"Don't forget tired. I'm a complete bitch when I'm hungry *and* tired," I replied sweetly.

"Not to mention when you're on your rag," grumbled Leo.

"True that. Ugh I must be due soon. When are our periods due?" I asked Jess. She and I have been in sync with our periods since about three months after we moved in together. We reckon Leo has started having PMS the same time as us since moving in with us too. If you can't beat 'em, join 'em I guess?

Jess just gaped at me with a confused look on her face.

"What?" I asked.

"I finished mine a couple of days ago. Haven't you had yours?" she said, wide-eyed.

Oh shit. Oh shit. Oh shit.

"OH. MY. GOD. Are you up the duff??!" Leo squawked loudly.

Oh shit. Oh shit. Oh fuck.

I must have had a completely pained look on my face because Jess touched my arm and said "Are you ok?"

"I haven't...had my...period," I managed to croak finally.

"Ohhh....it's all good," Jess said, taking charge. "We'll grab a pregnancy test while we're here, I'm sure it's nothing. Maybe your cycle has just changed or something," she said, smiling at me reassuringly.

My stomach flipped. *Oh my god was that a baby kicking??!*

We managed to make it home without me driving the car off the road and once we had dumped the groceries in the kitchen, Jess started unwrapping the pregnancy test.

"It says the best time to do this is first thing in the morning," Jess said.

"She knows that – she *is* a nurse," said Leo, "an up the duff preggo nurse to be exact!" he exclaimed gleefully.

"Why the hell are you so happy?" I snapped out of my stunned mullet daze and scowled at him.

"Hahaha it looks like your butcher isn't the best at wrapping his meat aye?" he laughed again. I glared at him. "Sorry, sorry. I've always wanted to be an uncle to your little goslings."

Mmmmm Ryan Gosling...

"ANYWAY," Jess interrupted, "do you want to do this now or wait until the morning?"

"Like I'm going to sleep either way...I guess I might as well do it now," I said and took it from her outstretched hand.

"Do you want me to come in with you?" Jess asked.

"Ummm, no thanks. I draw the friendship line at you watching me pee on a stick," I replied and made my way into the bathroom.

Oh shit. Oh shit. Oh shit.

I pulled my undies down and sat on the toilet, test in hand.

Shit how am I meant to do this? Do I stick it in between my legs? Or do I piss into a container first?

I looked around and couldn't see anything suitable to pee into – and I didn't think Leo would appreciate me using his shower cap - so I stuck the test between my legs and let it flow.

Oh that's disgusting! I thought as my urine cascaded over my hand. *But hmmm. So warm...*

I leaned forward and peered down between my legs to make sure the flow was actually going on the stick. I couldn't see anything except for the pee hitting my hand so I spread my legs more and bent forward further, squinting into the toilet bowl.

As I did I lost my balance and started toppling forward. I started panicking, mid stream, and brought both hands up and reached out towards the bathroom cabinet in an attempt to steady myself, test still in hand. Unfortunately my wet, piss covered, test clutching right hand was no help in stopping my impending plunge and I keeled forward, smacking my forehead on a sharp edge of the cabinet handle on my way down.

I felt the sharp pain and a trickle of blood start flowing down my forehead as I lay in a crumpled heap on the floor, undies around my knees. Leo and Jess must have heard the commotion and the muffled 'uumph' as I hit the ground because the door burst open and the both stood gaping at me.

Leo started laughing at what I'm sure was a ridiculous sight. "What are you doing you silly bitch? You don't have to try and top yourself just cause you're preggers you know. But if you're going to, could you at least do it with some pants on??"

Leo disappeared while Jess was helping me off the ground, my cheeks flaming red. I realised I was still grasping the pregnancy test in my right hand.

Should've used Leo's bloody shower cap...

"Leo you need to have a look at her head! It's pissing blood!" Jess yelled out as I pulled my knickers up with my left hand to give me some sense of dignity back.

"It's ok. Head wounds always bleed a lot. Ewwww I need to wash my hand!" I cried, putting the test down on the cabinet and turning the tap on. I caught sight of my blood covered face in the mirror.

Shitballs that is bleeding quite a lot.

Leo reappeared carrying a cloth and some gauze. He put the cloth on my forehead and applied pressure, still smirking. "You know what your mistake was Goose? You should have pulled your undies all the way down to your ankles – undies around the knees are too constrictive."

"Ewwww Leo!" Jess exclaimed, "We sooo don't want to know how or why you know that!"

Leo laughed and released the pressure on my forehead then pulled the cloth away. "Hilarious! You're going to need some stitches. Oh my God - I want to be a fly on the wall when you tell people what you were doing when you split your head open!" he said in another fit of laughter.

"Goose," Jess said gently. I turned to her. She gestured to the test that was still sitting on the bloodstained bathroom cabinet. "Your test must be ready. One line is negative and two lines means you're pregnant," she said, consulting the back of the box.

Oh shit. Oh shit. Oh shit.

I felt more blood trickle down my forehead. I brushed it away and reached for the stick, attempting to ignore Jess' concerned look and Leo's utterly gleeful one.

SO should've used his bloody shower cap!

I looked down at the test, silently willing there to be only one line.

OH FUUUUUUUUUUCK.

"Well?! Spit it out!" Leo screeched.

Numbly I handed the stick to Jess who glanced at it then passed it to Leo who started hollering in excitement when he looked at it and saw the dreaded two lines.

High School Sex Education: FAIL.

Jess put her arm around my shoulders, hugged me and led me out to the kitchen table and sat me down. "It's going to be ok Goose. You will be a great Mum!"

Well that was the worst thing to say apparently because with that comment the floodgates opened and I burst into tears.

"I'm not ready to be a mum!" I wailed, "I like sleeping in!

Leo laughed. "Is that the only reason you can think of for why you don't want to have a baby??"

"No!! There are heaps of reasons!" I cried.

"Like what?"

"I don't know! Heaps!" I replied, hiccupping.

"Oh shut your flaps woman and stop whinging. Actually, you probably should've shut your flaps a few weeks ago," Leo sniggered.

"Oh my God my FLAPS!!" I wailed again, "I'm going to have to GIVE BIRTH! It's going to fucking hurt! I've seen the YouTube videos!!"

Jess gave Leo the evils and turned to me. "You really need to calm down babe you're making your head bleed more by being all worked up. Come on Leo, let's take her to the hospital to get these stitches done."

"Ooh yes please. Corey is on night shift tonight," Leo replied, referring to the new and apparently hot nurse he had been roster stalking for the last two weeks.

"Do you want me to call Chops and tell him to meet us there?" Jess asked gently.

The dam burst again. "Oh no, *Chops!* What am I going to tell him??" I said between sobs. "We've only been together like, five months! I've only *just* had a shit at his house for God's sake! And we haven't even talked about moving in together let alone having a baby....oh no, he's going to dump me then I'm going to have to be a poor solo mum eating jam on toast and 2 minute noodles for dinner so that I can afford to buy nappies. Oh crap... AND I'm going to get fat and I'll have saggy tits and loose flaps!!"

Leo just about pissed himself laughing. "Good on you Goose - you just figured out the other reasons. Besides after all your rooting I bet you already have loose flaps."

Jess elbowed him in the side sharply and threw him another filthy look.

"Ouch! Calm down - you bitches be crazy!" He turned to me. "Look Goosey Goosey gander it will be ok. Chops is not going to dump you, he's a good guy and he loves you. He's like the Maverick to your Goose," he said.

I sniffed and wiped my eyes. "You do realise that Maverick and Goose weren't gay don't you? They were just mates," I corrected his obviously misguided Top Gun analogy.
"In my fantasy they are," he laughed. "Besides, you won't have to eat jam on toast and 2 minute noodles just so you can

buy nappies - I'll spring for a pie every now and then too. Nah seriously Goose, I bet Chops is going to be all good with it," he rubbed my shoulder reassuringly.

Mmmmmm pie....I think the baby is hungry...does that mean I get to eat two?

Leo burst out laughing again. "Shit I just realised, how bloody hilarious is it going to be if you're having *TWINS?!*"

I so *totally* regret not using the bastard's shower cap.

~~~~~~~~~~~~~~~~~~~

The next day I called in sick to work, partly due to the fact that I hadn't had time to make up a good enough story to tell people as to why I had a gash on my head that required 6 stitches and partly due to the fact that Leo is a bigmouth and told half of the hospital staff that I was pregnant, therefore I needed the day to figure out how to break the news to Chops.

I decided I would cook a mean feed of his favourite lasagne and then once we had had a nice relaxing dinner I would break the news.

So I sat at his kitchen table, nervously waiting for him to get home from work. Prozac smooched around my legs, purring. I stopped rubbing his head when I heard the front door open.

Here goes nothing...

"OUCH! What the hell?!" Prozac had launched himself full force at my leg and taken a meaty bite out of my calf. He then gave me the death stare, tail flicking as he sauntered past

Chops who came into the kitchen. Maybe he had finally figured out I had blamed him for that epic fart.

"Yum that smells so good! I'm starving!" Chops exclaimed as he plonked his work gear on the floor by the door.

"Your bloody cat just took a chunk out of my leg for no reason!" I grumbled.

"Haha, he's obviously used to you now. Shit, what happened to your head??"

"Oh, um, I, um, I, I – I'm pregnant," I blurted out.

Damn it!

Chops sat down in the chair opposite me. "Holy shit."

We sat in silence for what felt like an eternity and then he laughed.

"Well, I guess that means my boys are still swimming after you smashed me in the nuts when we first hooked up."

I blushed at the reminder and then just gaped at him. How could he be so casual about it?!

He must have seen the look on my face so he reached across the table and put his hand on my arm. "Are you ok??"

"Ummmm....I just can't believe you're being so *calm*. Aren't you a bit gutted?" I managed to squeak.

"Nah. I mean, yeah I guess it's a bit earlier than I would've liked but hey, it's all good. We'll be right babe."

"But we haven't even really talked about having kids! What if I get fat and you're not attracted to me anymore? We don't even live together! What if we move in together and then you feel trapped because I'm fat and ugly and I'm a shit mum? Oh no, what if we move in together and the cats hate each other and they piss all over the furniture?!" I could feel myself getting worked up.

"Goose, come here," he pulled me by my arm so I stood up and walked around the table and sat in his lap.

"Whoa, eating for two already?" he laughed. I blushed and went to get up but he pulled me back down. "I'm joking babe! You need to stop overthinking everything. I don't care if you get fat - I love you, you'll always be beautiful to me. And you will never be a shit mum, I think you'll be awesome. So just stop stressing, ok?"

I took a deep breath and nodded.

"Good. Can we eat now? I'm starving. And you can tell me how you hurt your head over dinner."

I groaned. *Shame...*

"Ok," I said, still in shock at how easy the whole discussion had gone. I finally smiled and got up.

"Choice. Now cook me some eggs bitch!" he patted my bum and laughed.

And so with that particular conversation over, I figured my life as I knew it was about to change forever.

And eating for two? Well, that was just a bonus.

September

"Happy birthday to you, happy birthday to you, happy birthday dear Goosey, happy birthday to you!" everyone sang as I blushed and felt myself sweating as I blew out the candles on my cake. Twenty eight candles can give off a fair bit of heat apparently.

Twenty bloody eight. This year's sedate birthday celebrations were a far cry from last year's drunken debauchery that ended with the whole embarrassing Ben saga starting. I had moved in to Chops' two bedroom house a week ago so we were having a quiet night of pizza and drinks to celebrate my birthday - although Leo informed me they were celebrating the fact that I had moved out. Such a charmer that one.

Wow. I've just realised how different *next* year's birthday will be. *Holy crap. I'm going to have a baby this time next year.*

I was shovelling chocolate cake into my gob to stifle my panic when Dee plonked herself down next to me, wine glass in hand.

"So you're telling the parentals tomorrow babe?"

Chops and I were going to my parents house the next day to have a birthday lunch with my family and we were going to break the baby bombshell on them then – Renee included. I had rung Matt and told him but sworn him to secrecy until I'd broken the news to Mum and Dad. He was absolutely devastated that he was going to miss seeing 'the look on bitchface's face' when she found out - am guessing not seeing her all year hasn't made his heart grow fonder.

"Yeah, and then we will go see his sister and his Dad next weekend," I replied, restraining myself to not lick the icing off the plate. Some things are best done in the privacy of the kitchen after everyone has left.

"I'm so happy for you Lucy Goose! You're life is turning out just the way you wanted!" Dee said as she hugged me.

"Oh yeah, apart from the getting knocked up after a few months and not being married part," I joked.

"Haha, speaking of married and getting knocked up – guess who just had a baby?!"

"Who?" I asked.

"Amy freaking Wallace. You know, from school?! I can't believe she managed to get someone to root her, let alone marry her! You should see the kid, totally looks like a munter."

I laughed. "You're such a bitch Dee. She wasn't that bad." Then I had a mental picture of the angry ginger and shuddered. "Ok yeah I guess she was," I laughed. "Besides, we haven't seen her for years – how'd you find that out?"

"She's my friend on Facebook. Have you signed up yet? Seriously if you haven't you sooooo have to."

"What's Facebook? And why is she your friend if you don't like her?"

"Oh Goose HEL-LO! You haven't heard of *Facebook*??"

"Oh! That must be the website Matt was talking about too. I'll have to have a look."

"Totally. I'll send you the link. You will LOVE my profile pic I look totally hot in it. Oh, you know who else I'm friends with on there? Jason!"

"Your ex Jason?! The one you hate cause he dumped you right before your birthday party because he'd hooked up with the gym instructor we thought was a lesbian?"

"Hmmph. Yes, that Jason. According to his relationship status he's single now though so maybe she does prefer muff after all. Haven't found out the goss yet he only accepted my friend request this afternoon. I'm going out after this so I'll have a good look at his profile tomorrow."

"Relationship status? Friend request? Profile? That all sounds a bit too confusing for my liking!" I laughed.

We were interrupted by Chelsea and Damian who came over to say goodbye. They were followed reasonably quickly by Leo and Jess and then lastly by Dee who had a hot date with some barman she had met at a club last weekend.

I looked at the clock. *9:30pm and the party's over. I am officially a nana.*

Chops came up from behind and put his arms around my waist as I was eyeing up, I mean clearing, the dessert plates off the coffee table. "I'm shattered. Time for bed?" he asked, yawning.

"Yep, you go on I'll just tidy up first," I smiled and headed into the kitchen with the plates as he walked off towards the bedroom, knowing full well he'd be asleep within two minutes of his head hitting the pillow.

Not that I minded - I had a hot date waiting for me in the

kitchen. Chocolate icing AND leftover cake...boom chicka wow wow...

~~~~~~~~~~~~~~~

"Shit, that's a pretty sight," Chops said, laughing, as he came into the spare room the next morning. I was on my knees half under the bed with my bum up in the air singing the Milkshake song in an attempt to coax Milkshake from her hideyhole in the back corner.

She had taken up permanent residence there since the day we moved in as Prozac had not taken too kindly to having his space invaded by a newcomer (apparently her milkshake *doesn't* bring all the boys to the yard). So as a result, there was a scene that closely resembled a feline Mortal Kombat in the lounge and my poor baby was now flatly refusing to come out from under the bed.

"I think you're going to have to stop feeding her in here and take the litter box out. Then when she gets hungry enough and needs to go to the toilet she will have to come out," Chops said as I backed out from under the bed and turned around to face him.

And then I burst into tears. "You want me to leave her to STARVE all alone in here??" I squawked. "It's all because of YOUR cat that she won't come out!"

I went to push myself up off the floor in a huff and in so doing, stuck my hand right smack into the bowl of jellymeat I had brought in to entice Milkshake out.

Damn it!

Chops looked at me and he was quite obviously trying not to laugh which made me even more upset.

"What's so funny?! You think it's *funny* that I just stuck my hand in cat food?! You think it's *funny* that my poor baby is too shit scared to come out from under the bed? Nice one," I exclaimed with a sob.

"Oh Goose," Chops sighed and came over and sat down on the floor next to me. "I don't think it's funny. Well I *do* think it's funny that you stuck your hand in cat food because let's face it, that *is* funny. But Milkshake will come out eventually and Prozac will get used to her. You just need to give them some time."

Deep down, even in my overly emotional, hormonal state I knew he was right. I sniffed and wiped my eye with my cat food covered hand without thinking.

DAMN IT! Could this get any more embarrassing?

Chops snorted with laughter and stood up, helping me up with my clean hand. I guess I could kind of see the funny side of it and I half smiled.

"You're awesome Goose. You just need to take a chill pill ok? Everything will be fine. Although maybe you should go and wash your hand and rinse your eye now - you stink like fish!"

"Chicken and salmon to be exact. And, I'm sorry to say my friend, that so do *YOU!*" I quickly wiped my cat food smeared hand onto his face, massaged it in then laughed as I took off down the hall before he could react.

"Ugh *yuck*!!!" he exclaimed. "I'm so gonna get you for that!" he yelled as he chased me down the hallway to the bathroom.

"Whatever Fishlips!" I yelled back and then squealed as he caught me around the waist and spun me around.

"You know you want some Fish and Chops!" he laughed as he buried his Jellymeat covered face into my boobs and shook his head left to right so that the cat food squelched as I squealed.

Mmmmm why did he have to mention fish and chips I'm hungry now...

"I love you Goose," Chops said as he came up for air, "even if you do smell like rotten fish."

"I love you too," I replied, smiling, "even though your cat's a psycho."

"We better get ready if we are going to get to your parents on time," Chops said as he let go and turned the shower on.

"Oh shit did you have to remind me?" I groaned. "Lunch with Renee and my parents. Oh AND we are telling them about the baby - awesome. It's going to be a whole new level of shitty. Ooh! I hope Mum is cooking a roast!"

"I'm sure Renee won't be *that* bad," Chops said, "she might be really happy for us."

I snorted as he got in the shower. "Yeah right."

Oh but if we had only known just how bad she would be...

~~~~~~~~~~~~~~~~

"We have some news," I said nervously after we had eaten lunch and were sitting down with a coffee. I could feel Renee's eyes burning into my face and I blushed.

Mum had outdone herself with a roast lamb and a triple chocolate birthday cake for dessert but unfortunately I had forgotten to wear my eating pants - so my jeans were feeling uncomfortably tight and I could feel my stomach muffin-topping over them (I blame the baby, it really wanted that second piece of cake). I shifted in my seat to try and get comfortable.

"Oh darling!" Mum squealed and clapped her hands in excitement, "you're engaged!!?"

"Ummm, no." Awkward. I deliberately didn't look at Chops to see his reaction.

"You're pregnant aren't you?!" Renee spat. "Either that or you're just getting fat!"

I blushed even more, partly with embarrassment and partly with anger brewing.

"Yes I am," I said through clenched teeth. "Pregnant I mean," I said to my parents. I thought I had better clarify that one.

"Oh darling!" Mum said and rushed over to hug me with tears welling in her eyes. "Oh I'm so pleased! I'm going to be a grandma! Roy we're going to be grandparents!!"

Dad got up and hugged me while Mum moved on to Chops, cooing and fussing over him. Dad shook Chops' hand and said, beaming "Congratulations, well done you two."

Well done??! Did my dad really just congratulate us for having a root and failing to use contraceptives correctly? Classic.

And then the Wicked Bitch really let loose. She slammed her cup down on the coffee table, spilling coffee over the side and launched herself out of her chair.

"You stupid cow!" she screamed. "I bet you did this on purpose because you know David and I are trying for a baby!"

Actually I didn't know that. And now I have a mental picture of them having sex ewwwwwwww.

"You have always been such a selfish little bitch! I'm the older sister, I should be having a baby before you! You've been with him for what, five minutes!? I HATE YOU LUCY!!" she continued screaming.

I so wish Matt was here to see this. Her nostrils are actually flaring... oh shit, don't laugh at her or she'll go completely postal and--

"Renee, that's enough. Apologise to your sister," my dad quietly commanded.

"I won't apologise! Come on David, we're leaving!" she grabbed her purse and stalked off, leaving her obviously embarrassed husband to stammer "I'm sorry. Thank you for lunch Pauline," as he quickly followed Renee through the door she had slammed on her way out.

"Well, that went well," Chops said jokingly, in an obvious attempt to brighten the dark atmosphere in the room.

I half smiled at him as Dad said "I'm very sorry about Renee. They've been trying for a baby since the wedding and I know she is upset about not getting pregnant yet - but even so that's no excuse to speak to you both like that. We are both very happy for you - aren't we Pauline?"

"Oh of course, I am so excited sweetheart! I just can't wait to knit some booties and little hats – oh and Glenys from down the road is going to be so jealous! Her daughter is so career-oriented she won't be getting any grandchildren out of her for a long time!" she said gleefully. "Now, how about another piece of cake with your coffee?"

Of course I couldn't say no to another piece of cake. Well, after a quick visit to the bathroom to undo my jeans that is.

Happy birthday to me.

October

"Hey babe. How was your morning?" Chops came in and threw his bag down on the floor by the couch. I looked up from the computer where I had been stalking a girl I used to go to university with (Dee was right, this Facebook thing is awesome!) and saw Chops in his work gear, his hair dishevelled and sleeves rolled up.

"Mmm hello yourself..." I got up and sidled up to him, waiting for that glorious smell of raw meat, blood and sawdust to hit my nostrils.

Hit me it did. Glorious it was not. I recoiled and screwed my face up in distaste as a wave of nausea hit me like a freight train.

"What's wrong?" Chops asked with a look of panic on his face.

"Oh my God-I'm going to be sick!!" I clamped my hand over my mouth and raced as quickly as I could to the toilet.

I just made it in time. I powerchucked my as yet undigested lunch into the toilet bowl with such force my eyes immediately started watering.

Chops had followed me in and as I was kneeling, bent over the bowl and moaning for death to come and take me like a hungover 20 year old, he pulled my hair back. I turned towards him and got another whiff of raw meat and vomited again violently.

"Go-" Another heave. Nice and Spicy Chicken noodles - not so nice on their way back up.

"-have a shower. Please." I managed to stammer. The smell was hideous.

"Okay. But are you going to be alright?" he asked in a concerned voice, smoothing my hair down.

"Yes! Just go! Please!" I cried, smacking his hand away and not wanting to look at him in case I got another whiff of the putrid stench.

He left and a minute later I heard the shower running and the shower door close. I got up off my knees and wiped my face with some seashell printed toilet paper and then flushed.

What the hell? I thought. *Normally I love the Eau de Rump Steak fragrance...*

I tidied myself up and reapplied my makeup, feeling much better instantly. Ugh apart from the manky vomit breath.

Chops came in wearing a towel with wet hair. He looked worried. "Are you okay now?"

"Yeah totally fine – I just seriously need to brush my teeth. That was so random, maybe the noodles I had for lunch were off or something?"

"I hope you're not going to start getting morning sickness," Chops said, "you've been so good up 'til now!"

"Nah, I'm almost 12 weeks I'm sure it's just a once off, I feel sweet as now. Apart from being hungry that is," I replied.

Chops laughed. "Legend. I'll go put my work gear in the wash and make us some lunch then. Maybe no more noodles for awhile though!"

It was not a once off.

The spew gates had been opened. But ironically it seemed to be only the smell of raw meat that caused the immediate and complete regurgitation of my entire stomach contents (*really helpful when living with a butcher*) the rest of the time I just had extreme nausea that unfortunately could only be momentarily fixed by eating.

So eat I did.

"I thought morning sickness was supposed to finish at 12 weeks, not bloody well start then," I whined through a mouthful of Salt and Vinegar chippies.

"Are you sure it's not twins? Apparently morning sickness is worse if it's twins," Laura asked, putting a coffee mug down in front of me. She was off work on maternity leave after having her baby, a little boy named Jacob.

Is she calling me fat??

"No, thank God, there's definitely only one in there," I replied, scoffing more chips. "We had the first scan last week."

"Awww, how did that go?" she asked, picking Jacob up out of a weird little bouncy contraption on the floor as he had started crying.

"It was ok – it just looks like a little alien or something to be honest. Chops just about fell asleep in there too. Said it was too dark and the hum of the machines was making him tired."

Jacob was really amping up now and I was struggling to hear Laura's reply over his high-pitched screams.

Shit I think I'd rather listen to effing Coldplay than this racket!

"Here, can you hold him while I heat his bottle up?" Laura asked and before I could reply and say hell no, she handed the howling baby to me.

Instant panic. I suddenly became acutely aware that I had held a grand total of two babies in my entire lifetime and both of those times the babies had been asleep. And yet here was this screaming, writhing thing in my arms who was literally turning red from the sheer effort of his piercing cries.

Oh my god oh my god oh my god. What the hell do I do?

I could hear Laura putting his bottle into the microwave and willed the microwave to hurry up and heat it.

"Sssssshhhhh," I said in a completely unsoothing, panicked and totally futile attempt to get him to calm down.

Can I put him back in that bouncy thing? Oh my God Laura please hurry up!!

I looked down at the baby in my arms who was quite possibly actually screaming his diddle off and felt nothing but complete and utter fear. Thankfully Laura reappeared with a bottle of milk in her hand and took him from me, immense relief passing over me as she said calmly "There you go baby, sshh sssh," and started feeding him.

It took all my restraint not to run screaming from the house so in an attempt to calm my frayed nerves and not offend my friend, shoved another handful of chippies into my mouth and pretended everything was fine.

Shitballs. What the hell have I gotten myself into??

~~~~~~~~~~~~~~~~

"I seriously am going to be the worst mother ever," I wailed to Jess over lunch at a cafe the next day. "I had no frigging idea what to do with that baby!"

"It'll be different with your own," she said reassuringly. "Once you hold yours it'll all come naturally to you I'm sure."

"God I hope you're right," I replied, not reassured at all, "otherwise my kid is going to need some serious therapy when it's older!"

"You'll be sweet Goose. Oh - I forgot to tell you I saw Rupert at the supermarket the other day. He was shopping with another umm, large lady, I'm guessing he must have found himself a girlfriend to move in with!"

I half smiled. "Man he would fully love to nick my undies now that I'm a fatty bombastic," I said grumpily.

"Oh you are not!" my far too exuberant friend said. "You look great!"

"Whatever. I told a patient at work that I'm pregnant a couple of days ago, she's this sweet little old lady and you know what she said? She said 'oh that's lovely Lucy. I had noticed you've put quite a lot of weight on. What are you, about 6 months along?' How embarrassing when I had to admit I'm not even 4 months yet! Bitch!"

"Oh Goose, don't stress about it. You'll always be pretty no matter what you weigh. And I'm sure you will lose it once you have bubs," Jess replied optimistically.

"Hmmmpf, don't mind me I guess I'm just having a bad day," I replied, "I'll snap out of it I'm sure."

"Honestly babe don't stress, I have faith in you," Jess smiled at me.

"Enough about me, how are things with Callum?" I asked her as we started getting ready to leave. Jess had started going out with a guy she met through a teacher at work a few weeks before. He was a bit too boring for my liking (he almost bored me to tears the night I met him by talking about politics – snore!) but even worse, he didn't laugh at my obviously awesome jokes. So not cool.

"It's okay, I don't really think he's 'the one' but-"

"LUCY!"

We were halfway to the exit when I heard somebody call my name. I turned in the direction that the voice came from and instantly felt the colour drain from my face.

My bad day was about to get a whole heap worse.

Charging towards me like a bull on steroids was Rob the Builder's shit-stirring, Tupperware-selling, bitch of a mother.

Oh shit...

"Oh crap, it's Rob's mother," I said to Jess under my breath.

"Holy shit! Don't worry I'll take the bitch on if she says anything nasty," Jess hissed back, fists clenched at her sides.

She finally reached us and I was already on the defensive, remembering how the last time I saw her went and knowing this could end up in a public brawl if Jess had any say in it.

I forced a smile onto my face as she reached us. "Hello."

"Oh Lucy," she said ever so sweetly and smiled, "I've been *hoping* I would run into you."

She had me baffled. She was being so uncharacteristically nice I didn't really know how to respond.

"I heard that you're pregnant and I just wanted to say congratulations," she continued and I warily listened, waiting for the bitch to unleash and tell me how fat and ugly I look and how disgusting it is that I got pregnant out of wedlock. But the bitch remained caged. And possibly heavily medicated.

"I just hope your partner treats you well as you deserve all the happiness in the world and I'm sure you will make a wonderful mum," she said wistfully.

What the hell?!?

I looked at Jess who looked about as confused as I felt.

"Oh Lucy, I do hope you know that if it doesn't work out with the baby's father then you would be welcomed with open arms back into our family. I wish things had worked out between you and Robbie, you could have been having this baby together-"

No seriously, what the hell?!?

"-you were our only hope. You should SEE the tramp he is going out with now. She's got tattoos and piercings and looks like something the cat dragged in, not at all a pretty girl like you Lucy," she almost looked as though she was about to cry.

I was dumbfounded. And devastated. It took all my strength to not burst into tears and/or smash her in the face. Who was this woman?!

"I, um, have to go," was all I could stammer.

"Okay darling it was so lovely seeing you, please make sure that man of yours takes good care of you, won't you? Oh and by the way, I'm selling Nutrimetics now so if you and your friends would like a wonderful Pamper Party please *do* get in touch with me," she smiled at us and held out a business card as Jess grabbed my elbow forcefully and started leading me away from her.

"Ok thanks," I mumbled numbly as we retreated through the door.

"What the fuck was that? Is she fucking crazy?" Jess said angrily. "I seriously feel like calling Rob and telling him to sort his mother's medication out before letting the crazy old bitch loose on society!"

"Um, they obviously already have," I replied, attempting to make light of the whole random encounter. "But seriously, please don't do that," I pleaded.

"I won't. I just can't believe she said that to you. You were their only hope? Bit bloody late you stupid old mole!"

I had been trying to hold the tears in but it was at that moment that I succumbed. I proceeded in sobbing all the way home with poor old Jess trying to console me while she drove... and the stupid thing was I knew I shouldn't be crying yet I couldn't stop. Frigging hormones have a lot to answer for.

As gutted as I was about what could have been, the past had to stay in the past. I had moved on and Rob the Builder had moved on. I had Chops and an unborn baby, he had the goth chick he had shacked up with. I was happy, he was happy, his mother wasn't. It was all good. Well, it would be after I stopped crying about it anyway.

And as for his shit-stirring, ~~Tupperware~~- oops I mean Nutrimetics-selling, bitch of a mother? Well, she could shove her wonderful Pamper Party up her fat ass for all I cared.

December

"Oh my God I'm sooooooooooooooo fat," I cried as I looked in the mirror in the changing room. "I bet that's why Chops hasn't proposed to me!"

"Why do you think he's going to propose? Ooh I like this top! I didn't realise this place had such cool stuff I've never shopped for clothes here before," Dee asked, pulling a top over her skinny little B-cups. I hate her.

I decided against reminding her that we were actually here shopping for baby stuff, not her.

"I kind of thought he might propose seeing as *I'm having his baby*. But apparently all the hints I've been dropping aren't working cause there ain't no ring on my finger! Mind you, my fingers are so fat I probably couldn't fit a ring anyway – look at them! They're like fat little breakfast sausages!!" I cried in despair and waggled my fingers at my friends.

"Oh Goose, give it time," Jess reassured me. "You're forgetting that you haven't even been together a year yet! He obviously doesn't want to rush into it."

Dee laughed and rubbed my protruding belly. "Although he knows how to rush some things apparently. Boom chicka wow wow."

I examined myself in the mirror. I was 20 weeks pregnant and looked like, in my opinion, a giant tub of lard. Even my maternity jeans were getting tight and to make matters worse, I had the beginnings of what looked like cankles threatening to engulf my entire lower legs. And I was *hot*, like someone had turned a heater on directly in front of me and was following me around with it in a successful attempt to make me look like a sweaty, revolting mess all of the time.

"This baby better be bloody cute after turning me into Harry Hippo! Look! I've even got stretch marks on my gut!" I lifted up my maternity top and pointed to my stomach as my friends shook their heads at me.

"Take a chill pill girlfriend," the Skinny B Cup bitch said as we left the changing rooms, "at least you don't look like *that*."

I looked over to the enormous she-man she had gestured to and immediately felt better about myself – mind you, shopping at K Mart will generally do that for a girl.

~~~~~~~~~~~~~~~

"Hey babe guess what," Chops said, coming into the kitchen and kissing me on the forehead, "Blair and Amanda have broken up."

"Aww that's sad! How come?"

I wasn't really sad to be honest, Amanda is actually a bit of a trollop (think Paris Hilton with a side of Renee) but I had to pretend to like her because she is Chelsea's cousin and had also been instrumental in getting Chops and I together.

"Not really sure, I don't know all the details. Don't think it's very friendly though. I offered him the spare room for a couple of weeks until he can find somewhere else to rent – I hope that's ok?"

Hmmm hot Blair in the spare room...ooh that's more than ok...

"Goose?"

"Oh, uh yeah, that's cool," I said, flustered and blushing. "Am totally dying to know why though."

"Oh no, leave the poor guy alone!" Chops laughed. "He'll be around later with his stuff. Just in time to watch the game and have some beers actually," he put his arms around me and rubbed my belly, smiling. "I can't believe we are going to find out whether the baby is a little Bartholomew or a little Agnes tomorrow."

"Piss off! Our baby is going to have a cool name."

"Are you telling me that Agnes isn't a cool name? Man, we really should've had this conversation before I knocked you up - I didn't realise you had such crap taste in baby names!" he said jokingly.

As I laughed I saw an opportunity. "Actually we haven't talked about last names have we? I'm guessing you want the baby to have Phillips as its last name?" I asked, ever so innocently.

"Yeah I guess I'd like to," he replied.

"I have no problem with that," I said, "I just feel a bit stink that the baby will have a different last name than me. I'd really like to have the same last name as my child." I stuck my bottom lip out for effect.

Take the hint damn it.

"Fair enough I can understand that," he replied, "we could always hyphenate it if that makes you feel better. Bartholomew James-Phillips has a nice ring to it," he laughed.

Grrrrrrrr...

"Fine.Whatever," I said grumpily and started stomping up the hallway to the bedroom.

"What's wrong?" he asked, following me.

"Nothing." I sat down on the bed and picked up a magazine.

"Ok...but it doesn't seem like nothing. Something's obviously bothering you – oh wait, you know I'm joking about Bartholomew aye?!"

Is he really that thick?? Alright then...he asked for it!

"You *really* can't figure out what's bothering me??" I exploded and stood up, throwing the magazine down onto the bed. "Ooh, how about the fact that every time I even mention getting married you make a joke or change the subject?? Obviously I'm good enough to have your baby but not good enough to marry - is that it??"

Chops sighed. "No, that's not it. You know that's not true you're just being irrational Goose."

"I'm being IRRATIONAL!? For wanting the father of my unborn child to actually *want* to marry me?!"

"No, for expecting it to happen so quickly! We haven't been together that long, I just assumed we could just take things as they go and when the time is right we could look at it then, I thought things were fine the way they are," he replied matter-of-factly.

"Oh I get it. Apparently FIONA was good enough to marry seeing as you obviously had no trouble proposing to her. But noooo, I'm just the crazy bitch who you were stupid enough to get pregnant and now you're stuck with!"

Okay, maybe I'm being a wee bit irrational now...

He was angry. "Bloody hell Lucy!" he exclaimed and stormed over to his bedside drawer. He opened it and pulled out something small then turned around to face me.

He was holding a jeweller's box.

Ohhhh shiiiit.

"I *do* have a ring and I *was* going to propose on Christmas Day," he snapped. "Of course I know how important it is to you to get married – contrary to what you believe I'm actually not stupid!"

Oops...

"But you just couldn't wait, you had to keep pushing it!" he continued.

I stood quietly while he ranted and decided bullrushing him to get to the box he was still holding was probably inappropriate given what the current argument was about.

"I don't know why you need a ring on your finger to make you happy because the fact is, I'm already happy. I've got you and we are having a baby – and that in itself already puts you miles ahead of bloody Fiona because I never even considered having kids with *her*. We only got engaged because *she* decided it was time to so *she* went and put an effing ring on layby and told me about it afterwards. What is the big obsession with getting a damn ring for you women?!"

"I'm sorry. I was being irrational," I said quietly, "but I thought if you didn't want to marry me then it meant that you have only stayed with me because I got pregnant. And I'm sorry I acted crazy but it's not just about a ring to me – I honestly want to be able to call you my husband and I want to be your wife. And if we're being honest, a ring probably wouldn't fit me at the moment anyway. Sausage fingers," I said, waggling my hand at him.

He laughed and came around to my side of the bed and sat me down next to him, still holding the jeweller's box.

"Goose I do want to marry you, of course I do. You might be crazy but you make me the happiest I've ever been and I'm looking forward to having a future with you and our baby and even a few more kids after this one."

"Whoa...calm the farm champ, only one more after this one," I said, smiling.

"I love you Goose, you crazy irrational bitch," he said and kissed me.

"I love you too," I replied and hugged him. "Umm, can I at least *see* the ring now??"

"Hell no," he said, "you can wait now 'til I'm good and ready." He stood up and put the ring box in his pants pocket. "That's your punishment for being impatient."

"Nooooo...I'll let you call the baby Agnes if you give it to me now?!" I laughed as he pulled me in for a hug.

"Nah, I'm actually thinking more along the lines of Tabitha or Demelza now," he said.

God help me I hope he's joking...

~~~~~~~~~~~~~~~~~

Chops and Blair came home from their pre-Christmas work drinks a week later, completely trashed and singing Rudolph the Red Nosed Reindeer to the taxi driver as he drove away. In an attempt to prevent them from waking the *entire* neighbourhood as they stumbled up the path, I met them at the front door and was surprised to see the newly single Blair with his arm around a very pretty brunette girl who only looked about 19.

Far out she's pretty...hmmmpf.

I looked her up and down in her tiny dress and stilettos and then looked down at myself in my polka dotted pyjama pants and extra large nightie that read 'Wake me at your own risk' (complete with a picture of a cartoon bulldog sleeping in a kennel) and immediately wished I'd stayed in bed.

What a skank. Grrr.

"Goose!" Chops exclaimed. "My beautiful darling Goose!"

They all managed to ascend the front steps without falling over and came inside. Chops grabbed me around my waist (as if such a thing actually exists anymore) and kissed me on the cheek. He reeked of beer.

"Goose this is Alicia," said Blair, introducing the mini-skirted skank.

She giggled and batted her eyelashes at me. "Hi!"

Ugh. Muppet alert.

"Hi," I replied, somewhat unenthusiastically.

"Well, goodnight you guys," Blair said as he and the still giggling Alicia stumbled off to the spare room.

I turned back to Chops who was leaning against the wall by the front door with a goofy grin on his drunken face.

"Goose! Take me to bed or lose me forever!" he quoted Top Gun and started laughing hysterically.

'I don't get drunk, I get awesome' doesn't apply to men – they just get bloody annoying.

"I'm guessing you guys had a good night then?" I asked as I took his arm and led him to our bedroom. He sprawled out on our bed like a starfish as I took his shoes off and tried to undo his jeans to help him get undressed.

"Yeah it was awesome," he struggled to sit up. "But it would have been better if you were there. You're so cool Goose all the guys love you. I'm so lucky!" he semi-slurred.

I became aware that some uh, interesting noises had started in the room next door. Chops suddenly stood up, his jeans falling to his knees as he strode past me towards the wardrobe, half tripping on his pants. I sat on the edge of the bed, not really sure what he was doing.

He pulled the wardrobe door open and peered inside, reaching for something out of the pocket of a jacket that was hanging inside.

The moaning and crying out from next door had gotten louder. If Chops noticed it he didn't seem to acknowledge it. Mind you it would be hard to ignore it - I imagine little old Mrs. McLellan in the house across the road could probably hear it *without* her hearing aids in.

Damn! What is he doing to her!? Lucky bitch! Hmm I wonder if he gives lessons...

My attention was turned back to Chops as he stumbled back towards me, pants now around his ankles, skinny white legs bare from his black Y-fronts down.

He knelt down in front of me.

Oh my God! Is he going to-

I got distracted by the moans from next door which had turned into full on explosive high pitched squeals of "Yes! Yes! Harder!" and realised our bedroom wall was shaking like a 6.8 magnitude earthquake from the deeds that were obviously being done against the headboard on the other side. I watched as the canvas wall art on our wall above the bed shuddered and shook.

Hmm, I wonder if I should take that down...

Chops, in his drunken state, apparently still wasn't even aware of the racket. "I love you so much Goose you are so amazing and you are going to be the best mum to our baby girl-"

Oh that's right forgot to mention we are having a girl! Woop woop!

"-I just wish my mum could have met you she would love you as much as everyone else does. You're the best Lucy James. Will you marry me?" he asked as he struggled to open the jewellery box.

"Yes!" I exclaimed but just as I was about to see the ring Blair must have finally hit a home run in his game of hide the sausage. We heard an almighty scream of "FUCK YESSSSSS!" along with low-pitched grunting, which was followed quickly by the crash of the canvas as it finally fell off the shaking wall and rebounded off the bed onto the floor.

Bugger. I guess I should've taken that down.

"Bloody hell Blair keep it down! I'm *trying* to propose in here man!" Chops yelled out.

A few seconds later the door flew open and Blair in all his hotness - and unfortunately with one hand grasping a sheet around his waist - came bursting in.

"Oh mate that's awesome. Congratulations champ," he said. He man-hugged Chops then turned to me. "Congratulations Goose, it's primo news," he said, then hugged me (with only one arm damn it) and kissed me on the cheek.

Ewwww I know where those lips have just been...

Speaking of where his lips had just been, I looked over to our doorway where the skinny little Alicia was standing in one of Blair's t-shirts, giggling. She came in and swooped on me, hugging me.

Ugh random sexed-up drunk chick hugging me! What the-

"Congratulations! I am so happy for you," she cried and then for no particular reason, burst into tears.

Geez he sure knows how to pick the crazy bitches! I stared at her in disbelief.

"I'm sorry," she hiccupped. "It's just so lovely. I hope I get to have a baby and get married when I'm your age."

What the hell!?? How old does she think I am!? Skinny little bi-

"Okay Alicia - we better leave the happy couple to celebrate," Blair winked at me, gesturing to Chops who still had his pants around his ankles, and led his still-crying new friend out of the room.

Damn could this proposal have gone any worse?!

Apparently yes it could. No sooner had I tried to force the beautiful Princess cut diamond ring on my fat little sausage finger (it didn't get past my knuckle) and texted Jess, Dee and Leo to tell them the good news, my future husband (who may or may not even remember proposing in the morning) had crashed out on the bed, Y fronts on display and snoring like a freight train.

"Ohhh! Yes! YES! Spank me big boy!"

Oh, *and* I was lucky enough to be wide awake to hear Round 2 of the earth-shattering Christmas celebrations happening in the spare room.

What a night.

~~~~~~~~~~~~~~~~

We were going to wait until Christmas Day to announce to our families that we had gotten engaged, but decided against that idea seeing as the last announcement we had made went down like a tonne of dog shit and ended with my sister screaming her hatred at me and storming off.

So instead we had rung my parents and Chops' dad and sister to tell them the news and everybody was really happy for us (in fact I think I could hear my mother looking up marriage celebrants in the Yellow Pages before I'd even hung up the phone).

But we had decided that we wouldn't be in a rush to have the wedding (first time for everything in our relationship!) and we had set a date for March 2009. I figured since the baby was due in April that would give me almost a year to lose all the extra weight I had been gaining during the pregnancy - apparently at 21 weeks a baby only weighs about 360g, so I was at a complete loss as to where the extra 12kg had come from. Okay, so maybe not a *complete* loss...it turns out Steak and Cheese pies and Big Macs aren't very good friends to have around for lunch every day.

And thankfully Renee had fallen pregnant too so she was due about 2 months after me - I reckon that she had been so pissed off that I was pregnant that after she found out she went home and rooted poor David and his ginger balls relentlessly for a few weeks until he finally knocked her up.

I have always wondered why people say a woman has 'fallen pregnant.' I mean, it's not like we accidentally slip and fall onto a random penis which then results in it unintentionally shooting semen into our vajayjays.

Well, apart from Dee that is - I am fairly certain *she* may have accidentally slipped and fallen onto many a random penis in her time.

But most importantly, in a completely astonishing turn of events, being preggers had turned my mean tempered troll of a sister into an almost unrecognisable person. On Christmas Day she was calm, friendly and dare I say it, actually quite NICE. All day I kept waiting for the exorcist within her to resurface but it just didn't happen, not even when I purposefully snaked the last piece of cheesecake -something that would normally make her see red and her head spin. Oh wait, no, that's me. Haha.

Matt reckons that they'll probably end up with a little farm full of Gingas running around cause David's gonna be knocking her up constantly if being pregnant means that she's not a total ball busting wench to him all the time. A farm full of Gingas...even the mere thought of it cracks me up.

2008
February

"You are just going to have to harden up and tell him it's time to move out!" I told Chops firmly as I straightened my hair. The 'couple of weeks' that Blair was going to be staying with us until he found a new flat was going on two months and I, for one, was sick of seeing hot half naked girls traipsing around my house while I was looking more and more like the Goodyear Blimp with each passing day.

"Besides," I continued, "we *seriously* need to get the baby's room sorted and we can't do that while he's in there."

"Yeah I know," Chops replied, "I'll say something to him in the next couple of days, ok?"

"Oh, you mean like you were going to last week?" I said sarcastically. I was beginning to suspect that Chops didn't mind seeing the hot half naked girls traipsing around our house - which was why he wasn't making him move out in any kind of hurry.

"I mean, how many girls has he brought home in the last 6 weeks?? Like, five?!" I exclaimed.

"To be fair, the third and fifth were the same girl, she had just dyed her hair in between times," Chops came to the man-whore's defence a bit too quick for my liking.

"Oh really?" I shot back, raising my eyebrows at him. How ironic that he hadn't noticed I'd had streaks put through my hair that very morning.

He obviously saw the look on my face and decided that retreat was his best chance of surviving the oncoming battle so he quickly said "I'll talk to him tomorrow, I promise. Go on off you go, have a nice night with your friends," and kissed me on his way out the bedroom door. "Oh, and your hair looks amazing by the way."

Ooh lucky save.

~~~~~~~~~~~~~~~~

"But the worst thing is, they're all about 20, giggly and *really* annoying," I told my friends about the whole Blair saga, "which is a shame cause he is actually a really cool guy he just has epically shit taste in chicks."

"Is epically actually a word or did you just make that up?" Leo asked.

"Hmm, I don't know," I replied, "but if it's not, it should be."

"Mate I need to meet this guy! He sounds hot!" Dee interrupted.

"He is pretty hot," Jess agreed.

"Ooh! I have a photo of him in my phone actually!" I exclaimed, pulling my phone out of my bag and scrolling through the photos.

"Why have you got a photo of him on your phone?" Dee asked.

"We were bored one night a couple of weeks ago and were taking photos of ourselves. So I took one of me and him – as you do," I laughed. "Ooh here it is!"

"Gee, that's not stalkerish at all," Leo laughed and had a look at the photo, "mmm mm. Not that I'm complaining of course."

Dee looked at my phone. "Damn. He is seriously hot! I think you need to hook a sister up Goosey!"

"No, he is *epically* hot," Leo laughed. "Ooh! Jess! He could move in with us since Stinky Stan is moving out!"

"Oh awesome plan, then I get stuck seeing all the little half naked tramps instead," Jess retorted.

"Oh but think of the eye candy for us Jessica – AND he might have hot friends! It'd be rude not to at least *offer* the poor homeless man a room for his insanely hot body to rest in. Ooh, we could make it a house rule that he isn't allowed to wear shirts!"

Jess shrugged. " As long as he does his dishes and actually has a shower unlike Stan then I'm all for it. And I guess it *would* save us choosing one of the mutants that came to look at the room today. Ugh."

"Sweet I'll text him and ask him!" I said happily.

And then we all had a moment of silence to imagine Blair without a shirt on. And then another to imagine him in the shower. It'd be rude not to really.

~~~~~~~~~~~~~~~~

Two nights later Blair, Chops and I were sitting in the lounge watching TV after dinner when Blair's cellphone started ringing. He looked at the caller ID, groaned and didn't answer it. I just couldn't help being nosy. "Who was that?"

He shrugged. "Nobody important."

"Was it Alicia? Or Maria? Or one of the other ones? I can't remember their names there have been so many," in a semi-sarcastic tone.

"Goose! It's none of your business," Chops admonished me.

"It's all good mate," Blair said to him. "If you must know, it was Lara."

"Who's Lara?"

"The girl that came home with me the weekend before last."

Ohhh Number 4. The blonde skank with the red bra.

"Oh yes I remember her. So why didn't you answer when she called?" The interrogation had begun.

"Goose! You are so nosy!" Chops interrupted again, exasperated.

"Because she's kind of annoying. She's really full on and keeps wanting to hook up all the time and I don't want to," he replied.

"Well, she is only about 19 isn't she?? I'm sure I was pretty annoying at 19 too," I said.

"What, you mean you're not now?!" Chops interjected. "Leave the poor guy alone."

I death stared him then turned back to Blair. "I'm sorry but I have to say it – why are you hooking up with these random young chicks that you obviously don't care about? They obviously really like you but you are treating them like crap. I always thought you were such a good guy-"

In fact I've heard how good you are...many, many times.

"-but you're acting like a bit of a dick. Is this the person you really are and I was wrong about you? To be honest I'm kind of disappointed in you."

Oh my god I sound like a nagging mother. I blushed and waited for him to go off his nut and tell me to mind my own business.

Surprisingly, he didn't. He slumped back in his seat and sighed.

"You're right," he admitted.

I am?? Why yes of course I am!

"I don't mean to treat them like crap, it's just easy, I guess. They all really like me-"

Oh yes. I've heard just how much they like you...

"-and after being treated like shit by Amanda for three years, it was kind of nice to be on the other side of it for a change."

Chops took that as his cue to leave the room. His friendship with Blair apparently didn't extend to deep and meaningfuls.

"But if you know how it feels to be treated like crap then why would you knowingly treat others like it? That's not cool. And why did Amanda treat you like shit anyway?"

Finally! The gossip I have been dying to know for weeks!

"Because I'm *just* a butcher, I didn't earn enough, wasn't smart enough, the list goes on. I was never good enough for her – apart from when she wanted to make other girls jealous. And then I was perfect and could do no wrong of course. I mean, I look at you guys and you obviously respect Chops heaps. I never had that with her."

"That sucks! I always knew she was an up-herself bitch!" I exclaimed. " I tell you she's soooo not all that with her yuck fake blonde hair and her try hard makeup!"

Blair laughed. "That's one way to put it."

"So why did you stay with her for so long?"

"I don't know. I guess we did have some good times, you know? It wasn't all bad."

"Well I think you're too good for her. Always did. Until you started man-whoring your way through all the teenagers in our direct vicinity anyway," I said with a smile.

He laughed again. "One of them was 25 you know, she just looked really young. You remember Alicia?"

I blushed. *Bitch! That's the one that called me old!*

"Hmmmpf. How could I forget? You've got some uh, special skills apparently."

It was his turn to be embarrassed. "Oh man. I'm so sorry Goose."

Hmm, is now a bad time to ask if he gives lessons?!

~~~~~~~~~~~~~~~~~~

"Awww that looks so cute!" I walked into the spare room where Chops was finishing putting a baby animals wall decal on the freshly painted baby pink feature wall.

"Yeah," he replied, "we better hope they got the sex right on the scan or we are going to have a little boy who loves pink."

Blair had moved to my old flat with Jess and an extremely excited Leo a couple of weeks ago. Being the wonderful person I am I had given him my old bed - sheets and duvet cover included - as the bitchy Amanda had pretty much left him high and dry without anything when he had broken up with her. And after the action that had gone down in that bed (no pun intended hahaha) since he had been staying with us I was pretty sure the mattress would have permanent dents in it and the sheets would probably have a permanent stench of skank anyway.

And we needed the space for the baby's cot. I was coming up 33 weeks pregnant and we had finally gotten the room sorted for our as yet unnamed baby. We were even due to start antenatal classes the following week. Oh yes, shit was getting very real very quickly.

But on the upside, the morning sickness and nausea had ended. The continuous eating had not.

"What do you want for dinner?" Chops asked, getting down off his stepladder.

"Ohhh you know what I really feel like??" I replied.

"What? You're not going to say something gross like sardines and bacon on toast are you?"

Mmm bacon...

"No. I really feel like fish and chips from that place we went to on the way back from your Dad's after Christmas."

"That's like 45 minutes away! What's so great about them that they'd be worth driving that far for?" he asked in disbelief.

"Oh man they were sooo good. They were really greasy and I just feel like something really greasy at the moment. Come on babe let's go for a drive. Please?"

"Oh, alright then," Chops gave in to the puppy dog eyes and pouty lip I was giving him.

"Yay! I'll just feed the cats and we can get going," I told him. Milkshake and Prozac had come to a point in their relationship where Prozac no longer ambushed and attacked Milkshake every time he saw her but there was still no love lost between them. I doubt they would ever be BFFs but as long as they tolerated each other I think that was as good as we were going to get.

"My milkshake brings all the boys to the yard," I did a booty shake and sang to the meowing cats as I spooned cat food into their bowls.

"Ok, let's go Dancing Queen," Chops came into the kitchen behind me.

I turned around, still shaking my booty. "You want a piece of this?" I drawled, rubbing my enormous stomach and hip thrusting at him while quoting Fat Bastard from Austin Powers: "Get in mah belly!"

Chops laughed. "God you're special."

"Whatever, you're just jealous of my moves," I replied with a final hip thrust and smacked him on the bum. I was actually puffing a bit from the exertion – mind you it was the most exercise I'd done in the last um, 33 weeks or so. "Now feed me before I turn nasty."

He shuddered at the thought. "Shit let's get going."

~~~~~~~~~~~~~~

45 minutes later we reached the fish and chip shop – which thankfully was open as I hadn't had the foresight to actually check it would be before we started on our mission. It was a rather harrowing drive that consisted of me yelling at Chops for driving like a boy racer and swearing that I was never going to let him drive with our baby in the car.

I swear to God the man thinks he's bloody Vin Diesel or something. Or Paul Walker.

Mmmm Paul Walker....

We got our fish and chips and walked down the road to a nearby park to eat.

"Yum it smells so good," I said as I started scoffing chips and tomato sauce. I started feeling full only about halfway through my piece of fish and felt a massive burp coming on so I let it rip.

"Nice!" Chops said.

"Pardon me," I said, "but this baby is taking up too much room! I can't even finish my food!" I threw a chip down in devastation.

"Was it worth coming all this way for though?" Chops asked, leaning over me and helping himself to the rest of my fish.

"To be honest, it was a bit greasy," I replied with a frown.

I'm still not sure why he just about choked on the piece of fish he was eating.

March

The night of our first antenatal class fell on the first anniversary of when we hooked up. I have to give Chops credit as he did remember the anniversary without having to be reminded (mind you I had mentioned it about oh, thirty four times in the two weeks prior) and he came home from work with a big bunch of flowers and a box of chocolates for me.

I consumed about half the box as an entree before we left and then we had a totally romantic dinner at Burger King before the class started. It was being held at a conference room at the hospital and Leo was on shift so he came down on his break to have a nosy at the group before the class started.

"Good Lord look at that woman!" he hissed under his breath, nodding his head towards a woman seated across the room from us. "I can see her bloody leg hairs from here! Let herself go much?!"

"If her legs are that bad, imagine what her pubes are like!" I whispered back. I neglected to mention I hadn't actually shaved my legs in about three weeks either.

The look of absolute disgust on his face was priceless. Chops came back from the drinks table with a coffee as the woman running the class clapped her hands and said "Ok everyone, one couple still isn't here but let's get started anyway. My name is Melanie and I am a midwife here at the hospital-"

"Oops I guess it's time to go! Bye darling have fun," Leo whispered, jumped out of his seat and made his way to the exit. As he was going out the door the late couple were coming in so he had to stand at the side to let them in. As they passed he made a face at me which, because I know him so well, I knew meant "Hello, hottie alert!"

I looked at the couple as they took the two empty seats in the circle next to Hairy Maclary and her partner.

Holy crap that guy looks like-

At that moment the man of the couple looked over at me with a surprised look and smiled.

Holy shit it IS him!

I felt my face turn a deep red instantly. The guy smirking across the room at me was none other than my high school boyfriend, Sean Harrison. The very same boyfriend that I had lost my virginity to in his parents bed all those years ago.

I hadn't seen him in about nine years but he looked almost exactly the same. Unfortunately the same could not be said for me as I was hugely pregnant, fat, and had cankles the size of the Grand Canyon. Yet the woman sitting next to him looked like she had just stepped out of a pregnancy magazine – all skinny with a bump and looked as though she was still wearing normal sized jeans. None of this elastic waistband shit for her. Bitch.

I tried to concentrate on what Melanie the midwife was saying to us. I caught the tail end of her sentence – "so ladies please introduce you and your partners and tell us a wee bit about yourselves."

Shit. Is he still staring at me? Shit. He is.

We were second for the introductions. First was a chick who looked a couple of years older than me called Karen and her husband Darren. Karen and Darren. If I hadn't been breaking out in a sweaty panic I would have probably found that amusing.

"Hi," I managed to squeak, blush on overdrive, "I'm Lucy and this is my fiancé-"

Ooh fiancé! I still love saying that!

"-Nathan." I could feel Sean's eyes on me and made the mistake of catching his eye. He was still smirking at me. "We, um, are having a, um girl and she is due on um, the 15th of April," I stammered. I sounded like a complete spoon.

The introductions continued around the room until it was Sean's partner's turn. She looked around at everyone. "Hi, I'm Natalie and this is my partner Sean. We are having a boy and we are due on the 15th of April too," she said and smiled at me.

I forced a smile back at her. Oh *of course* she was. Knowing my luck I would probably end up sharing a hospital room with her and her tiny little uterus.

After about 20 minutes of the midwife talking about things that we would be covering during the six week course she announced that we would have a 10 minute break to mix and mingle and get a coffee and a Gingernut (or four in my case).

No sooner had she said that, Sean was up and out of his seat like a rocket and making a beeline for me and Chops.

Oh shit oh shit oh shit.

"Lucy James. Goosey Goosey Gander. Shit it's been, what, 8 or 9 years??!"

"Hi Sean," I stammered, cheeks on fire. "Hi," I said to his partner. I was pleased to see that, while she was a crapload skinnier than me, she looked quite a bit older. Maybe there is truth to the belief that fat people look younger due to the fat cells plumping out our wrinkles. Whatever the reason is, I'll take it.

"Hi Nathan, I'm Sean," he held his hand out to Chops and they shook hands.

"Hey mate, you can call me Chops," he replied, "so I'm guessing you two know each other?" he asked me.

"Umm-" I started but before I got another word in Sean interrupted me.

"We go *way* back don't we Goose? We went to high school together," he said to Chops. "In fact, we used to walk ALL THE WAY home together quite often didn't we? And sometimes we would even GO DOWN to the dairy," he grinned cheekily.

"Uh huh," I squeaked, laughing nervously. If Chops or Natalie thought anything was odd about the conversation they didn't show it. We had a couple of minutes of small talk in which I tried to not sound like a retard until Melanie thankfully called us all back to the circle.

"They're a nice couple," Chops whispered.

I looked over to Sean and Natalie. Natalie was concentrating on what Melanie was saying about water births but Sean was still smiling at me. He winked when we made eye contact.

I blushed again. He always was a cheeky shit.

~~~~~~~~~~~~

"No frigging way! Sean Harrison?! Are you for real??" Jess squawked, reaching for the popcorn.

"Unfortunately totally for real! It was soooo awkward, especially when he told Chops and his partner that we used to walk *all the way* home together," I replied, blushing at the memory.

"What? You didn't live anywhere near each other!" Jess said, confused. Then she got it. "Ohhhhhh. So I guess he's still a smart ass then!?"

"So that was the guy that came in as I was leaving?" Leo asked, throwing an M&M into the air and catching it in his mouth.

"Yep, we went out at school for what, almost two years Jess?" I replied, shovelling a handful of popcorn into my mouth.

"Are you saving some for later Goose?" Leo asked sarcastically, referring to the 3 pieces of popcorn that had fallen down my cleavage into my bra. I scowled at him.

"Yeah, he was a year older than us aye?" she remembered correctly.

"Mate, you do alright for yourself Goose. He was a bit of a hottie!" Leo sounded surprised.

"Why do you sound surprised?? Are you saying you think I'm too ugly to score hot guys??" I demanded.

"Chillax your hormones girl!" he replied, "all I meant is that I'm impressed - you've had a very impressive line up from what I've seen. And so he was the one who took your V plates??"

I blushed at the thought. "Yeah. It was terrible. It was in his parents waterbed - I don't know if you have ever tried scoring in a waterbed but I don't recommend it."

"In his parents bed? Goosey you slapper!" Leo laughed.

"Shut up! Where did you lose yours??" I fired back indignantly.

"Unlike you, I was all class. In the back of a Mercedes Benz A Class hatchback that is," he replied, laughing. I threw a piece of popcorn at him.

"And what was his wife like?" Jess asked.

"Partner. They aren't married. She's skinny with this tiny little bump. I look like I'm having triplets compared to her - and she's due the same day as me!"

"Good old Sean Harrison. Man is that a blast from the past or what! It's such a small world – it'd be fun to see him again he was always a laugh," Jess replied.

"Hold your horses it's not like we are going to be inviting him to bloody BBQs or anything! Antenatal classes are going to be awkward enough without having to see him in social situations too!"

Leo started laughing again. When we looked at him he said "I'm sorry. I just can't believe you can't go anywhere without running into someone that you've rooted. It's like Six Degrees of Goose's Bacon around here!"

Shame! He's kind of right!

"Sssh!" someone behind us hissed. The movie was starting. I settled back in my seat, stuffed my face (ok, and my bra) with popcorn and lost myself in the Adonis that is Ryan Reynolds. Now *that* is a man who would know how to rock a waterbed.

April

"I'm so glad you've come for a visit before the baby is born!" Chops' sister Cherie said happily as she put a bowl of chips and dip on the coffee table. "I just can't believe I'm going to have a niece in a couple of weeks time!"

"I know it's gone so fast," I replied, shifting in my seat. My back was killing me. "I seriously hope I don't go too far past my due date I feel so uncomfortable as it is."

"Ahem," Chops said, clearing his throat. "Are you also forgetting whose birthday it is today??"

"Oh, yes happy birthday of course," Cherie said to him, waving her hand as though he was an afterthought. It was his 34th birthday - damn that's old.

"You look good though Goose," Cherie continued our conversation. "You've finished work now haven't you? And your morning sickness has finished now?"

"Yeah, thank God I finished yesterday." Chelsea had organised a massive farewell morning tea for me at work, complete with mini mince pies, sausage rolls and a chocolate cake covered in little bibs and nappies made out of icing.

"And yeah I haven't even had any nausea for the past two months – and I'm stoked I didn't spew anywhere in public. Now my biggest fear is that my waters will break while I'm at the supermarket!"

"You'll have to send Chops to do the groceries until you've had the baby," she replied.

"Yeah right," I rolled my eyes. "Last time he did the groceries we ended up with 1-ply toilet paper and budget brand shampoo. Ugh!"

She looked horrified. Obviously I'm not the only one who has standards when it comes to wiping our asses or washing our hair.

"Oh, but maybe I did that on purpose so you wouldn't make me do the groceries again," Chops interjected. "And in that case, my plan worked like a charm didn't it?"

She ignored him. "If it makes you feel any better, when I was pregnant with Nate I had *terrible* morning sickness and one night we were leaving the movies when I suddenly felt like I was going to be sick. I ran as fast as I could but didn't make it to the toilet and instead I threw up all over myself in the foyer."

"Ohhhhhhhhh you poor thing!" I exclaimed.

"Yeah and we had eaten Indian for dinner so that was a pleasant drive home," her husband Jon interjected. "It took weeks to get the smell out of the car. Mind you, then we had the baby and the car permanently smelled like crap or spew anyway."

Chops looked panic-stricken. I knew he was imagining his prized Subaru becoming a nappy infested family wagon and he wasn't liking the thought.

"Don't worry babe, I won't be letting the baby in the car with you anyway until you learn how to drive like a normal person," I said sweetly.

"Chops! Are you *still* a shit driver??" his sister asked sternly.

"No! There's nothing wrong with my driving!" he defended himself as Cherie and I gave each other a knowing look.

"*Anyway*, instead of talking about my driving which there is nothing wrong with, how about you tell them what you want to name our poor baby!" he said, trying to change the subject. "Cherie, you will hate it," he said smugly.

"It's a cool name," I said indignantly.

"So, tell us what it is then!" Cherie exclaimed impatiently.

"I really like Carter," I said hesitantly.

Before Cherie could respond, Chops interjected. "But I don't want it because it would sound like we named her after bloody Nick Carter from the Backstreet Boys. Shame."

I gave him the evils. "Well, the fact that you're 34 years old and you even know who Nick Carter is means that you're hardly a good judge of what is shameful." I turned back to Cherie. "And I thought Lynn for her middle name, after your mum. So Carter Lynn Phillips."

Tears welled up in her eyes. "I love it!"

"You do!?" Chops exclaimed. "Jon, help a brother out here! Don't you think it's a bit of a crap name?"

"Um, nah mate. I actually really like it. Nice to hear something a bit different. Besides, you should really listen to Goose, she's cooler than you," he said, laughing.

I smiled at him and then stuck my tongue out at Chops. "Told you it's a cool name!"

He stuck his out back at me. "I was just rarking you up anyway I was always going to let you have it. To be honest I'm just grateful that you didn't want to call her Timberlake!"

Damn it now why didn't I think of that??

"So what did you guys think of Sandra??" Cherie asked later that night as we got into the car. Their dad had taken us all out for dinner (best lemon meringue pie I have EVER had) for Chops' birthday and also to meet his new 'lady friend' that he had been seeing for a few weeks. She was a widower too and met at a Charity Fundraiser walk to raise money for Cancer research. They looked as though they were totally into each other. Middle aged love connection = super cute.

"She seems really nice," Chops said, "what do you think?"

"I like her," Cherie replied, "and I can't remember the last time I have seen Dad that happy so that's got to be a good thing!"

"They were very cute together," I said, shifting my massive weight in the front seat. I got to ride shotgun, mainly because nobody wanted to see the lemon meringue pie come out at the same speed it went in. Although Jon was driving so it was a much more sedate drive than if Chops had been rally car driving us home anyway.

"I think she was really scared of meeting us," Cherie observed.

"Scared of *you* maybe," Chops said, "Dad would have warned her about you - I'm the nice kid. Oww!" he exclaimed as Cherie thumped him on the arm.

"Ooh Chops! It's a song for you!" I cried excitedly and reached for the volume button to turn the radio up and blasted Backstreet Boys 'The Call' through the speakers at the back. "They must have heard you love them *so much* that you're naming your baby after one of them!"

April 13th. Two days until due date. Freshly waxed and ready for birthing action.

"Excellent Lucy. The baby's head is down and in the perfect position. It could be any day now," my midwife Merryn smiled at me as she finished the internal exam and started removing her gloves.

I pulled my knickers back up. It's true what they say about pregnancy – any dignity you have goes out the window. *And* I hadn't even pushed the bugger out yet, I really would have none left by the time this was over.

"Yesterday would have been nice," I moaned, "I just can't believe how uncomfortable I am."

"You're doing great Lucy. Have you got any questions or concerns you want to talk about? Do you want to go over your birth plan again?" Merryn was really nice. She was about 45 and had four teenaged kids. Crazy bitch – I can't believe she would voluntarily go through this four times.

My friend Emma the midwife had recommended I use her seeing as I didn't think it was appropriate that my friend be my midwife. Actually if truth be told, it was more that I didn't want my friend to imagine my gaping muff every time she looked at me in the future.

"Well, I have definitely decided I want to try it without drugs," I replied. "They were talking about all the options in antenatal class and I really don't think I'll like an epidural. And pethidine sounds awful - I don't want my baby to come into the world all drugged out."

"Ok, cool," Merryn said, making a note of it in her book.

"Oh, and um, I was wondering what happens when I push. Um, I heard that people generally um, accidentally, um-"

"Shit?" Merryn asked, smiling.

"Um yeah," I blushed, "I was leaning more towards poop but shit will do. Haha," I laughed nervously. "Even the thought of it embarrasses me. I mean, Chops and I have only been together just over a year. I still get embarrassed taking a dump with him in the house!"

"You're so funny," she smiled, "but don't stress about it. It does happen but I'll get rid of it. I'm very quick and very discreet - he won't have any idea," she told me.

I exhaled with relief. "Ok, thanks. That's great. Now it's time to get this baby out. I seriously need to go to the supermarket!"

"Get a hot curry for dinner and have sex," she laughed at the obviously horrified look on my face. "Honestly, it's worth a try!"

~~~~~~~~~~~~~~~~~~~~~~~

April 17th. Two days after due date. I was seriously ready to rip the lazy little minx out myself, especially after hearing that Sean's partner Natalie had their baby, a 7 pound boy named Rafe three days before our due date. Of course the lucky tart had to go early while I was still wallowing in my own fat like an angry hippo.

The curry didn't work. And in a decidedly shitty turn of events it gave me wicked diarrhoea that had me on and off the toilet the entire day afterwards. In fact, it took two whole days before I could fart with confidence again.

The attempt at sex was awful. There's nothing like being massively pregnant to make a girl feel completely unsexy - I'm surprised poor Chops could even find the right place to stick it through all the blubber. And there is nothing enjoyable in hearing your partner express concern that he might accidentally poke your baby in the head with his penis.

Oh, and apparently "don't worry, it's not like it's big enough to do that," was not the appropriate response to allay *that* particular concern.

So curries and sex were off the cards for further attempts at bringing on labour and, after Googling what other things I could try, I decided that as I hate pineapple and even the sound of Castor Oil made me want to heave, I wasn't going to be boarding the labour train in a hurry – I was stuck at the damn station until further notice.

~~~~~~~~~~~~~~~~~~~~

April 19th. Four days after due date. Eight days since my last supermarket visit. And my back was bloody sore so sitting, standing, lying down – *everything* was uncomfortable. Oh and our baby was obviously planning on being a gymnast because apparently staying still was no fun at all.

I still wasn't asleep by 11pm that night. I was absolutely shattered as I'd been having cramps all day and had tried to keep my mind off them by doing housework (now *that* is desperation in its highest form). Chops, on the other hand, had been snoring since about 9:45pm.

Hmmmpf lucky prick.

I sighed and tossed back the covers dramatically and managed to swing my legs around off the side of the bed to stand up.

Holy shit what's that?! Is that a- oh my God! Owwwwwwww!!!!

I felt what was like one of the cramps I'd been having all day only about twenty times stronger. Bloody hell, did it hurt like a mofo.

"Chops!" I shrieked.

He sat bolt upright, eyes glazed over. "What? Is it happening?"

"I think so! I think I'm having a contraction!"

"No shit! Ok! Umm, what do we do?" he jumped out of bed and looked around with a panicked look on his face.

"Owwwwww," I moaned and doubled over with the pain as another contraction hit me.

"Holy shit, sit down!" Chops raced around to my side of the bed and sat me down on the edge. He started rubbing my back.

"Call the midwife," I managed to squeak. Finally it passed.

"You need to time how far apart they are," I said to him. "She will ask how long they are and how far apart they are."

"Ok!" He scrambled over to his side of the bed and grabbed his watch.

"Fuuuuuuuuuuck!" I moaned as another one started.

"I think they're quite close together," Chops said.

"No. Shit. Sherlock!" I finally gasped.

I heard him ring Merryn but was only half aware of their conversation. I heard him say a panicked "Ok see you soon."

"Goose." he said gently and took my arm as I came out of another contraction. "We need to go. The midwife will meet us at the hospital."

"Don't forget my bag." I said as he put my slippers on my feet and helped me up.

Shit, where did I put my bag?

"Yep, got it. All good. Let's go!" he said in a tone that could only be described as nervous excitement - or perhaps he was shitting himself with fear. Join the club.

He helped me into the front seat of his car and backed out the driveway as I started writhing in pain again. I opened the window for some fresh air as I had broken out in a full body sweat.

We started making our way to the hospital which was normally about a fifteen minute drive but I figured we would be there in about eight minutes with the way Chops drove.

Ummm no. There was no channelling of his Fast and the Furious counterpart this time - nope, instead he was driving like a frigging nana. He stopped as a light turned orange even though there wasn't another car anywhere to be seen in any direction.

"What the hell? You choose *now* of all times to drive Miss fucking Daisy?!" I screamed at him. My voice echoed in the quiet night air out of the open window.

Before he could defend himself the light turned green and another contraction started with a vengeance.

"It's ok baby, we're almost there," he said soothingly, patting my leg.

"It's not ok-owwwwwwwwww," I cried. Then all of a sudden everything became very muted. I was aware that Chops was talking but I had no comprehension of what he was saying. And I really didn't care.

I didn't know how much time had passed but I realised that we had reached the hospital carpark. I could see the bright red light of the emergency sign as he pulled the car to a stop outside.

I saw Merryn standing at the entrance with a wheelchair and saw her running over towards us, pushing it in front of her.

I was aware that she and Chops were helping me out of the car and into the wheelchair and I could hear them talking hurriedly as they pushed me towards the lifts to take me to the birthing unit. I heard snippets of what they were saying and I could hear an approaching ambulance siren but otherwise everything was eerily quiet. Except for the random cow I could hear mooing.

Where is that coming from? There are no farms around here...

I heard it again, so distinctly. The low, deep sound of a cow mooing –and it sounded like it was in pain.

Oh the poor cow. I hope it's not hurt...

I heard it again and at the same time I realised I was no longer in a wheelchair, I was being helped onto a hospital bed.

"Chops," I squeaked through a dry mouth, "where's the cow? It sounds hurt."

"What? What cow?" he looked confused. Just then I heard it again and came to the realisation that there was no cow. It was me.

"Moooooooooooooooooooo."

Oh my God. I sound like a dying cow...

But even after realising it I couldn't stop it. The noises I was making were coming from deep in my throat and were completely involuntary. I would normally be highly embarrassed by sounding like a farmyard animal on its way to slaughter but the pain of the contractions were so intense I didn't give a flying crap what anyone thought.

"Ok Lucy you are doing so well sweetheart," Merryn said, "how about we check how dilated you are so we have an idea of how long this will take. I'm guessing it won't be long."

I broke out of my semi trance by an overwhelming desire to go to the toilet. "I need to go to the toilet! Now!" I said, trying to push myself off the bed.

"Do you need to do number ones or twos?" Merryn asked.

"Twos! I need to do a shit! Now!!" I exclaimed.

"No you don't darling, you're feeling like you need to push. Let's check down below and see if you are ready to!" she replied excitedly.

She helped me lie back on the bed and checked. "Just what I thought. You're about 9cm dilated. But your waters haven't broken so I'm just going to break them for you and then we can get this baby out!"

She moved away from the bed and when she came back into my eyesight she was holding up a long silver hook that was glinting under the fluorescent lights. I felt the blood drain from my face as I realised the hook (that closely resembled the murder weapon from I Know What You Did Last Summer) was about to used up my poor vajayjay.

I closed my eyes to avoid watching the massacre and a second later I felt a massive gush of liquid explode between my legs and all over the bed. As painful as the constant contractions were, I think the feeling that I'd just pissed myself in the most extreme way was the worst part. Oh wait, the baby wasn't out yet. I take that back.

"You're doing so good babe," I heard Chops say as he was rubbing my shoulder.

From somewhere in between my legs I heard Merryn say "Ok honey when you're ready you can start pushing."

I gave a massive push and the noise that came out of my mouth was unrecognisable. The dying cow had died and instead I had turned into some maniacal baboon on a rampage.

I don't know how long I had been pushing for when I heard "Stop pushing! You need to stop pushing Lucy!" Merryn's head appeared above the bed.

"I can't stop!" the urge to push was just too strong.

"You have to stop Lucy or you are going to tear. Listen to me!"

"I CAN'T STOP!"

"GOOSE! FOR FUCK'S SAKE STOP PUSHING!" Chops yelled at me.

Well, that was the straw that broke the camel's back. Or in my case, the labouring elephant. I burst into tears.

"Why are you yelling at me?" I sobbed through my tears. But at least I had stopped pushing.

"I'm so sorry babe. But you needed to listen to Merryn. It's ok, I'm sorry," Chops said in a gentle voice while he rubbed my back, "you are doing so good, you're amazing."

A couple of minutes later Merryn piped up again. "Ok Lucy you're good to go again but I need you to lie on your side, ok? And Nathan I need you to hold her leg up, she is going to struggle against you but you need to hold it up while she pushes, ok?"

And then it was all on. I was still crying, tears streaming down my face as I grunted and pushed with all my might while poor Chops struggled to hold the massive weight of my leg up. I had no idea how long I had been pushing as all I could concentrate on was the searing pain down below.

I heard Merryn call out "Good girl! The head is out! One more big push Lucy to get these shoulders out. You're almost there!"

Trust my kid to have the shoulders of a Quarterback. One more push and I felt my entire vagina erupt into burning flames as the shoulders passed through and then all of a sudden I felt immense relief as I felt the rest of the baby slide out. It felt like the most massive crap I'd ever done.

And that massive crap was my child. I moved onto my back in time to see Merryn holding our little girl up, covered in my yucky poon juice and shrivelled up like a little old man.

Chops had let go of my leg and was gripping my shoulder.

"Meet your daughter," Merryn said, smiling, as the baby started wailing.

Oh my god. I just gave birth. I am a giver of life. I am a mother. Holy shit does she have-

"Looks like you have got yourself a little redhead," she continued.

We have a GINGA!??!? What the-

Apparently Karma is indeed a bitch and my years of hassling redheads had finally resulted in the ultimate payback – I had given birth to a carrot top.

I looked at Chops - he was beaming at our daughter, red hair and all. Merryn asked him if he would like to cut the umbilical cord and I watched as he did. My legs were shaking but a couple of minutes later I was handed my baby, who had stopped screaming and was wrapped up in a pink hospital blanket and was gazing serenely up at me.

"For someone that kept you waiting she sure came out in a hurry," Merryn said.

"Why? What time is it?" I asked. It was still dark outside so I knew it wasn't quite morning yet but figured it wasn't far off sunrise. Hmm, maybe her hair wouldn't be ginger in the daylight.

"Just after midnight," she replied.

"Really? Wow. That felt like hours!" I was shocked.

Chops kissed me on the forehead and touched her head. "Hello Carter Lynn Phillips. She's perfect Goose. You're so amazing."

"Careful now," I joked, "saying that to me was how I ended up pregnant in the first place."

"You did brilliantly Lucy, no tearing at all," Merryn said, who was back in position between my legs examining my girly bits. "Oops I better weigh her."

She took the baby and popped her on the scales. "Wow, you've got yourself a 9 pounder! 9 pound 2 ounces to be exact," she said, smiling. "You did exceptionally well not to need stitches after that effort."

Oh shame. Leo was right about me having loose flaps!

"Unfortunately though, it's not quite over yet," Merryn said. "Daddy, can you please hold the baby - we need to get the placenta out now."

Sunday 20th, April 12:09am: my vagina feels like it's just birthed a monster truck and I am bleeding like a stuck pig - but I am the proudest I have ever been of myself. I am a mum. I have a baby. We are a family.

Now I just need to find out if there is a support group for mothers of Ginga children...

Four days later I was at home, sitting on my bed crying. And not the few tiny tears rolling silently down my cheeks kind of crying - it was the full blown sobbing, hiccupping, I want to bury my face in a pillow until I die kind of crying.

The first day after having the baby was awesome. Luckily she had decided to grace us with her presence on a Sunday morning so we had constant visitors for the entire day which was tiring but I didn't care, I had a beautiful baby girl to show off.

Leo was the first visitor as he was doing a night shift so after getting the text he came hurtling up to the maternity ward on his break at about 2:30am. The nurses weren't going to let him in (seeing as it was about eight hours past visiting hours) but because he was in uniform and sweet talked them they let him in for a couple of minutes. He then got curtly asked to leave after his roaring laughter at seeing my daughter's hair colour was so loud he had disturbed the woman sleeping in the room next to me. "There are always hats Goose!" he called as he was being escorted out of the room by a sour faced nurse.

Oh yes, there will be hats. Many, many hats.

My Mum and Dad were the next to arrive at about 9am and I'm quite sure the whole ward had the pleasure of hearing my extremely excited mother arrive about five minutes before she got to my room.

Dad's quiet excitement at becoming a Grandad was so lovely and Mum bawled her eyes out while announcing "She's so beautiful! I need photos! Take some photos Roy! I need photos to show the ladies in my book club - they are going to be so jealous!" and then "Now darling, are you sure you want to call her Carter? It's just that she doesn't really look like a Carter. How about something pretty - like Sophie? Or Grace?"

Jess came at about 10:30am with Blair. She was carrying flowers and chocolates which I ripped into straight away (the chocolates, not the flowers) as the cold scrambled eggs and toast I had been given at 7:30am really hadn't cut it. Blair and Chops did the male bonding thing while Jess cuddled my sleeping baby with tears in her eyes.

"She's just so beautiful," she gushed. "I am so happy for you Goose!"

"Thanks babe. Oh my God though, what do you think of her *hair*??"

Jess rubbed her hand softly over Carter's soft hair. "Oh Goose it's beautiful. Random, but beautiful. And at least it's not that really *ugly* ginger, it's pretty. Strawberry blonde!"

I retract my past statement of 'there's no such thing as strawberry blondes, only Gingas in denial' - yep, I've officially changed my mind and there is *totally* such a thing as strawberry blonde hair. And my baby girl has got it. Haha.

Cherie, Jon and their boys, along with Chops' dad arrived at lunchtime just as a completely unappealing sandwich and soup arrived for me. They stayed for about an hour, with Cherie crying and taking copious amounts of photos of Carter with her two boys, Carter with Grandad, Carter with Chops (I flatly refused to be in any photos as I did not want any to find their way onto Facebook without my prior approval).

Nate and Eli, who at just turned five and two and a half years old, would probably rather have chewed off their own legs than be at a hospital seeing a newborn baby so they left rather quickly after Nate decided a raucous game of hallway tenpin bowling was how he would like to pass the time and another grumpy looking nurse had snapped him collecting up empty water jugs to use as pins. I am so glad I had a girl.

Surprisingly, my sister and David came to visit too and she was still being as nice as pie. She even hugged me and told me how happy she was for me. I still really didn't know how to take this new person she had become – she's like a vicious looking dog tied up to a pole outside a shop, you give it a wide berth and don't get too close for fear of losing an arm.

Dee popped in that afternoon while Chops was out on a Big Mac mission (new mothers need red meat for strength you know) but as it turned out she couldn't stay long as Merryn arrived to check up on me and Carter decided it was time to scream the place down. I can't say Dee looked devastated when Merryn said she was going to help me breastfeed so suggested she might want to come back and visit another time – in fact am pretty sure I heard the same grumpy nurse tell her to slow down as she hauled ass towards the exit. All before I'd even flopped a boob out.

Ah, breastfeeding. If I'd had any sliver of dignity remaining after the birthing process it was well and truly gone after three days and nights of very unsuccessfully breastfeeding my baby. I had nurses and midwives constantly coming into my room, yanking my boob out, shoving my screaming baby's face onto it and then repeating the process with the other boob until I was sitting there bare chested and blushing.

Don't get me wrong, most of the nurses were lovely and very supportive. But there was this one nurse who actually sighed loudly when we couldn't get Carter latched on properly on the second night – but the icing on the cake had to be when I made an offhand joke about how much easier shoving a bottle in her gob would be and another nurse frowned disapprovingly and then proceeded in giving me a ten minute lecture about the benefits of breastfeeding over bottle feeding and that 'breast is ALWAYS best.'

Oh, and did I forget to mention I'm a shit cow?! Apparently my breast milk was a bit slow to start - as in, hadn't started at all. My milk jugs were empty, my milkmakers weren't making milk.

Hence why, four days after Carter was born I was at home, sitting on my bed, hiccupping and sobbing, wanting nothing more than to bury my face in a pillow until I died.

At that particular moment I had an electric breast pump attached to not one, but both of my boobs in an attempt to get my baby juice flowing. None of those petite little hand pumps for me, nope I needed a heavy duty commercial milking machine apparently. And it was orange. I fucking hate orange.

In and out it went, suctioning my poor useless boobies into a horribly abnormal shape, all the while making a horrendous suctioning and whirring noise. I looked and felt like a cow who's udders were hooked up to an automatic milking unit and every time it sucked one of my boobs out into an elongated sausage I cried even harder.

"Goose?" I hadn't heard the tap at the bedroom door. I turned to see Chops in the doorway with a concerned look on his face.

"Don't look at me!" I cried, trying to cover my chest with a pillow while the big orange beast kept futilely pumping away to a regular rhythm.

He flicked the machine off at wall and I scrambled to unsuction the cups of my boobs and do up my pyjama top. He came and sat on the edge of the bed and put his hand on my leg.

"Goose, I think it's time we get some formula," he said gently.

Through my sobs I exclaimed "So you think I'm useless too?! I'm such a shit mum I can't even do the one thing mums are supposed to be able to do!"

"No!" he replied. "I think you're exhausted. And you're stressing yourself out trying to breastfeed but what's to say your milk still doesn't come through in another four days? Or eight? And I hate seeing you this unhappy. I mean look at you, you're absolutely miserable aren't you?"

I nodded, still hiccupping.

"And what did Merryn say to you yesterday?"

"That it doesn't matter if a baby is breast fed or bottle fed as long as it's loved," I sniffed, wiping a tear off my cheek.

"Exactly. So how about I go get some formula and bottles? I want my girls to be happy. I don't give two shits whether you breastfeed or not and I don't want you to put so much pressure on yourself. Besides, I wasn't breastfed and I turned out ok," he said with a smile.

"That's debatable," I managed to joke with a half smile.

"Smart ass," he replied and pulled me in for a hug. "You are already the best mum in the world. You really think Carter is going to grow up and think any less of you because you didn't breastfeed her? As if. She's going to grow up thinking you're the most awesome mum in the world because you love her and didn't listen to what those bloody bitchy nurses said."

"Uh huh," I mumbled. Deep down I knew he was right. Deep down I wanted to smash those bloody bitchy nurses in the face.

"So I'm going to go to the supermarket now ok?" he asked.

"Ooh wait," I said, cheering up immensely at the thought, "can I??"

He laughed. "Go for it. Oh and we need some new toilet paper too, some cheap bastard bought bloody 1-ply again!"

~~~~~~~~~~~~~~~~

Note to self: NEVER go out without the baby until I am skinny.

My eagerly anticipated return to the supermarket (which now could not be marred by my waters breaking in the fruit and vege section) was instead ruined by Rhonda, the lovely old checkout chick who I always chatted to when I was there. She had made a beeline for me when she saw me and said "Ooh hello love! How long until this baby of yours is due? It must be any day now?"

I was mortified. And I was far too embarrassed to admit that the baby was in fact four days old and my large stomach that she was so eagerly gesturing to was housing nothing more than the remnants of far too many pies and chocolate biscuits – so I just blushed to my full height of redness, smiled and said "Yes any day now!" and made a mad dash away from her. Oh the shame.

Right, the diet starts tomorrow. Well, after I've eaten all the junk food in the house so it won't be there to tempt me anymore.

May

"You're looking so good," Dee said to me. Carter was two weeks old and praise the lord, asleep in her bassinet.

I snorted. "That will be because I actually managed to have a shower and put makeup on today!"

"Has it been pretty tough?" Dee asked.

"Hard out. Honestly since Chops went back to work there are some days that I don't have a shower until like 4 o'clock in the afternoon. My friend Laura came around the other day and she sent me off to have a shower while she looked after the baby. That was the first day I had a shower before lunchtime! I feel like a bloody minger!"

Dee laughed but she seemed preoccupied.

"So anyway, what's new with you?" I asked as I offered her a Toffee Pop (so much for getting rid of all the junk food in the house).

"Umm," she said, "well I do have some news."

"Ooh yes?" I asked.

"Well, things haven't been going that well at work lately so I quit a couple of weeks ago. It was my last day on Friday."

"I wondered why you were visiting on a weekday! Wow, that's huge! What was going on at work?" I asked, concerned and still surprised.

"Ummm, well, you know how a couple of years ago I slept with my boss? Alex?"

"Yeah. Oh no, did everyone find out?"

"Well, yeah," she looked sheepish. "But it wasn't just that one time two years ago. We've been sleeping together pretty much off and on since then."

"Oh Dee..."

"So yeah, not overly proud of it. His wife obviously got suspicious and found out so she had a massive moose at me in the reception area a couple of weeks ago and called me a homewrecking slut in front of some clients. So the shit hit the fan and I pretty much got asked to resign as it wasn't seen as 'favourable behaviour within such a well respected company'."

"Oh shit. Why didn't you tell me babe?"

"Umm *hello* Goose you had plenty of other stuff to be worrying about in the last few weeks - you didn't need to be adding my stupid crap into the pile!" she replied. "It's all good, honestly."

"So did his wife kick him out?! Are you guys going to keep seeing each other?" I asked.

"No, she actually hasn't. Silly bitch. They're going to work through it apparently. No way, it wasn't ever going to be a long term thing, it was just a bit of fun that went on for far too long. But wait, there's more," she continued, "I've decided to go over to London and live there for awhile. I leave next Thursday."

"Holy shit!! No way!"

"Yep, I just need to get out of here, I'm over it."

"Wow. So you leave next Thursday?! When are you moving out of your flat?"

"Already have, am back at the parentals until I go. So you better find a babysitter cause I'm having going away drinks this Saturday and you totally have to be there."

"Um, ok, I'll see what I can do. So what are you going to do when you get to London?"

"I sent your brother a message on Facebook so I'm going to crash on his couch when I get there and then get myself sorted."

"Oh God Dee, please don't root my brother!" I said, half joking.

"Haha. Of course not," she laughed a little too loudly. I could tell by the guilty look on her face that that particular ship had probably sailed a long time ago.

"Holy shit *have* you rooted my brother??!" I exclaimed.

That sheepish look was back on her face. "Well, um yeah. But only once. Okay, maybe twice. Fuck alright it was three times ok? But it's all good it was a long time ago and we were both consenting adults."

"How long ago?" I demanded. Not that it really mattered as I am not my brother's keeper or Dee's for that matter (geez now *that* would be a big job) but now the nosy side of me was dying to know.

"Oh, um, back when we were about 20..." her voice trailed off.

"So he was 17?! OH MY GOD Dee! Did you pop his cherry??!"

"Well not exactly...oh ok yeah maybe...but it was an accident. And besides, your brother is quite hot Goose!" she defended herself as though his hotness was more than enough reason to have bumped uglies with my 17 year old brother.

"Ugh! Shut up!" I waved my hand at her. "Fine, fine. It's all good. I just can't believe I didn't know!"

She laughed. "The first time was at your flat too! After a party one night-"

Oh no. No more details please-

"-on your dining room table."

"Oh ewwwwwwwwwww. Thank God I left that table behind!" I cried, "that table has seen more ass than a Donkey farmer!"

"Actually, speaking of your brother and donkeys-"

NOOOOOOOOOOOOOOOOOOOOOOOOO!!!!!

~~~~~~~~~~~~~~~~~~~~

"Ooh yeah check me out," I sidled up to Chops with my hand out, waggling my fingers at him. He looked up from his laptop and stared blankly at me. "What?"

"My RING egg! I finally managed to get it on my finger!" My cankles had decreased to a relatively normal size and therefore my fingers had also lost some of the sausage-like qualities they had before I gave birth. Truth be told it was still a bit tight though.

"Oh that's awesome. It looks great. I have good taste," he smirked.

"Well, *obviously*. You hooked up with me didn't you?!" I stuck my tongue out at him.

It really was more than just a bit tight. I possibly should have guessed that when I had to force it onto my finger though.

"I think I'll take it off now, I'll wait until I've lost more weight before I start wearing it all the time."

"Have you lost weight?" Chops asked.

"Are you serious?! I've lost 6kg since she was born! Ok, granted a lot of that was water retention but still, are you saying you can't tell?!" I stuck my lip out.

"Oh. Yeah of course I can tell darling you look awesome. But then I don't notice your weight you always look beautiful to me," he replied with a crock full of shit.

"Pffft whatever. My jelly belly and thunder thighs are kinda hard to miss. But it's all good I've started walking I'm going to be skinny again if it kills me – and besides it's less than a year until the wedding so I need to get my ass into gear."

"I think walking to the dairy to get lollies kind of defeats the purpose though," Chops stupidly interjected.

"So you DO think I'm fat?!?"

"Oh shit. No. Of course not. I just meant that maybe – ooh shit look at the time, Carter needs her bath," he changed the subject mid sentence and took off down the hall.

Hmmmpf. I bet he does think I'm fat.

I started pulling the ring off my finger but it wouldn't budge.

Oh shit oh shit oh shit. Oh shit, is my finger turning purple??

I tried twisting the ring while pulling it off but it still would not budge. I looked down at my finger and realised it was definitely starting to swell from the pressure of the ring. My poor finger looked like a really overweight person wearing a too-tight belt.

Soap! That'll get it off!

I charged down the hallway to the bathroom where Chops was running the water for Carter's bath and pumped some soap out from the dispenser. I rubbed my hands together furiously in an attempt to get my finger slippery enough for the ring to slide off.

But slide off it did not.

"What are you doing?" Chops asked curiously. Awesome, just what I need – to explain to my fiancé who already thinks I'm fat that I'm *so* fat I can't get my ring off.

"Ummm, just washing my hands," I tried to keep the panic out of my voice. My finger was really starting to pulse now.

"Is your ring stuck?"

"No!" I blushed. I twisted the ring again, there was no moving the damn thing. It was well and truly attached to my swelling finger. "Ok, yes! I can't get it off and it hurts!"

"Let me have a look," Chops said as I ran my hand under the tap to rinse off the vast quantity of soap that I had dispensed. I smelled like I'd rolled in a lavender bush.

"Oh shit that's really on there," he said upon closer inspection.

"Oh gee really? You're soooo observant you should be on CSI," I said sarcastically.

He ignored my sarcasm. "Let's try some butter. If that doesn't work it might have to be cut off."

"My finger?!" I burst into tears, partly out of total embarrassment and partly out of fear.

"No Goose! Not your finger, the ring!" he started laughing and then thought better of it. He put his arm around me. "Come into the kitchen - let's try some butter."

I sniffed back a sob. "We don't have any butter! I used it all when I made the chocolate chip cookies yesterday!" I wailed.

I neglected to mention that I ate most of the cookie dough before it made it to the oven in cookie form – in hindsight I really shouldn't have been surprised that I got the ring stuck on my chubby little finger.

"It's ok, margarine will do," he said, grabbing the container of margarine out of the fridge. "Calm down babe, it'll be ok." He started massaging it into my finger, thoroughly coating it in the greasy spread.

"It's not working!!" I exclaimed, panicking.

"Give it a minute. I think it's coming. I'm going to start sliding it back towards your knuckle so you need to keep your hand really still ok? It might hurt a bit."

Can't hurt any more than my ego does right now...owwwwww!

"There it goes!" Chops smiled and held the margarine covered ring up triumphantly, after managing to drag it over my knuckle. My finger felt like it was on fire. "It just needs a good clean now, no harm done."

"Thanks," I mumbled, cheeks as red as my finger.

"No worries babe," he smiled. "And don't stress, we can always get the ring resized and get it made a bit bigger if you want."

Asshole! He DOES think I'm fat!

"Shush, shush," I hushed the baby, rocking her in my arms. It was one o'clock in the morning and she had been screaming for a good hour and a half and counting.

"Put her in the stroller I'll take her for a walk, maybe that'll put her to sleep," Chops said, yawning.

"I just don't understand why she's still crying!" I exclaimed. "I've tried everything!"

Chops yawned again. "Maybe she's got a sore tummy or something."

I yawned too. Why is yawning contagious?

"Shush, shush," I hushed her again, sighing. "You go to bed you have to be up in a few hours for work," I said to Chops.

"Are you sure?"

"Yeah," I replied, "I'm going to take her for a drive that always puts her to sleep."

"Ok, thanks babe," Chops kissed me on the forehead then kissed Carter. "Be a good girl and go to sleep for Mummy." Then he took off in the direction of our bedroom at a somewhat hasty speed, obviously before I could change my mind.

I looked down at our screaming bundle of joy and attempted to forget how tired I was. I tried the bottle in her mouth again but she just moved her face away, still crying.

"Ok Miss Carter, looks like we are going for a drive."

I strapped her in to her baby capsule and popped a hat on her head (to keep her head warm - not to hide her hair this time) and carried her out to Henrietta. I plugged the capsule into the base, hopped into the front seat and started the car.

I looked down at myself. I was wearing a pink nightie with no bra on, mismatching pyjama pants and my ugg boot slippers. What a stunner.

PLEASE don't let me be pulled over by a cop looking like this...

After driving aimlessly around the streets for 15 minutes and singing Britney's greatest hits to my restless baby I realised the crying had stopped. I turned the music down and I heard a post cry sigh from the backseat.

Goddamn rear facing baby capsules! I couldn't see if she was asleep in the rear vision mirror and the risk of stopping the car and having her start wailing again was too high. So I kept driving. After another five minutes I hadn't heard a peep from the capsule so decided it was probably safe to start heading home.

I drove back into the driveway and parked. I pulled on the handbrake ever so quietly as I didn't want to risk any noise at all in case it woke her. I stealthily took off my seatbelt and got out of the car, pushing my door shut gently – but of course the damn thing didn't shut properly so I had to reopen it and close it a second time. I stopped and listened, shattered nerves on edge. I heard nothing.

I breathed a sigh of relief and then slowly and quietly opened the back door of the car. There was my flame haired angel, fast asleep in her capsule like a picture of pure innocence, far from the inconsolable beast she had been only half an hour earlier. Despite my complete exhaustion and desperation for sleep I couldn't help but smile at how peaceful she looked. Lucky tart.

I unhooked the capsule as gently as I could but accidentally bumped it against the back of the passenger seat.

Shit! Don't wake up don't wake up.

She stirred in her seat and opened her mouth. I flinched, waiting for the screams to start again. But it was just a yawn.

I breathed another sigh of relief as I managed to get her inside the house and into our bedroom without her waking up. Chops was dead to the world in bed, snoring.

I undid the capsule buckle like a ninja and started gently removing the harness off one of her shoulders to get her out and into her bassinet. Bad idea - she immediately started crying again.

Damn it!

But thankfully it didn't last long. After a quick little cry she fell back asleep and as there was no way I was going to risk waking her again, I covered her back up with her blanket and decided leaving her sleeping in her capsule for one night didn't constitute child neglect. The hideous purple Winnie the Pooh hat I took off her head possibly did though – would have to remember to put that in the 'ugly arse clothes that she is never to wear again ' pile in the morning.

I crawled into bed and looked at the clock. I groaned. 2:09am. I closed my eyes and willed sleep to come and take me quickly.

Man, this parenting thing is bloody hard.

~~~~~~~~~~~~~~~~~~~~

I woke up three and a half hours later to her cries. I looked over through half closed eyes and saw Chops holding her, capsule still on the floor where I had left her in it.

"Sorry! I just thought I should try and put her in the bassinet!" he said over the deafening sound of her crying.

"Damn it Chops! She was fine in the capsule!" I felt like crying.

"Sorry honey,' he said apologetically, "I have to get going to work. I'll make a bottle though - hopefully she will go back to sleep after you give her it?"

Yes, and maybe I'll stab you in the eye with a fork later. Never wake a sleeping baby you halfwit. Grrrrr.

I threw my covers off in a huff and took our crying baby from him while he headed out to the kitchen to heat a bottle.

'**contraception:** noun \ˌkän-trə-ˈsep-shən\   the deliberate use of artificial methods or other techniques to prevent pregnancy as a consequence of sexual intercourse.'

Lesson well and truly learnt. I'm never having sex again.

~~~~~~~~~~~~~~~~

Oh good Lord that baby is ugly.

"Thanks," I said to Karen from my antenatal class and smiled at her, taking the coffee she handed to me. I couldn't take my eyes off the baby that was sitting in a capsule by the feet of the woman formerly known as Hairy Maclary, Lydia. And it kept staring at me too. In fact, I could swear it was frowning. Can one month old babies frown?

Jesus it's like freaking Chucky. Stop staring at me you little freak.

I was at the first antenatal catch up for our class since our six week course. All the babies had been born and Karen had organised a morning tea gathering for all the mums at her house. There is nothing more awkward than sitting amongst a group of women who have nothing in common apart from having a root at approximately the same time of the year. Oh, actually yes there is - sitting next to the partner of the first guy you ever gave a blow job to while amongst that particular group of women is fairly high on the awkward-o-meter.

I was sitting on the couch with Carter on my lap in between Natalie (Sean's partner) who had little Rafe in her arms and another woman called Rachel. Rachel had a little girl called Sophie (my mum would approve) and she seemed nice enough. Mind you it's hard to tell what a person is really like when all you have to talk about is what colour their baby's shit is and whether or not that shade of green is considered normal.

Mind you - nosy bitch that I am - I had found out that Natalie is 32, a receptionist at a gym (free gym membership – explains a lot) had met Sean at a pub and have been together for six years. Rachel, on the other hand, was 27 and a rival for me for how short a time she was with her partner Jared before she got pregnant. She thinks it's quite possible Sophie was conceived the first time they had sex as she found out she was six weeks pregnant six weeks after they got together. That would suck - at least I had a few months under my belt before I got knocked up.

"Damn...is it just me or is Lydia's baby really freaking ugly?!" Natalie hissed at me under her breath.

I was so shocked that she had voiced my innermost thoughts that I gaped at her open mouthed for half a second and then I burst out laughing. A couple of the other mums looked over at me and I blushed. Lydia left the scary baby in the capsule and her and a couple of the other mums went up the hallway with

Karen, who was showing them her baby Jackson who was asleep up the other end of the house.

"Is it a boy or a girl?" I whispered. It was wearing white so unfortunately there was no telltale blue or pink clothing to help me out. I had been emailed the class list of names and phone numbers and what the babies' birthdates and names were (Karen was very organised apparently) but I really hadn't paid much attention.

"It's a frigging girl, would you believe? Her name is Gretchen," she whispered. I looked at the baby again and shuddered. Poor kid, as if being ugly wasn't bad enough her parents had to name her Gretchen?

"Does it do anything? Other than sit there and frown?" I said. Just then she opened its mouth and started crying a high pitched cry, baring four sharp pointy teeth.

"Oh my God!" Natalie whispered the same time that I hissed "Holy shit!"

"It's got fucking teeth already!" she exclaimed under her breath. "It's like a vampire baby!"

Rachel laughed and leaned forward to join our conversation. "That's some freaky Twilight shit aye?" she whispered, "I wonder if she breastfeeds?"

Natalie nudged me to alert me to the fact that Lydia had walked back in the room. We all watched in amazement as she picked Gretchen up out of the capsule, unhooked her bra, pulled up her t-shirt and shoved the baby onto her boob, teeth and all.

I made myself turn away. "We shouldn't be so mean!" I whispered. "I mean I can hardly talk – I've got me a random

Ginga!"

"True that. And Rafe's got these random Dumbo ears," Natalie laughed.

Haha he kind of does...

"Sausage roll ladies?" Karen appeared in front of us like a pastry bearing angel, holding out a plate of sausage rolls.

"Ooh yum! Don't mind if I do!" Natalie said, laughing and taking two sausage rolls. Rachel took one and I restrained myself and only took one - but Karen could obviously tell I was the gannet of the group and put the plate on the coffee table right in front of me.

Mmmmm sausage rolls...

I brushed flaky pastry off Carter's head and reached for another sausage roll. Maybe this antenatal thing wasn't so bad after all.

June

"Cheers!" we all clinked our glasses together. We were having a small party to celebrate Chops and I surviving our first six weeks of parenthood relatively unscathed. It was almost 10pm and most of the people that had come for dinner and drinks had already left.

As if on cue, the baby monitor crackled and we heard Carter cry out.

"I'll get her," Blair volunteered, putting his bottle of beer down on the coffee table and heading off towards the bedroom. He came back in a moment later, carrying my red-faced, wide-eyed baby who was no longer crying but was staring up at Blair in adoration.

My girl already has good taste...

I watched as Blair cooed over her and followed Chops into the kitchen, presumably to get her a bottle. "Awww he's going to make such a good daddy someday," I said to Jess and Leo.

Leo snorted. "Yeah and we all know who wants him to be her baby daddy, aye Jess??"

Jess blushed and smacked him on the arm. "Shut up dick!"

I looked at Jess' embarrassed face and Leo's smug one.

"Oh my God! How did I miss this?" I exclaimed. "Jess – do you fancy Blair???"

"Fancy him? Shit it's been like Grey's Anatomy at our house lately with all the sexual tension going on," Leo chortled, "I told her she just needs to sort her shit out and make a move but she won't. And he's just as useless as she is!"

"Whatever. I'm so not his type," Jess said, still blushing.

"As if! You're just a chicken shit," Leo continued. "I know you're not supposed to screw the crew but MY GOD Jess you seriously need to jump him. It's soooooo obvious you both want to."

I was in shock. Had having a baby made me completely oblivious to everything around me??

"So why haven't you guys hooked up yet??" I demanded. "Oh man it would be SO awesome if you guys got together!" I was already picturing their wedding and babies - man, they would have some good looking babies.

"Leo's full of crap. Yeah ok, maybe I like him but it's not like he feels the same way."

"But when did this start??!"

"Well obviously I've always thought he was hot-"

Well, duh. You're not blind.

"-but I guess a couple of months ago after I'd broken up with Callum and he started seeing that girl Karla I got *really* jealous and realised I, um, I kind of like him."

"Kind of?!" Leo interrupted. "Your panties just about drop every time he walks in the room!"

She blushed again. "I didn't realise it was that obvious."

"So what's stopping you?!" I interjected, "he's not seeing anyone at the moment is he? And you're single. Leo! We so have to hook them up!"

"Goose, no! Please! It will be so embarrassing if he doesn't like me! I have to live with the guy!"

"And I have to live with the two of you creaming your pants

over each other and doing nothing about it!" Leo exclaimed, "I'm with Goosey Gander on this one! But we need to get the ball rolling Goose I've got to get to work soon."

I clapped my hands in glee. Oh I do love matchmaking...

Chops and Blair came back into the lounge carrying Carter, a bottle of formula and a beer each.

"Chops!" I screeched. "I need to talk to you in the kitchen!"

"Oh crap, I know that look," he said, groaning.

"Just come!" I demanded, dragging him by the arm and leaving Blair to feed Carter.

"You won't believe what I just found out!" I exclaimed, once we were in the kitchen with the door shut.

"Probably not."

I didn't let his lack of enthusiasm deter me. I was onto my third Margarita so I was amped. And awesome. "Jess likes Blair! Like *really likes* Blair, if you know what I mean. And Leo reckons Blair likes Jess too! Can you find out if he does?!"

He groaned again. "Goose, I'm not getting involved. *You* can ask him if you really want to know. Or better yet, how about Jess asks him and you retract your nose from out of their business??"

I pouted at him. Talk about making it sound like I'm a nosy bitch!

"You suck. Fine. I'll sort it out myself!"

I stalked back to the lounge where Jess, Leo and Blair were laughing about something.

"Ah, Goose, we were just saying that Carter must have your

ass she is farting something chronic," Leo said.

"Ha ha," I said. I was on a mission now - a matchmaking mission and I had the targets in my sights.

"Blair, give the baby to Chops and come and sit on the couch next to Jess please." He looked confused but obviously knew well enough to do what I said without arguing.

"Goose-" Jess said, blushing.

"Sssssh Jess. It's for your own good!"

"Leo, Chops, come with me. Right Blair, Jess – something has come to my attention and it needs to get sorted before you leave tonight."

They looked at each other, both blushing now.

Ooh yeah how did I not notice that before?! They are sooooo into each other!

"I can see just by looking at you that you both have feelings for each other. So we are going to leave you in here for a bit so you can have a chat about that. Come on you two," I said to Leo and Chops and shepherded them out of the room.

Once we were in the kitchen Chops, who had put the baby bottle down and was burping Carter, said "Goose you're a shocker. I can't believe you just did that to the poor buggers."

"Well, you didn't want to help me, I had to do something! Their future happiness depended on it!"

"It's about time they sorted it out," Leo said in my defence. "I hope they sort it out quickly though I need to leave for work in a minute and my bag is in there."

"Ooh, I wonder what they're talking about!" I pressed my ear to the kitchen door. I couldn't hear anything.

Damn it!

I then had what was possibly not my brightest idea of the evening. I dragged a chair from the dining room table across to the door that connected the kitchen to the lounge.

"What are you doing??" Chops asked, alarmed.

"Looking in the window! I want to see what's happening!" I whispered, referring to the small frosted glass window above the door frame. I never understood why anyone would put a window there but I was now very excited that they had.

Ooh I wonder if he's kissed her? So exciting!!!

"Goose I don't think that's a very good idea-" Leo said at the same time Chops said "Don't be stupid!"

"It's fine!" I hissed and clambered up onto the chair. I had to stand on my tiptoes to see through the window and then I inched closer to the glass to get a better look. I could see them talking, their heads close together.

"Ooh Leo I think he's going to kiss- oh SHIT!!" I exclaimed as the chair skidded backwards on the linoleum floor and I lost my balance. The chair went crashing backwards, taking me with it as I plummeted ass first to the ground. A second later my bum connected with the hard floor and I heard an audible crack (no pun intended) before feeling intense pain shooting through my lower back.

"Owwwwwwwwwwwwww," I cried out as I heard Leo burst out laughing.

The door to the lounge flew open and Jess and Blair came barrelling in to see me sprawled out on the kitchen floor.

"What happened?" Jess exclaimed. Chops was kneeling down next to me to try and help me up, Carter still over his shoulder.

"Here, give her to me," Jess said, taking Carter from him.

"Goose broke her ass! She broke it trying to spy on you!" Leo managed to say through his laughter.

"It's not funny!" I cried, "it fucking hurts!" I smacked Chops' hand away as he tried to help me up. "I can't get up!

"Lucky I'm going to the hospital now aye Goose I can give you a ride – that is unless you want to be picked up in an ambulance and have to tell everyone that you broke your ass because you're such a drunken nosy bitch!" He was practically doubled over in laughter.

"Do you think you've broken something?" Chops asked, concerned.

"Do you need to go to the hospital?"

I want to die....

The pain was worse than childbirth. "I think so," I admitted, more embarrassed that I have ever been in my life.

"It's okay mate, you go with her. We'll look after Carter," Blair said. I could swear he was trying not to laugh.

"Okay, thanks guys. Come on Leo, let's get her into the car."

"As long as I don't have to carry her, I saw how much pizza she ate tonight!" Leo continued laughing at my expense.

Bastard. If only he had broken my fall.

~~~~~~~~~~~~~

Four hours later we returned home from the hospital. Arriving with Leo had been somewhat handy as he had managed to bump me up the queue and get seen by a doctor faster. I guess the prick does have some uses.

"Come on Goose," Chops said, helping me out of the taxi outside our house.

"Byeeeeeeeeee. Thank you Mr. Taxi Driver!" I slurred. I was drugged up to the hilt on pain medication and I felt awesome.

"Let's get you inside and into bed," Chops said, half dragging me up the stairs.

"Oh is that right you dirty boy?" I giggled. "You want a piece of this?" I gestured to my lady parts and just about fell over.

He helped me get upright again as the front door opened. Jess was standing in the doorway and came out to help Chops get me up the steps.

"I would've come and picked you up!" she said as we got inside the hallway.

"It's all good we got a taxi," he replied as they led me in to my bedroom. "How's Carter been?"

"Just had another bottle now she's sleeping like a log. Do you want me to stay in case she wakes up so you can get some sleep?"

"No, it's cool thanks Jess. I should get a few hours before she wakes again."

Blair appeared in the doorway. "So what's the verdict?" he asked.

Ooooh he's pretty. Oooh look at those forearms. Bet he's got a really big-

"BLAIR!! Did you kissssssss her?" I slurred. "She's sooooo

beautiful, isn't she?" I patted Jess on the head but missed, just about falling over again.

"They gave her some mean as drugs, Tramadol I think it's called. Am pretty sure she's been hallucinating on the way home - she thinks she's Lindsay Lohan. But anyway, she fractured her coccyx."

"He said *cock*!" I whispered loudly and then giggled profusely.

"So she broke her tailbone? How do they fix that?" Jess asked him.

"Just pain relief really, she'll be sore for a few weeks. That'll teach her for being a nosy bitch."

"I'm not sore! I'm awesommmmmmme!" I drawled.

"Oh and she has to sit on this doughnut ring until it heals, the hole will stop her tailbone from hitting anything hard," he said, pulling the pillow out of a bag.

"Cock in the hole!" I exclaimed and giggled again.

"Okay I think it's time you get to sleep," Jess said and helped me lie face down on the bed.

"But I'm not tirrreeeddd," I grumbled into my pillow.

Oh wow, that's so soft. It feels like a cloud. Am I on a cloud?

"I'll see you tomorrow Goose," I felt a hand on the back of my head and heard Jess speak but she sounded like she was really far away.

Where is this goose they're talking about? I think they're quacking up hahahahaha.

"Thanks guys," I heard Chops say. "Hopefully Lindsay and her broken ass sleep it off."

I AM Lindsay Lohan. I knew it!

Dee: So how's motherhood treating you babe?

Lucy: It's good. She's sleeping heaps better. I've been really sore lately though I broke my tailbone a couple of weeks ago

Dee: What?? How'd you do that?!!

Lucy: Oh, I kinda fell off a chair and landed on my bum

Dee: Hilarious!! Reminds me of that time you walked into the lamp post outside Tequila Mockingbird!

I groaned. Why does everyone have to remember every embarrassing thing that I do?? I was chatting to Dee on Facebook – the first time since she had moved off Matt's couch and into her own flat in London so there was a lot of gossip to catch up on.

Lucy: God, don't remind me. Anyway guess who hooked up??

Dee: Who??

Lucy: Jess and Blair!!!!!!!!!!

Dee: NO WAY!! Lucky bitch!! When did that happen??

Lucy: A couple of weeks ago. They are sooo cute together ☺

Dee: Man, I'm jealous. That guy is so hot!

Lucy: Hard out!

Dee: Speaking of hot guys, you will be pleased to know I never had to sleep on your brother's couch...I slept in his bed...hahahahahaha

Lucy: Oh no! Poor Matt! Haha ☺

Dee: Nah, jokes. His flatmate was more than obliging to let me sleep in his though. You should have seen this guy Goose he's from Sweden and looks like a bloody movie star

Lucy: Nice. So how's your new flat?

Dee: All good, a couple of my flatmates are muppets but I don't see them much cause they work nights

Lucy: Oh cool and how's your job going?

Not long after Dee had arrived in London she had managed to score a job at a swanky hotel on reception. She had then subsequently been scoring non-stop by the sounds of it.

Dee: Boring as hell but the pay is really good. Am going to Paris for the weekend! ☺

Lucy: That's awesome. So have you seen Matty J lately?

Dee: Yeah I caught up with him last night actually. His girlfriend is really pretty

His girlfriend?!?!

Lucy: What girlfriend?!

Dee: Hasn't he told you?! Her name is Dora and she's from Spain

Lucy: Like Dora the Explorer?!? That's freaking hilarious

Dee: Who's Dora the Explorer?

Oh shame. I have officially become a loser. Shit if I start singing a Wiggles song next I will shoot myself.

Dee: Hey babe I have to go and get ready for work

Lucy: Oh sweet as. Talk soon!

Dee: Defo. Kisses for Miss Carter xxxx

So my brother has a girlfriend and hadn't told us. Little shit. I was in the middle of writing him a semi-abusive message when Chops arrived home from work.

"Hey babe," he said coming over and kissing me on the forehead. "Is the little munchkin in bed?"

"Yep. She should be awake soon though."

"Cool. How's your arse?" he asked.

"Fat."

"Obviously not fat enough to cushion your fall."

"Oh ha ha you're sooo funny. It's still tender. But a bit better," I smiled at him.

"Sweet," he replied. "I better go have a shower. Are we still going to go to the hospital to see your sister?"

"Oh yeah. I guess we better."

Renee had given birth to their baby the day before so we were going to visit them and meet my new nephew. They had called him Eugene - seriously, who calls a little Ginga baby Eugene? Actually, who calls *any* baby Eugene these days??

I finished my message to Matt and then examined my Facebook profile picture. It was such a great photo of me – unfortunately it was almost two years ago when I was still skinny and fairly hot. Leo reckons I shouldn't be allowed to use it now as it's false advertising – mind you he also thinks anyone that uses a picture of their children or pets as their profile picture must be total mingers. My profile picture was taken on the night of my 27th birthday, the night I hooked up with Ben.

Hmmm Ben...I wonder if he's on here??

I typed his full name into the search bar and a list of about seventeen Ben Bruce's came up on the screen - in hindsight it was probably quite lucky he was a fucktard as Lucy Bruce just sounds stupid.

I scrolled down the list of names, examining the thumbnail pictures next to them. I found one that looked like it could be him and clicked on it.

There he is. And that's a good picture of him. Hmmpf. Assholio.

Bingo! His security was obviously not set properly because I could see *everything* on his page. Relationship status: single. Haha what a loser.

I trawled through the pictures on his page (many of them were of him and various girls – what a man whore) and read all the posts until I suddenly realised that Chops had walked back into the lounge, carrying Carter who had obviously woken up from her nap.

"Are you *still* on Facebook??" he asked.

"Oh, uh yeah. Just writing a message to Matt, apparently he has a girlfriend he hasn't told me about!" I replied, hoping that the red hue spreading across my cheeks wouldn't alert him to the fact that I had actually been cyber stalking another man.

"How DARE he not tell you!!" Chops laughed. "Well, I've changed her bum so do you want me to give her a bottle before we go to the hospital?"

"Uh huh," I said, quickly closing all the tabs on the laptop and closing the lid before he could see what I had really been doing.

Time to go and meet Eugene. God, it just sounds like something out of Winnie the Pooh - oh hang on, that's Eeyore. Whatever, it's still a dumb name.

~~~~~~~~~~~~~~~

Well imagine my surprise (and slight irritation) upon arriving at the hospital to find that the little Ginga Ninja Eugene was NOT a Ginga Ninja and actually had dark brown hair. How the hell did I end up with a redhead and Renee didn't – especially considering her husband is a complete Fanta Pants!?

Karma fully had given me a double smackdown. So, from this day forth, I shall never utter an unkind remark about anyone of the Ginger variety (although mainly for fear of being the recipient of a second one in the future).

Eugene was actually pretty cute, as cute as Renee and David's offspring could be anyway. I asked if Eugene was a family name from David's side, fully expecting them to say it was a great Grandfather or something as ancient as that but no, apparently they just liked it. Ugh. Poor kid.

We stayed at the hospital long enough to take a couple of photos of Carter and Eeyore (a nickname that I will not be informing Renee of as I quite like having an unbroken nose) but after about twenty minutes I could see the old Renee starting to resurface as she started snapping at David for taking too long to get a vase for the flowers we had brought her. I took that as our opportunity to leave just in case she truly unleashed her old self and threw the vase at him.

Poor Fanta Pants, the bitch is back.

August

"Owwww! Carter don't pull Mummy's hair!" I tried to extricate a clump of my hair from my daughter's vice like grip as she smiled at me.

"Ah ah ah," she replied, her big blue eyes staring at me ever so innocently.

"Are you laughing at me you little minx?" I replied, tossing my finally freed hair over my shoulder as she lunged for it again and kicked her legs into my stomach.

"How about Mummy goes and gets a hair tie while you sit there," I said as I put her into her bouncinette and handed her a rattle.

"Ah!"

I went to my bedroom and pulled my hair up into a messy bun on top of my head. I examined my reflection in the mirror. I was pleased that I could finally tell that my post baby diet was working, partly due to the fact that I had stopped eating all delicious food (have I mentioned how much I hate salads?!) and partly because I had started back at the dreaded gym. My will to live was just about gone – and truth be told I would probably murder my own mother for a Big Mac and large fries.

I had lost 12kg since giving birth (still had about 8kg to go mind you) and was finally wearing non-maternity clothes again. I looked okay with clothes on – but naked was a *whole* different story. That shit was never gonna look the same again.

Now the only time my stomach looks flat is when I am lying down as all the excess fat spreads sideways - oh and my poor boobs! Don't get me started on them...so I had come to the realisation that while I would never look any good naked ever again, at least with a heavy duty push up bra and industrial strength suck in undies I would at least look half decent clothed.

I could hear Carter gurgling and shaking her rattle. I looked at the bedside clock.

Oops better get going!

I made a bottle, put it in the nappy bag then scooped Carter up from the bouncinette and grabbed my purse.

"Come on gorgeous girl, let's go see your friends!" We were going to Natalie from antenatal's house for morning tea and as usual was probably going to be late.

I got a whiff of something unpleasant. "Ewww have you done a poo Miss Carter?" I said at the same time I became aware that the back of her top was damp. I turned her around and saw a dark greenish brown stain all the way up the back of her bodysuit.

"Uggghhh that's disgusting," I almost dry heaved when I saw that the same stain was all over the seat of the bouncinette too and then I realised I was on sole clean up duty of the poo explosion, aisle 3.

"Ah ah ah," she gurgled and smiled her toothless grin at me again.

"Now I *know* you're laughing at me you little tart! Pooooo weeee!!!!"

∼∼∼∼∼∼∼∼∼∼∼∼∼∼∼∼

We got to Natalie's about half an hour late as the poopsplosion didn't just require a change of clothes it also required a bath - I resisted the urge to put my stinky baby out on the deck and hose her down from a distance as I figured that probably wouldn't win me any Mother of the Year awards.

"Hi Carter! Hey Goose!" Natalie said as I carried her inside to Natalie and Sean's lounge.

"Hey Nat," I replied dropping the nappy bag on the floor and putting Carter and her capsule on the floor by my feet. Damn that thing weighs a tonne. "Hey Rachel," I said to Rachel who was sitting on the couch giving Sophie a bottle.

"Hey Goose, how are you?"

"Good, now that I'm finally here. Geez I think I need a vodka after the crap I just cleaned up - if I win Lotto I'm so going to hire someone to change nappies! It's the worst thing about motherhood by far."

"Nah I vote for the sleepless nights," Rachel said.

Natalie came back into the lounge carrying a coffee for me and a plate of sausage rolls.

Damn it there goes the diet! I'll just have one to be polite...

Seven sausage rolls and a caramel slice later:

"You don't think it's mean that I didn't invite the others do you?" Natalie asked. "I just really can't cope with all the fake nice crap and everyone talking over each other. I mean, seriously, who knew having babies would evoke such competitiveness??"

"I know! The way Lydia talks you'd think she's got a bloody Doogie Howser on her hands! Gretchen's only what, three and a half months old and she's already a genius apparently!" I laughed.

While we had been to a few group catch ups it was fairly obvious quite early on that the other women in the group weren't really on the same page as the three of us. I think it was when we saw one woman, Elise, holding her baby Lillian over a bucket to do wees and another woman Dawn tell us that her daughter Harmony would never be allowed to watch TV as shows like Barney the Dinosaur and the Wiggles have 'been proven' to cause brain damage that really made us click - as we realised we are by far the coolest people in the group. With the coolest babies too of course.

And I don't know about brain damaging but I admit Barney is frigging annoying – but he's still the best damn babysitter around.

I love you, you love me, we're a happy family. With a great big hug and a kiss from me to you – damn it, now I've got that damn song stuck in my head.

"So, have you guys had sex since you had your babies?" Rachel blurted out.

Whoa that came out of nowhere!

"Uh yeah. We did a couple of times before I fractured my tailbone and then obviously we couldn't while that healed but we have a few times since that's been better. Why??" I replied.

"We've tried a couple of times but both times it was so painful," Rachel said. "Was it sore for you the first time?"

"Umm not really...it was uh, different though."

"What do you mean?" they both asked.

"Well, I don't know, it just felt a bit loose I guess. Like he was parking his car in a garage that could've fit a truck and trailer you know?" I blushed.

Rachel laughed. "Really? Did Chops say anything??"

"No of course not. I asked him if it felt different to him but of course he lied and said it felt exactly the same. Yeah right, it was like he wasn't even touching the sides and was just in there, flapping around in the breeze."

They burst out laughing. "Maybe you need some of those little balls you can get that you shove up there and you have to clench your muscles to stop them from falling out?" Rachel said.

"Mate the way my punani is at the moment a basketball would probably still fall out!"

Natalie was still laughing. "Oh well, at least you are giving it a go *we* haven't had sex yet."

"Really?" Rachel asked.

"Hell no. I'm so not ready for any action down there yet."

"Wow, does Sean mind?" I asked. The Sean I remembered would probably have been gagging for it by now.

"Yeah, he's starting to get a bit pissy about it and makes a few smart ass comments. Actually, he even said that he bet YOU wouldn't be holding out on Chops and probably gave it up a few weeks after you gave birth."

I blushed. *Shame. He always did know me well.*

"Mind you, it probably doesn't help that we didn't have sex for the last five months of my pregnancy either."

Holy crap!

"Why not?!" I asked.

"I don't know, I was always just too tired and felt sick all the time I guess."

"So he hasn't had sex in almost nine months?! That's like, about nine years in man time isn't it??" Rachel exclaimed.

"God when you put it like that I feel a bit mean. I'm just scared that it's going to hurt! You just said it did for you!"

"It might not for you though. You might need to brush off the cobwebs first though," Rachel joked.

"Besides," I interjected, "you never know - you might get lucky and have gaping flaps like me and not even feel it!"

~~~~~~~~~~~~~~~~~~~~

"So how are things with Blair?" I asked Jess, puffing through my sixth minute on the crosstrainer.

"Really good! He's so awesome! It is a bit weird already living with him though, it's kind of like we've skipped the whole 'dating' part of the relationship and gone straight to living together. Not that I mind, it's just different to every other relationship I've had. And oh my God Goose, the sex is *amazing*. He is so hot!!"

Ohhh I can only imagine...

"Oh yay! I'm so happy for you guys!" I exclaimed through puffs.

"I am a bit pissed off though, bloody Amanda has started texting him again. I'm guessing you told Chelsea that we hooked up aye?"

"Oh yeah I did. Sorry!"

"It's all good, doesn't bother me. But obviously it bothers her. I can't tell if she wants him back or not or she's just trying to shit stir. I mean they broke up *months* ago!"

"Did he tell you that she's been texting him?" I asked.

"Yeah, he's been really honest about it. And I think he's happy with me but I have to admit I am a little worried."

"I don't think you need to be, she treated him like shit so I highly doubt he'd go back there. Besides, he's totally into you babe!"

"Hmm. How did you get rid of Fiona? She was hard out texting Chops for awhile there aye?" she asked, hardly even breaking a sweat while I was red faced and breathless.

"It kind of sorted itself out really when she went overseas. As far as I know he hasn't heard from her since she's been gone."

"Oh right. I wish Amanda would take a flying jump and piss off too," she grumbled.

"Man is it time to get off this effing thing now??" I asked.

"Yeah I've had enough for today too, do you want to go next door and get a coffee? Do you have to hurry home?"

"Nah Chops'll be holding the fort I'm sure. Let's go girlfriend," I smiled.

We grabbed our stuff and ten minutes later were seated at a table in the cafe next to the gym with large coffees and bacon and egg croissants (all that exercise made me hungry).

"Goose, do you know that chick over there? At your 2 o'clock. She keeps looking at us but I don't know who she is."

I turned to look at my 2 o'clock and saw a man with a beard stirring his coffee.

"2 o'clock not 10 o'clock! She's up at the counter about to be served," Jess told me.

I looked over to the counter and saw a girl with blonde hair with her back to us placing her order. I kept watching her and not long after she turned around and I saw her face as she made eye contact with me and then looked away.

"Nah, she does look familiar though. Maybe she's just staring at me because I look like such a sweaty hog at the moment," I said and turned back to Jess.

"She just looked over again. Maybe she's a lesbian and likes a bit of sweaty hog action, " Jess joked.

I looked over to the girl again who was collecting her takeaway coffee and watched her walk out the door. It wasn't until I saw her walk past the front window of the cafe that it finally dawned on me who she was.

"Holy shit it's bloody Fiona!!" I hissed at Jess.

"No way! We were only just talking about her! I thought you said she was overseas??"

"I thought she was!"

"I wonder if Chops has heard from her since she's been back?"

"Hmmmpf. You better believe I'm going to find out!"

~~~~~~~~~~~~~~~~~~

"So, why didn't you tell me Fiona was back from overseas??" I demanded when I got home. My plan to be cool, calm and collected had failed to come to fruition.

Chops looked surprised. And was that guilt on his face?!

"How do you know?" he answered.

Bzzzzzz. Wrong answer dickhead.

"So you HAVE heard from her?? Were you planning on telling me??"

"I've had a couple of texts from her. I didn't think it would be a big deal, she got home a couple of weeks ago I think. How did you find out anyway?"

"I just saw her at a cafe if you must know!"

"Cafe? I thought you were going to the gym?"

"That's not the point! Why didn't you tell me? Have you *seen* her?" I asked angrily.

He sighed. "No I haven't seen her. I don't see what the big deal is, you know she's no threat to you."

"Do I?? And how do I know that? My future husband has been texting his ex fiancée without my knowledge - that really makes me feel soooo secure in the relationship *Nathan!*"

"Don't overreact *Lucy*. She was only texting to congratulate us about

Carter – she actually wants to come around and meet her and meet you properly. She's only trying to be nice."

Nice?! Is he really that dumb?!

"Oh awesome. Why doesn't she come around for brunch tomorrow while she's at it??" I replied sarcastically.

"I guess I could ask her. Are you sure that you don't mind though? I guess it would get it over and done with."

Oh man he IS that dumb! Why don't I think before I speak?! Crap! Okay, be the bigger person here it might not be so bad - hang on, I just saw her I AM the bigger person here. Damn it!

I decided the 'keep your friends close and your enemies closer' track was the way to go.

"Of course," I purred innocently. "It would be nice to meet her properly and have her meet our daughter."

And have her see everything she hasn't got...

"Okay, I'll text her after I mow the lawns," he smiled and kissed me on the top of my head.

"Text her now darling," I said sweetly, "if she's coming I'll have to make sure I've got everything I need to make something yummy." I smiled angelically at him.

Bitch Slut Skank Whore!

I heard Carter cry out from her room so I left Chops texting on his phone and picked her up from her nap.

"Hi baby girl," I soothed but her cries continued. "Who's a hungry bubba?"

I went out to the kitchen and handed Carter to Chops while I made her a bottle.

"Did you text her?"

"Yep I'll let you know when she replies." I had finished making the bottle so he handed her back to me. "I'll go get these lawns done, okay?"

"Sure," I smiled, sticking the bottle in Carter's mouth. I watched Chops as he went out the back door, leaving his phone on the kitchen bench – it was like a lighthouse, beckoning me like a ship in the dark night.

Don't be a crazy stalker bitch...oh crap! Like I can resist it!

I heard the lawnmower start in the front yard so I balanced Carter and the bottle against my chest and grabbed the phone with my free hand. I quickly opened it to the message inbox.

A COUPLE of messages?!?!?!

I counted the messages from Fiona. Unless the definition of 'a couple' had been changed from two to about twenty two, unfortunately Chops had been stretching the truth just a bit.

Asshole!!!!!!

I quickly read the messages. Okay, so they seemed harmless enough to the untrained eye but I still had my suspicions about her – man, does she really have to use so many damn smiley faces?!? – so after reading them all I listened to make sure the lawnmower was still going and then checked the sentbox to see Chops' replies. Again, nothing incriminating, but did he really have to be that nice to her? She cheated on him after all!

Just then his phone buzzed and a little envelope icon flashed up. It gave me a fright and I immediately hit the back button, which was not actually the back button and instead opened the message.

I'd love to ☺ What time? Can I bring anything? ☺

Crap! She's coming! And he's going to know I was looking at his phone!

I frantically tried to figure out if I could make the message appear unread but had no idea how to. I figured honesty may have to be the best policy to get out of this one. And I figured I might as well reply to the text while I was there.

About 11am no need to bring anything see you then ☺

I figured 11am would give me plenty of time to make myself beautiful AND cook an awesome brunch. The back door opened and I was caught red handed with Chops' phone in my hand. I blushed.

"I uh, heard your phone buzz so I checked the message I hope that's ok? Fiona is going to come so I replied for you and just said to come at about 11am," I told him innocently, like I hadn't been poring through his messages like a crazed stalker for the last 10 minutes.

"Sweet as," he said, drinking a glass of water. "Hi baby girl," he said to Carter who was straining her neck to look at him. "I'll just finish the back lawns and I thought I'd have a couple of beers and watch the game if that's cool with you?"

"Of course," I said sweetly. "I'll pop out to the supermarket soon and grab a couple of things for brunch."

"You're awesome," he said and went back out to continue mowing the lawns.

"Come on Missy Moo let's go to the supermarket," I said to Carter and then got a whiff of her rancid nappy.

"Ewwwww, once Daddy comes back inside to change your bum that is!"

~~~~~~~~~~~~~~~~

We took a detour on the way to the supermarket and stopped by Jess and Leo's house. They were both home and luckily Blair was out on a run so there would be no man ears (Leo's don't count) to eavesdrop on our conversation.

"So then I said we should have her over for brunch tomorrow so he bloody well invited her and she said yes!" I moaned to my friends.

Jess was bouncing Carter on her lap and giving her kisses while Leo came back in with a coffee and a Coke Zero for me and Jess.

"Well that was a stupid thing to do," Leo said matter-of-factly. "Do you want us to come for moral support?"

"Whatever Leo - you just want a free feed!" Jess laughed.

"Well, that too. Blair sure as hell doesn't love you for your cooking ability Jess."

"Ooh Jess has he told you he loves you??" I interrupted.

She blushed. "Yeah."

"Oooooooooooooohhhhh that's so cool!!!"

"Anyway back to the problem at hand," Leo said. "I reckon you should put laxatives in her food. That'll teach the skank to leave your man alone!"

Oh man why didn't I think of that!?

"Leo! No Goose, don't listen to him. You're far too mature to do that!"

"Am I?"

"Yes! Don't lower yourself to that level," she gave Leo the evils. "Just cook awesome food and show her your gorgeous baby and that will piss her off enough! What are you going to cook anyway?"

"I've got a pumpkin in the fridge so I thought I might make a pumpkin soup with bread and then Eggs Benedict or something like that," I replied.

"Yum! I love your pumpkin soup," Jess said.

"And you know what would go well in pumpkin soup don't you?" Leo asked.

"What?" I asked.

"Starts with 'L' and ends in 'axatives'" he said, laughing.

"LEO!" Jess chided him.

Tempting, oh so tempting...

~~~~~~~~~~~~~~~~~~

But I didn't give in to the temptation. I decided to be mature and not give in to the evil little Goose that was pecking me on my shoulder telling me to give Fiona the screaming shits. I mean, surely she would be on her best behaviour. Maybe she really did just want to be nice?

She arrived at about 11:10am. I had taken extra care applying my makeup and straightened my hair in preparation for her arrival. I let Chops answer the door and stood out of sight in the doorway of the lounge to hear their greeting.

"Hey you!" I heard her exclaim. Then I think she hugged him.

Did she just kiss him? Dirty slapper!

"Hey Fee. Goose?" he called. "Fiona's here."

I paused for a second so that they wouldn't guess I was hiding right by the door then took a deep breath and walked into the hallway.

Here goes...

"Hi Fiona," I said, smiling. "Nice to meet you."

"You too Lucy! I've heard lots about you."

"You can call me Goose, it's fine."

"Okay. And where's this little girl of yours?" she said with way too much enthusiasm for my liking. I noticed she was holding a present, wrapped in baby pink wrapping paper. "Oh, I brought her a present too."

"That's so nice of you," Chops said. "She's sleeping at the moment but should be awake soon."

"I'll give you this then, Lu-I mean Goose," and handed me the present.

"Thanks," with as much enthusiasm I could muster.

"Chops, show me the baby's room I'll be quiet I promise! Oh, I just can't believe you're a daddy!" she exclaimed.

"I'll just go get lunch sorted," I said grumpily to nobody as they had already gone into Carter's room.

I went back into the kitchen and stirred the soup and started cutting a loaf of bread to go with it. I heard them come into the lounge and Chops offered her a drink to which she said something and giggled. A second later he came into the kitchen and opened the fridge.

"You ok?" he said, coming over and putting his hand on my shoulder.

"Of course," I beamed at him, hacking at the bread like it was her giggly face.

"Cool, it smells awesome babe."

"Thanks." I started spooning soup into the bowls.

He went back into the lounge carrying her drink and I headed over to the fridge to get the sour cream out. I peeked around the corner and watched him hand her the drink. She looked up at him and said thank you and I could swear she batted her eyelashes at him while she touched his forearm.

Well that was it. If I had been in a cartoon that would have been the point that my face went bright red and steam started hissing out of my ears. The skanky bitch was going down - in a screaming heap of runny shit.

I stalked over to the medicine cabinet and jerked the handle open, forgetting it had a kiddy lock on it. I struggled to get it open.

Goddamn kiddy locks!!!

I finally got it open, knelt down started looking through it.

Come on I know it's in here somewhere...yes! I triumphantly pulled out a bottle of liquid laxatives that Merryn had given me for constipation while I was pregnant.

Maybe I shouldn't do this...maybe she is just super friendly?

That particular thought was interrupted by her laughing out loud to something Chops had said followed by "Oh Chops you're *sooo* funny!"

He's not that funny bitch. Too damn right I should do this - she's totally in there flirting with him.

So I unscrewed the cap and read the instructions: 'Keep out of reach of children, take 1 or 2 teaspoons when required and no more than 3 teaspoons per day. Fast acting - may take up to three hours to take effect.'

Okay 6 teaspoons it is!

I quickly stirred it into one of the bowls and topped them all with sour cream. I pulled Fiona's special bowl to the front so I knew which was which.

"Goose, Carter's awake I'll go get her," Chops called from the lounge.

"Wait! I'll go!" I called and raced into the lounge. I wanted to make sure her ginger mohawk was tamed before Fiona saw her. "Back in a tick!"

"Good girl," I cooed to Carter as I picked her up out of her cot. What a perfect day to wake up happy. "Now be an even better girl and pull the bitch's hair."

I went back out to the lounge but Chops and Fiona weren't in there. I walked through the kitchen to find them sitting at the dining room table waiting for me, three bowls of soup already on the placemats.

Oh shiiiiiiiiiiiiit.

"I brought the soup in babe I figured you don't want it to go cold. I assumed they were all the same?"

"Uh-huh," I said, eyeing up the three bowls and internally working through what order I thought Chops would have picked them up from the bench. Surely he would have picked up the front one for our guest first, wouldn't he? Damn it! He's a man - like there is any logical order to anything they do.

"It smells amazing Luc-Goose," Fiona said.

"Thanks," I squeaked, realising there was a very good chance I was about to sit down in front of the tainted bowl of soup.

"Awwww look at you, you gorgeous girl!" she said and I realised I was still holding Carter.

"Oh, um, you guys start. I'll get Carter a bottle and eat afterwards."

Or not eat at all...

"No babe, you cooked it I'll feed her while you eat," Chops said and took Carter from my arms.

Damn it!

"Oh, um, ok." I sat opposite Fiona and picked up my spoon. "Bread?" I asked and offered her the plate of bread.

"Thanks, wow this soup is delicious! It's got a really different taste, what's in it?"

Phew...she must have the front one.

"Um, bacon and lentils," I said, relaxing a bit as I watched her eat.

"Oh, it must be the bacon, I'll have to get the recipe!" she said enthusiastically.

Haha if you only knew...

I took a small sip of my spoon. I felt safe enough to start eating it - mine tasted exactly like it always did. Which was AWESOME, if I do say so myself.

After we finished the soup and Carter had finished her bottle I left them in the lounge while I put the Eggs Benedict together. As I was drizzling the hollandaise sauce over each stack, Chops came into the kitchen carrying Carter.

"Where's Fiona?" I asked.

"Just popped to the loo, that looks great babe!"

Oh crap! I didn't think the laxatives would kick in that fast! My poor toilet!

When Fiona came back in a few moments later I searched her face for the residual effects of diarrhoea induced watering eyes and/or pain but saw nothing out of the ordinary. She must have just gone for a wee.

"Wow that looks awesome. You better be careful or I won't want to leave!" she giggled.

Oh yes you will bitch...in approximately 2 hours and 10 minutes.

Chops put Carter in the bouncinette by the table while we ate and she was gooing and gaaing over her rattle and acting like a perfect angel baby. I'd be jealous of me and my little family if I was Fiona.

After we ate our Eggs Benedict I made coffees and took them into the lounge.

"Owwww!" Fiona cried. "Wow she's got a good grip on her for such a little baby!" she half joked as she unsuccessfully tried to loosen Carter's fist from around a clump of her hair. She finally got it loose and Carter immediately grabbed another clump, smile on her face.

Yes! That's my girl!

About an hour later she finally left. She thanked me for lunch and Chops walked her out to the front door while this time I watched from a new hiding place just inside Carter's bedroom door after putting her back to bed.

I watched as she touched his forearm again and giggled as she said goodbye, no doubt batting her eyelashes again.

Grrrr, the dirty dog deserves everything she gets. I hope the laxatives take effect while she's driving home and she shits her pants!

I came out of Carter's room after he had shut the front door.

"Thanks for that honey, I know it must have been hard for you," Chops said. "To be honest though, I'd rather not invite her over again. It was nice to see her but I kind of feel like that part of my life is over and needs to stay in the past. So if she texts again I'll just tell her that."

Maybe he's not so dumb after all!

"You could tell she was hitting on you, couldn't you?" I asked, surprised by his comment.

"Oh, uh, yeah I guess I could," he said sheepishly. "I can't believe you noticed and didn't go crazy bitch on her and slash her tyres or something haha."

"Haha," I replied, smiling. Oh if he only knew.

"Dawg, dirty dawg, dawg, dirty dawg,
Oohh, you're a dirty, dirty,
Dawg, dirty dawg, dawg, dirty dawg
Oh, you're so damn dir-ty," I sang.

Chops started laughing. But I wasn't finished.

"Yo, yo, why you wanna act like a tramp, a wet food stamp,
I think it's time for me to break camp
Had a crush on my man the first time we met.
Now what you see is what you get
Lost more than a mil on a gambling bet
So here's the Chuckwagon for the dog in you,
Here's the Kennelration and the Alpo too," I rapped, complete with gangster dance moves and homie hand gestures.

Chops was pissing himself laughing. "Where the hell did *that* come from?"

"That is now Fiona's theme song - courtesy of New Kids on The Block, circa 1993."

He was still laughing. "God I love you. But please, don't give up your day job!"

I feigned hurt and stuck out my lower lip. "Yo homie, don't be a hater. You're just jealous. I'm like Eminem - but with boobs. Feminem even."

"And such nice boobs they are," he said and copped a feel.

Hahaha it's obvious he hasn't seen me naked in awhile!

~~~~~~~~~~~~~~~~~~

"*Owwwwwwwwww!!*" I cried as I writhed on the toilet.

GOD HELP ME! OH THE PAIN!! KILL ME NOW! PLEASE!!

Apparently six teaspoons of liquid laxatives doesn't take the full three hours to take effect - it hit me with full force after exactly 2 hours and 34 minutes. Apparently Chops used man logic and *didn't* take the front bowl to give to our guest...

What an absolutely shitty idea *that* had turned out to be.

September

"But I don't see why we have to invite *those* cousins, I mean when was the last time you even saw them??" I demanded.

"That's not the point, I can hardly invite two of my cousins and and their partners and not the others," Chops replied.

"Why not?? You don't have anything to do with them. Why should we waste four of the spaces on our guest list for people we don't want to invite?! That's four people we *do* like that we can't invite!!" I said grumpily.

"They will expect to be invited Goose! I'm sure there are relations *you* don't want to invite that your mum expects you to, isn't there??"

"Only my sister." I grumbled. "Besides, I just don't see how we are going to get this guest list down to 100 people. It's just not going to happen!"

"Well, it has to. The venue only holds 100 so I suggest you start culling off some people – *not* starting with my cousins," Chops said matter-of-factly.

"Could we at least not invite your cousins' partners then?"

He gave me an exasperated look.

"Fine," I replied, sour faced.

"Good," Chops smiled, obviously ignoring the look on my face. "Now go and have fun dress shopping. Carter and I are going to watch the game."

"We are already arguing about the guest list," I said to Jess and Leo.

"Well, aren't weddings and having a baby supposed to be the most stressful times in a relationship?" Jess said. "And you've already got through one of them so once you get through the wedding you'll be sweet."

"True. And I've got the best bridesmaids a girl could ask for," I said, putting my arms around my friends as we walked into the first dress shop.

Leo cleared his throat. "Brides*man* thank you!"

"Haha yes bridesman," I smiled at him, "and I'm not even making you wear orange!"

"Oh shit, you haven't told us what Renee said yet! Are we going to have the displeasure of having her as a bridesmaid with us??" Jess asked.

My mother had, of course, insisted I ask Renee to be one of my bridesmaids seeing as I had been one of hers. I decided against informing her that, unlike my witch of a sister, I had enough friends to make up numbers and I *really* didn't want her as part of my bridal party. I mean, imagine if she tried to get revenge on me for the um, unfortunate incident at *her* wedding? (Of which the video was now at over 100,000 YouTube views – classic!)

So I did what Mum asked. I sucked it up and rang Renee and asked if she would be one of my bridesmaids. I'm not sure if she could tell that I had my fingers crossed when I asked but she said she would think about it and let me know.

"I meant to text you! She said no!!"

"Oh thank God I don't think I could've coped spending that much time with the Bulldog. Why'd she say no? I would've thought she'd jump at the chance to make your life miserable!" Leo said.

"Just too busy with Eeyore and she will be back at work by then so didn't think 'she would have the time to commit to it.' So it's just you guys and Dee." I breathed a sigh of relief. "Oh and my gorgeous little flowergirl of course. How cute is it going to be if Carter is walking by then?!"

"She will be so gorgeous! Awww she can have little pigtails with ribbons in them!" Jess clapped her hands in delight.

"Hi. Which one of you is the bride?" a skinny, heavily made up salesgirl approached us, smiling.

Holy shit that's me! I'm a bride! Boom!

"That's me," I said. "And this is one of my bridesmaids and my bridesman."

She giggled. "Cool. Have you got an idea of what kind of dress you would like?"

"Maybe a halter neck? I definitely don't want strapless I don't think I could go bra-less these days," I replied. "And I still have back fat so I really don't want that muffin topping over in a strapless dress." That vision was still all too clear from Renee's video.

"Are you planning on losing weight before the wedding?" she asked.

Is she calling me fat?!

Leo snorted. I death stared him.

"I've lost about 15kg since I had my baby, I have about 5kg more to lose I guess," I replied, blushing.

"Awww you have a baby?! That's so lovely."

"Hmm. Thanks."

"Okay then let's get started," the salesgirl said. "I'm just going to take some measurements so if you could please come over here and pop your arms up for me that would be awesome. When is your wedding date?"

"14th March. If we can agree on the guest list that is!"

"All of us important people will be there Goosey don't worry about all the other plebs," Leo said. "Who are Chops' other groomsmen? Apart from Blair?"

"We don't need to worry about whether a groomsman and bridesmaid will hook up aye Jess? You've got that covered for us," I laughed.

"I'll take one for the team if he's got any other hot ones!" Leo interjected.

"Good luck with that," I said to him. "He's having his brother in law Jon and his best mate from college, Gav. And they're both married with kids."

"Dumb. Some friend you are," he replied.

"Awwww poor Leo. Is it going to fall off from a lack of action and neglect?" I asked sarcastically.

"You laugh - but a man has needs you know," he said.

The salesgirl cleared her throat. I had almost forgotten she was there. She had finished taking my measurements - poor bitch probably needed to find a longer measuring tape.

"Um, if you don't mind me interrupting your conversation, my flatmate is gay and I think you guys might get on really well. Do you want me to give him your number?" she asked.

"I think you've got the wrong idea. I'm not gay," Leo said to her.

"Oh, oh no. I'm so sorry," she stammered.

I snorted. "Leo you're a prick. Don't be mean to the poor girl."

"I'm sorry, I couldn't resist. The look on your face was priceless," he said to her, laughing.

"So you *are* gay?" she asked warily.

"As gay as Wentworth Miller from Prison Break. So to put it simply, yes, I like cock. And I'd love it if you gave your flatmate my number. As long as he's hot," the ever classy Leo replied to her.

"Noooo! I told you! WENTWORTH MILLER IS NOT GAY! He can't be!" Jess exclaimed.

"Whatever Jess, he's as gay as they come. Just you wait!"

~~~~~~~~~~~~~~~~

We left about an hour and a half and eight dresses later. There was one halter neck dress I really liked but unfortunately I quickly figured out where Carter got her Quarterback shoulders from as I felt like an extremely white version of the Incredible Hulk in it.

Jess voted for an off-the-shoulder Sweetheart Chiffon dress with ruching (apparently that is good for hiding lumps and bumps) but I wasn't sold on it.

Oh well, at least I had six months left to find a dress. *If* we can agree on the bloody guest list that is.

"Happy birthday to you, happy birthday to you, happy birthday dear Goose, happy birthday to you!" my friends sang to me.

I blushed in the dim light of the restaurant. I was surrounded by all of my closest friends and we had just had dinner and drinks to celebrate my turning 29 the day before.

29 - how did that happen!? Only one year until I'll be 30. Now *that's* a scary thought.

It was also Chops and my first night away from Carter for the whole night. We had booked a hotel room for the night and my mum was in her element on Nana duty at our place.

"You're not texting your mum *again* are you?" Chops asked.

"You make it sound bad that I'm worried about our baby! I just want to know she's okay," I replied indignantly.

"Of course she will be. She's five months old babe she will be lapping up all the attention from her Nana. Come on, we're all going to head next door to the pub for some more drinks."

I followed everyone next door and then my phone beeped to signal a reply. After Carter was born I had decided it was time to grow up and change my Darth Vader ringtone to something a little more respectable. Well, that and Matty J had texted me once during the night and in my sleep-deprived state I had freaked out and thought it was an intruder who had broken in to kidnap my baby. So after jumping out of bed all Ninja styles holding my bedside lamp as a weapon to find an empty room, a boring old beep it was.

She is still fine darling. You would think I have never looked after a baby before! I did have 3 of you remember? And you all turned out ok!

Renee didn't...oops I've offended Nana.

Sorry! I won't text again I promise! Have a good sleep see you in the morning ☺ I replied and then put my phone away.

Oh I hope she remembered to change her nappy before she put her to bed...

"Goose!! You sexy bitch!" Sean came over to me and put his arm around me, slightly slurring his words. It was the first time my friends had met my antenatal friends (apart from Jess who of course remembered Sean from school) and it was going really well. Apart from Chelsea, who doesn't always play well with others.

"Hey Sean," I replied. "Thanks for coming." I extricated myself from his drunken grip.

"I wouldn't miss it for the worrrrlllldd. I forgot how awesome you are Lucy Goosey. I'm sooooooo glad we're friends again," he drawled.

Chops came over at that moment, put his arm around me and handed me another glass of wine. "Hey Sean."

Oh shit oh shit, Sean please don't say anything about us having sex in the back of your Mum's car. Or on the stairs at your brother's flat. Or on the beach on New Years Eve...

"Chops! Mate! You've got yourself a good woman here. I remember back at college-"

Oh shit oh shit.

"-we all knew Goose would make someone a good wife someday. She's got such a massive-"

Oh SHIT.

"-heart. You're a lucky man Chops!"

Phew. That could've gone a LOT worse.

"Thanks mate, I think so too," he replied, smiling at me and hugging me tighter.

Natalie came over then. "Sean there you are! Hey Goose," she gave me a hug. "Happy birthday. But I think we better get going, I think *someone* has had enough to drink," she said, gesturing to Sean. "And the babysitter is having trouble settling Rafe. I'm pretty sure he's teething."

"Oh poor baby. I wondered if Carter was the other day too. Either that or she was just being an angry ginger," I laughed.

"Speaking of teething, imagine how many teeth Gretchen has got by now?!" Natalie exclaimed. "She's probably got a whole mouth full of chompers!"

"Haha true! Thanks for coming Nat. I'm so glad you met some of my friends before the wedding," I replied.

"Man, that Leo is a crack up! Your friends are great."

"Yeah they are! Thanks so much for coming," I said.

"Thanks for inviting us. Enjoy the hotel tonight..." Natalie winked at us and Sean's eyes almost popped out of his head.

"Goose! Remember that time back at college when we-"

OH SHIT!!

I blushed in panic as I knew exactly what he was referring to. "Oh Nat! I really hope your first day back at work goes well on Monday!" I interrupted him quickly before he could unearth any of our dirty little secrets.

"Thanks chicken. Have a great night."

After they walked away Chops pulled me closer to him and kissed me. "I think Sean has a bit of a crush on you, Miss James."

"Nah I don't think so," I blushed. "He's just really friendly. We always got on well at school."

And got it on well hahahahaha.

"I don't mind if he does. It just goes to prove how lucky I am to have such a gorgeous woman to take back to the hotel room and do naughty things to tonight," he said suggestively.

"Oh, who's that?" I replied innocently. "*I* don't do naughty things, I'm pure and innocent."

"We'll see about that!" he said and grabbed me around the waist, making me squeal.

"Get a room Sluttypants!" Leo called out.

"We have a room!" I called back.

"Then go use it you horny bitches!"

Three wines and several Vodka shots later we did. Sluttypants was on form if I do say so myself, loose flaps and all...and Chops, well *damn* is all I can say. My butcher's got a pork sword and he knows how to use it.

~~~~~~~~~~~~~~~~~

Our night of passion was quickly forgotten the next morning when I found myself in the middle of the most horrendous hangover I have ever experienced – and you know it's a bad one when even a Sausage and Egg McMuffin doesn't make you feel better.

We made our way home late morning to find Carter in the Jolly Jumper and my mother finishing off an epic clean of my kitchen - she had even cleaned the microwave. I take back every bad word I have ever said about my mother. She's a legend.

While I had been looking forward to seeing my smiling, giggling little girl I had to admit I was also really looking forward to her naptime. Who knew having a baby and a hangover would be so hard? In fact I actually had to get Chops to take her out of the Jolly Jumper as the constant jumping was making me feel sick and the squealing was making my head hurt even more.

Then just to rip my undies, Carter chose that particular day to not have a nap and instead cried the *entire* afternoon. Chops suggested she may be teething but I knew the truth – the little tart was punishing me.

It was quite possibly the longest day ever and when I finally got her settled at 9pm that night I came to the conclusion that a) I am not 21 anymore and b) I can no longer handle nights of drunken debauchery and still function the next day. And that's only with *one* kid – how do people do it with more than one??

So it's official. I am ~~never drinking~~ again. I am never having any more kids.

October

"Hello little lady, and good morning Mum," said Elise when we entered the baby area at Carter's new daycare. "And how is mum feeling about her first day back at work?"

Elise was the manager of the Under 2 area and was a lovely motherly type of woman. There were also two other women who worked in the baby area who seemed really nice - but that still didn't make it any easier to leave my six month old baby with them for an entire seven hours until Chops would be there to pick her up.

"Umm, I'm ok," I said as chirpily as I could muster while I fought back tears. Who knew I would turn into such a sap!?

Elise could obviously tell that I was lying through my teeth and patted me on the arm. "It's ok love. Carter will be in safe hands and she's had three visits with us so she will settle fine, I'm sure of it." She held out her hands for me to pass Carter to her.

"Uh huh," I replied, gripping onto my smiling baby for dear life.

Elise managed to extract Carter from my grasp and said "Ok little lady say goodbye to Mum, she doesn't want to be late for her first day back at work."

I kissed Carter on the head and felt the tears about to erupt.

"Ok, um her blankie is in her bag, and her bottles, oh and she doesn't like them too warm, oh and sometimes when she goes to bed she kicks her covers off and then wakes up because she gets cold-"

"No problem we will be fine won't we missy?" Elise interrupted my pointless raving and spoke to Carter who was perched on her hip. She took her hand and waved it at me. "Wave goodbye to Mummy!"

Carter giggled as Elise waved her chubby little hand. "Now off you go Mum, have a great day and we will ring you if there are any problems, which I'm sure there won't be."

I managed to make it to the foyer of the daycare centre before the tears spilled over and I'm sure the receptionist thought I was a right cot case as I streaked past her, tears flowing freely and snot pooling in my nose. But then again, maybe she'd seen it all before – surely I'm not the only neurotic mum to ever have cried after leaving her poor defenceless baby at daycare for the first time.

I sat in my car out the front of the centre for a good ten minutes while I cried. When I had calmed myself down I looked my reflection in the rear vision mirror and groaned - what a waste of time it had been to apply mascara as it was now all over my face. I'm bringing sexy back.

Oh harden up Princess! I told myself. *You're only going back to work two days a week!*

Oh yeah, forgot to mention that all the emotional basket case behaviour was all over Carter going to daycare only two days a week – imagine what a sobbing lunatic I would be if I was going back to work full time!

My cellphone rang. I looked at the caller ID and it was the daycare's number.

Oh my God what's happened to my baby!??!

"Hello Lucy speaking??" I answered breathlessly.

"Hi Lucy it's Elise. I just wanted to let you know that Carter has settled fine and is having a lovely time reading a book with Janine at the moment."

I sighed with relief and almost started crying again. "Thank you Elise."

"No problem, now you get yourself off to work and have a good day love."

Oh shame does she know I haven't even left yet?! I blushed and looked around but couldn't see anyone peering at me out of the windows.

Then I did what I was told and gave myself a quick tidy up, got rid of all mascara and snot remnants and drove the five minutes it took to get to work.

And you know what? I survived. And I actually kind of liked it. Well, apart from when I realised that my return to work happened to coincide with Helen's biannual smear test. I had only just recovered from the last one.

∼∼∼∼∼∼∼∼∼∼∼

A couple of weeks later, I came home from work to find Chops in the kitchen cooking dinner with Carter in the Jolly Jumper. She gave me a big smile when I walked in the back door.

"Hello baby girl, awww look at you with your big red cheeks!" I said after giving her a kiss. "Man I hope she's not cutting some more teeth I haven't gotten over the first ones yet," I said to Chops.

"She might be. She was hard out chewing on a rusk before," he replied.

"You didn't give her a rusk while she was in the Jolly Jumper did you?! What if she choked on it??"

"Chill out woman - she was in the high chair!"

"Ok then," I grumbled. I got a whiff of meat. "What are you cooking?"

"My latest sausage invention for you to try. Beef, chilli and dark chocolate."

The sound of it just about made me want to throw up, not to mention the smell. Meat and chocolate?? Ewwww. "Oh, um, ok. Sounds uh, interesting."

"Are you ok? You look a bit pale," Chops asked.

"Yeah I'm just tired I think. I'll go have a shower before dinner if that's ok. My feet are killing me."

"No worries. Me and C-Dog have got everything under control, haven't we little chicken?" he said to Carter who was still happily jumping in the doorway.

Awww that's so sweet I want to cry!!

What a sap. Someone seriously needs to give me a cup of concrete.

~~~~~~~~~~~~~~

I was wrong. Beef, chilli and dark chocolate sausages are *amazeballs*. I want to eat hundreds of them. Every night. But I must stop or I won't fit my wedding dress. In fact, I have put on a kilo and a half since the last time I weighed myself. Damn you chocolate sausages.

"Hey Goose, you don't happen to have a tampon I could borrow do you?" a nurse from work, Kelly, asked me in the staffroom.

"Sure," I replied, grabbing one out of a box in my locker. "But hey, treat yourself and keep it chick. Don't really want it back."

Kelly laughed and took it from me. "Thanks heaps. Trust me to get my period at work and be unprepared."

"Uh huh," I said, suddenly very distracted. I watched as Kelly walked off towards the bathroom and turned back to my locker. The box of tampons was half full.

When did I have my last period???

I wracked my brain trying to remember but all the days and weeks seemed to merge into one. I started to get a bit panicky.

Surely I've had it recently. Come on Goose, remember!

But I couldn't remember.

Shit!!!

I pulled my cellphone out and texted Jess. She would remember, I'm sure she would. That's what best friends are for — unless your best friend is me, then you're on your rag and on your own.

Hey chick do you remember when I had my last period??

I waited impatiently for a reply and scoffed my lunch down. I'm such a stress eater. My phone finally beeped.

No...I remember you whinging about it but not sure when that was. WHY?!?!?!

Just wondering. Didn't write it down but it's all good ☺ I replied. All good my ass - I started stressing BIG time. Where is chocolate cake when you need it?!

I made it through the afternoon, only because I had come to the conclusion that I was overreacting and no doubt my period was due any day now. I decided I would take a pregnancy test home just in case but was absolutely sure I would have my period by the next day.

Yep. All good.

~~~~~~~~~~~~~~~~~~

Later that night once Carter was in bed, Chops and I were sitting in the lounge watching Lost (Chops liked it – I was well and truly lost and had been since the second season).

"Hey babe, you don't happen to remember when I had my last period do you?" I asked casually. Surely he would remember – men always remember when they can't have sex for 5-7 days.

He looked at me with his eyebrow raised. "Um, no. I do remember you whinging about it but I can't remember how long ago that was. Why?!"

Why does everyone think I whinge all the time?!?

"Oh, uh, I'm sure it's nothing. I just can't remember when the last one was and I didn't write it down. I'm sure it's nothing, maybe they're still a bit up the wahzoo after having Carter," I said, trying to make light of it.

"You told me that they were regular again after having her. Shit, do you think you need to do a pregnancy test??" His brow had furrowed and I swear he had started sweating.

"No, no. I'm sure I'm overreacting. Maybe if I haven't got it in a few days I'll do one," I said, hiding my stress very well under the circumstances.

"Okay..." he looked at me again, as if trying to gauge my stress levels from behind the serene look on my face. "Shit. Imagine if you are," he said, shaking his head.

I don't want to! I can't be!

"Nah, I'm sure I'm not, I feel fine," I replied, figuring the more I said it aloud the more it would turn out to be true.

"Ok sweet as," Chops said simply and then turned his attention back to the TV.

And I went to the kitchen to bake a chocolate cake.

~~~~~~~~~~~~~~

"Ooh yummy! Open your mouth here comes the plane! Where's the plane going to? Carterville!"

Carter giggled and smacked her marmite sandwich down onto the tray of her highchair and slid it across sideways leaving a poo-like dark brown smear across the tray.

"Mmm nice one! Now open your mouth Mummy has got some yummmmmmy fruit for you!"

She did as she was told and I put a spoonful of pureed peach and pear in her mouth. Her face immediately screwed up as though she had eaten a dozen extremely sour lemons - she actually resembled her Aunty for a second there.

Then she spat it out. Half of it landed on top of the brown smear on the tray and the other half hit me square on the cheek and through my hair.

"Ewwwwww poor Mummy!"

Carter giggled again and threw what was left of the smooshed up bread in her hand on the floor.

"Let's try that again," I said wiping the puree off my cheek. Damn it, I had only just washed my hair this morning. "Here you go Miss Carter...here comes the plane!"

The plane got to its destination but the airport was closed. Carter had her lips firmly pursed shut and she wasn't opening them for anything. I nudged the spoon up against her mouth but she didn't budge. After the third nudge she tried to grab the spoon off me, sending more puree all over herself and me. I finally got the spoon away from her and she threw her head back and burst into tears. I decided against the idea of shoving some puree in her mouth as she was wailing because some had landed on my upper lip and after tasting it, I decided I couldn't blame her for not wanting to eat it. That stuff tastes like crap.

"Oh ssshhh baby. Mummy knows it's yucky! How about some banana custard instead?" I knew she wouldn't turn that down, that stuff tastes goooood.

Carter stopped crying and watched me put the tin of puree in the sink and get a tin of custard out of the pantry. Her big blue eyes weren't even teary from her outburst. What a Hollywood.

"Gaaaaaaaa!" I opened the tin and she started smiling and wriggling in her seat. Yep, she knows the good shit when she sees it. She hoovered the custard down happily and in about 30 seconds flat - she really is a chip off the old block.

"Good girl. Just you wait 'til you can have a pie, now *then* you will think you have died and gone to heaven!" I said to her as I put a pie in the microwave to heat up for my lunch.

It had been a day and a half and I still hadn't got my period. As much as I wanted to bury my head in the sand, the unknown was also threatening to do my head in – that and I had eaten the entire chocolate cake I had baked so my waistline was under threat too.

So I bit the bullet.

"Stay there missy moo, Mummy's just going to the loo," I said to Carter. I'm a poet and I just didn't know it.

I unwrapped the pregnancy test and shoved it between my legs and started weeing.

Far out I forgot how warm that is...

After a much more successful attempt at peeing on a stick than the first time (I still have a small scar on my forehead from that epic fail) I wrapped it in toilet paper and washed my hands in the bathroom. I went back to the kitchen and stuck it on the bench while I got my pie out of the microwave.

I squirted tomato sauce on the pie and took a bite, burning my tongue in the process. Patience was never a virtue of mine, especially when pastry was involved.

I drummed my fingertips on the bench and stared at the little stick – surely it had been long enough? I took another bite of pie and turned to Carter. "Cross your fingers little lady. Mummy loves you but I DO NOT want another one of you right now."

I took a deep breath, had another bite of pie and picked the test up.

OH SHIT. Noooooooo!!!

There were two lines.

I burst into tears, mouth half full of pie and sauce. I swallowed and tried to calm myself down but all I could think was that our wedding plans would be ruined as there was no way I would be waddling down the aisle with a baby on board sign stuck to my ass.

I sobbed and looked at the pie on my plate and figured I might as well finish it before I called Chops to break the news. So I stood there at the kitchen bench, stuffing my face with pie, the dreaded white stick at my side and my six month old daughter now throwing pieces of banana on the floor one by one and smiling at me.

Holy hell I'm having another one. Another pie, that is.

~~~~~~~~~~~~~~~~~~~~~

Three days later I was still reeling from the shock.

After telling Chops that I was up the duff yet again (which he took remarkably well considering all I wanted to do was smash him in his seemingly bionic testicles) I told Jess and Leo the news. They both took great pleasure in laughing about it until Leo realised that meant we would have to cancel the wedding and he wouldn't get to be my bridesman. In true Leo styles he threw a bit of a tanty – oh yes, because it was all part of my plan to ruin *his* big day apparently! I then rang Merryn the midwife who, after initially laughing, had suggested we have a scan to figure out the dates.

I'm not quite sure why everyone finds it so damn funny. *I'm not laughing.*

The day after I had done the test I had suddenly remembered the drunken night of my birthday and realised that as I didn't know when I had fallen pregnant (I will never be falling on his damn penis ever again that's for sure) I may have already been pregnant *before* my birthday - which then could mean that the poor baby was in extreme danger of being a mutant from my excessive alcohol consumption that night. Like I didn't have enough to worry about.

So off to the scan we went, partly to find out how far along I was and partly to allay my fears that I had drowned the baby in wine and vodka.

"Do you know the dates of your last period?" the radiologist asked.

"No. That's why we're here. How early can you tell if a baby has foetal alcohol syndrome??"

"Goose! Stop stressing. The baby will be fine, it was only one night," Chops said firmly.

"Okay, I'm just putting the gel on your tummy so it will feel a bit cold," the woman said as she squirted a large gob of the gel onto my already expanding tummy.

She put the scanner on my stomach and I heard the familiar whirring of the machine.

"Oh." The radiologist spoke quietly. She reached for a box of tissues next to the machine and handed them to me.

"What?! Oh my God is the baby dead?? I *did* kill it didn't I???" I wailed, straining my neck to see the screen.

"Um, no...have you felt particularly sick recently by any chance?" the radiologist asked.

"No, why??"

"What's wrong with the baby?" Chops demanded.

She gestured towards the screen. I felt the colour draining from my face because I could see what she was pointing to on the screen as clear as day.

No no no no no-

"Nothing's wrong. You're having twins! Can you see the two embryos there?" she replied, pointing.

TWINS!?!

The room was silent for what felt like a year. Then Chops broke the silence.

"Holy shit. I must have like, Superman sperm or something!" I could hear a smile in his voice and turned to look at him.

I burst into tears, clutching the box of tissues the radiologist had given me. How could he joke at a time like this?!

"Ssssh, don't cry babe. We'll be ok," he soothed and rubbed my shoulder.

"No we won't!"

"I'm sorry, I'll give you two a minute in private," the radiologist said. "I'll come back and do the measurements properly soon but at a guess I'd say you're about seven weeks along."

"Thank you," Chops said to her as she hastily exited the door and switched on the light on her way out.

"How can you be so calm about this?" I screeched through my tears.

He shrugged. "I don't know, can't do much about it. So, I must have knocked you up on your birthday aye? That was about seven weeks ago."

Happy birthday to me...

I cried harder. "We're going to need a bigger house! And a bigger car! And I'm going to get soooo fat! Like a fucking orca whale!" I wailed. "Three kids?! How can we be so unbelievably shit at using contraception!?"

"I bet three kids will be pretty good contraception," Chops said, laughing.

"I can't believe you can joke about this! We are going to have *three kids under two years old*!" I sputtered as something dawned on me. "Oh my God we are going to have to sell Henrietta! And probably your car too! We're going to have to buy a PEOPLE MOVER aren't we?!"

That stopped him laughing pretty damn quick.

~~~~~~~~~~~

So there you have it. I'm seven weeks pregnant with two babies. Two babies that will scream. And cry. And shit.

Two babies. Holy crap.

Oh how life can throw a curveball. And there are just so many questions that I don't know the answers to, like:

Do they even make suck-in undies big enough to fit orca whales?

Would our relationship (and my sanity) survive having three kids?

Would my vajayjay ever be the same? (Oh wait - that ship not only sailed, it bloody well shipwrecked after the first one.)

Would Carter like being a big sister? Oh man. Imagine if it's two boys. Shit - I hadn't thought of that possibility.

Would I have to give in to the dark side and drive a Mum bus?

Was I, *not* my witch of a sister, going to end up with a farm full of Gingas?

Well played Karma, well played.

Made in the USA
Coppell, TX
16 April 2022